THE TIGER'S EYE

The Tiger's Eye

angels in mumbai

XULON PRESS ELITE

Scott B. Delaney

Xulon Press
2301 Lucien Way #415
Maitland, FL 32751
407.339.4217
www.xulonpress.com

Printed in the United States of America

Paperback ISBN-13: 978-1-6628-0910-1
Dust Jacket ISBN-13: 978-1-6628-1387-0
Ebook ISBN-13: 978-1-6628-0911-8

This book is dedicated to
the beautiful people of India.
I am forever grateful for the hospitality,
love, and respect that I have been shown
over the many years of work in
this amazing country.

A special thank you to my wife, Jenny,
not only for her patience and support
during the writing process,
but for her insightful suggestions
that have had a powerful influence
on this book.

O white-robed Angel, guide my timorous hand
to write as on a lofty rock with iron pen the
words of truth, that all who pass may read.

- WILLIAM BLAKE, "SAMSON",
POETICAL SKETCHES

Whoever shuts his ears to the cry of the poor
will also cry himself and not be heard.

- PROVERBS 21:13

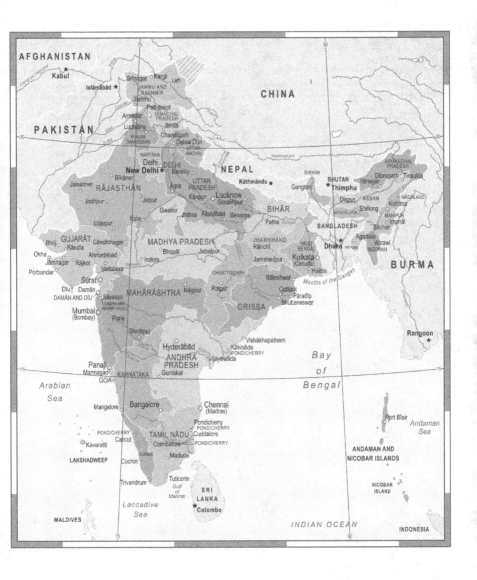

vii

PROLOGUE

MUMBAI, INDIA
1:45 P.M.
JUNE 2, 2022

an absolutely amazing study of contradictions. This is India! Beautiful and Filthy. Highly educated and desperately illiterate. Vegetarian and Non-Vegetarian. Indescribable wealth and abject poverty. Hindu and Christian. Muslim and Sikh. Tea or Coffee. Milk or No-Milk. I could go on forever.

Walking through the Dharavi slum in Mumbai always reminded me of the most extreme side of the contrast compendium. Today was no different. As we made our way through the tiny alleyways that led from the busy main street into the heart of the Mumbai slum, the smell of raw sewage and fermenting rubbish filled my nostrils, causing me to reflexively gag on a couple of occasions. The walls of the poorly constructed shantytown seemed to bend and sag in areas, making it seem that this unnatural world might completely swallow us, never to spit us out again. We weaved our way through the labyrinth of poorly built shanties and filthy hovels, tiny pop-up salty snack carts, candy and produce vendors, stray dogs and cattle, and scurrying children with tattered garments and matted hair. Manoj motioned for us to keep up the pace. Manoj Gupta, having spent over fifteen years as a missionary in this section of Mumbai, knew these tiny passages as well as many of those that dwelled here.

I could not help but feel a bit claustrophobic as we continued through the cramped, yet bustling and electric maze that made up this area of the slum. Bodies darted in and out of tiny doorways, through windows, bumping into me over and over again in passageways barely wide enough for one-way foot traffic. Each time one of the residents collided with me or my daughter, a quizzical stare would stop them in their tracks for longer than comfortable as they carefully eyed the light skinned and light-haired intruders, both of us clad in much more expensive clothing than was typical in this part of Mumbai. We had never ventured this far into the depths of Dharavi, and for the first time, I was acutely aware of how well the Oscar award-winning movie Slumdog Millionaire had portrayed this amazing and mysterious entanglement of steel, concrete, wood, rock, brick, dirt, and exposed wiring that formed this world famous slum.

On a couple of occasions, I was reminded of the overwhelming sinking feeling I had experienced while making my way through the abandoned mine back in Creede, Colorado only a couple of years back; heart racing wildly, dizziness coming and going, uncontrollable sweating, labored breathing, stomach cramping. It had never occurred to me prior to my time in that titular, cold, dark mine shaft that I had a fear of cramped spaces. Of course, the darkness and complete quiet of the mine might have also exacerbated that fear, but these tiny alleyways that snaked their way through acres of filth and squalor had a similar effect. Prayer had been the best answer for me as I searched the mine, and as we continued to move through the maze, I whispered prayer upon prayer for protection, for the people that lived here, for peace in the middle of this scary and unsettling environment. Once again, prayer was the right answer.

My thirteen year old daughter, Alisha, caught up with me and reached for my hand. This was uncharacteristic for my uber-confident and self-sufficient baby girl, but very much welcomed. As my father would always remind me, "The nut didn't fall far from the tree with that one." She was obviously struggling in this strangely inhumane and unfamiliar place just like I was.

This was my third visit to this particularly rundown area of these sprawling slums since we joined the Global Calling Ministry team and moved to India. Unfortunately, the sounds, smells, and sights had not become any more bearable. The percussive sound of car, rickshaw, and truck horns created a cacophony of noise that literally pounded my ear drums to the point of severe headache and palpable anxiety. The Dharavi slum started as a tiny fishing village in 1884, growing in popularity due to its proximity to the rail lines on either side that provided residents with convenient and affordable transportation in and around Mumbai. In a city where rental costs are among the highest in the world, Dharavi provided a cheap rental option for those moving to Mumbai to earn their living. Each tiny room had three essential items. Number one was continuous electricity, often poached from power lines that ran above the shanty city. Number two was a cooking gas stove that also served as a source of heat when needed. And number three, arguably the most important worldly possession to slum dwellers, was a big screen television, the bigger the better.

As we continued through the tangled mess of humanity, wandering feral animals, twisted steel dwellings, dented and dirty food carts, and cramped huts, I inadvertently stepped into what looked like a small puddle of water but was actually an almost eight inch deep pothole filled with muddy sludge, the residual byproduct of a wetter than average monsoon season. I twisted my ankle just badly enough to make the rest of the walk to meet the good Dr. Nehru much more difficult.

My near fall caused Alisha to drop my hand and she stopped just a few feet ahead of me, turning back in my direction. "Dad, how much longer before we get to the temple?" We had already walked in the sauna like maze for over thirty minutes, her reddened cheeks and sweat soaked Roxy t-shirt confirming this fact. This was certainly not turning out to be the ideal afternoon in the mind of a teenager, or her father for that matter.

It was hard to believe that it had already been three years since I, along with my colleague and trusted friend, Trevor Haas, braved an epic winter storm to rescue my family from the abandoned silver mine in Colorado. That brutally cold, eerily dark mine shaft, where my family had been imprisoned by an evil mercenary and his dangerous band of henchmen, was turned into a terrifying prison that still haunted our entire family. Nicolai Virshenko, a military trained assassin, had been hired by a greedy and morally corrupt, secret society to kidnap our family in what turned out to be a foiled attempt to disrupt the successful and fast growing Christian based ministry known as 'The Call.' Trevor and I, along with my wife, Beth, my son, Cade, my daughter, Alisha, and several other church leaders, had all become targets due to our leadership and affiliation with this rapidly growing movement. Remarkably, my daughter seemed to be dealing with this unimaginable trauma better than any of us. Her seventeen year old brother, Cade, had not fared as well, still struggling with the difficulties associated with post-traumatic stress.

Since the escape from Niki's hideout in the Mountains near Creede, Colorado, Alisha's faith had blossomed, and once our family moved to India, she took a strong interest in the 'Global Calling Ministry,' the worldwide extension of 'The Call' movement. Alisha was now a curious and excited regular on many of my trips through the slums of India, but today the intense heat and humidity put a damper on much of her usual zest for ministry and adventure.

"Only another couple of alleys over, I think." I sat on a concrete block and rubbed my ankle for a minute or two and asked Manoj if he had any idea. I wasn't completely sure, but the hand drawn map that had been given to Manoj by Dr. Nehru's fourteen-year-old son had been fairly accurate to this point. His cartoon-like drawings and descriptive roadmap creation made finding directional landmarks very easy. We were coming to what looked to be a dead end. Alisha glanced over Manoj's shoulder at the map, the arrows showing we were to take a right at the neon green water tank. In the margin, a note gave additional information that read, "the tank is sitting on top of a run-down restaurant that leans over the small alleyway to the building's left." Once again, his description left no room for question. I stood up and followed Alisha and Manoj, now with a mild and uncomfortable limp, to the right, down the larger alley as the map had instructed. Manoj estimated that we would reach the community's common area in another two hundred or so steps.

"Mr. Andrew, you can tell we are getting close. Can you see how much nicer this area looks than the rest of the slum?"

"You know what? Now that you mention it, I can definitely see a difference. No trash. Buildings seem to be in much better shape." I looked around with a heightened sense of the remarkable cleanliness in this area of the slum.

"I am telling you. This is because of Dr. Nehru. He has provided the people with a new sense of pride for Dharavi. And your ministry has indeed contributed greatly to the effort."

"What do you mean? Global Calling?"

Manoj stopped and turned to look back at me, "Do you remember the water refurbishment project?"

"Yes. When was it? Maybe a year back?" I vaguely remembered a mention of this from Rajiv in one of our ministry update meetings.

"Yes, sir. Not quite one year." Manoj placed his hand on my shoulder as he continued. "Dr. Nehru used the promise of clean drinking water as a metaphor for a cleaner Dharavi. For months, the people that live here removed mountains of trash. Many craftsmen also donated their time for much needed construction and renovation. You can't even recognize the place." He smiled with obvious hometown pride.

As we emerged from the tiny alley, the common area was not much of an area at all. The total size of the square could hardly be more than two thousand square feet, the size of a small house back in the States. In the center of the space, a crude yet colorful open-air temple had been constructed with its clay colored concrete floor raised about eight inches above the grassless dirt yard. No more than twenty chairs in various shapes and sizes were set up in four rows facing a small lectern at the far end of the temple. Obviously, this was where Dr. Nehru would address the crowd that was expected to gather at 2:15 for the weekly service, which was traditionally followed by a meal of Naan bread, Dal Makhani, Aloo Tikka, and Gobi Manchurian for all that attended. And, back by popular demand, Manoj, and his sister Dharvana would make up a large batch of their famous sweet mango lassi, a blend of yogurt, water, spices, and fruit that was especially popular among all the children that attended.

In the far corner, immediately behind the left most column of the poorly constructed temple structure, six preteen slum residents were engaged in a game of gulley cricket. Because of the cramped space on this miniaturized pitch, the makeshift wickets, two roughly sawed off PVC pipes that might have been pulled from a nearby rubbish pile were set only fifteen to twenty feet apart, not the typical twenty two yards that one would find in an actual cricket stadium. The cricket bat for this neighborhood match was an oversize plastic whiffle ball bat and the ball being used appeared to be a dirty, well-worn tennis ball. As I watched in surprisingly gratified amusement, I noticed that they had created a boundary by placing rocks in a semicircle that almost reached the corner of the temple and extended to the left and right wall of the common area in a relatively haphazard arc. As Manoj would explain later that afternoon, balls hit over the boundary in the air would receive a score of six runs, balls that rolled over the boundary would receive four runs and any hit that was not caught in midair by the fielders would require that the batsman run back and forth between the wickets with the opportunity to gain as many runs as possible before either the ball was back at the batter's wicket or the runner was tagged out.

I watched a couple of overs and noticed that one of the neighborhood kids, standing behind and to the side of the far right boundary, would carve notches in a piece of wood with one of the sharper rocks whenever runs were scored. This was the score keeper for the match, and he was very serious about his responsibility. On several occasions, a player would run back to his position, looking over his shoulder, with a dramatic pointing of the index finger, appearing to question his carefully inscribed scoreboard. The scorekeeper would summarily shoo the player away with the hand holding the rock writing utensil and turn the scorecard upside down indicating that scoring was not subject to player review at any time. This kid did not mess around. The scorekeeper was infallible, and the players had to defer to his expertise. Period.

As the teams switched again from fielding to batting and vice versa, I walked around one of the rear columns that held up the thatch covered roof of the small building and noticed Dr. Malik Nehru approaching us from the alley that entered the courtyard from the opposite direction of where we had come in. "Hello, Dr. Nehru," I said with a sense of relief that we had once again been able to navigate to our desired location without any real trouble. Just a sprained ankle and a buildup of sweat and body odor that was less than desirable.

"Good afternoon, my friend from the West. It is always great to see the world famous Andrew Morrison." Dr. Nehru greeted me with a hug in his uniquely bombastic way. "We are thrilled to have you join us for today's event. I hope that you all have come with a hefty appetite. The Dal is a special recipe from my favorite Indian restaurant here in Mumbai. Maybe not quite Bukhara worthy, but close. Might be a little spicy for you Yanks with the sensitive tummies, but you will like it." His formal education in Great Britain had created a somewhat dry sense of humor, but a sharp wit that always lightened the mood.

"Sounds delicious." My daughter had appeared at my side, appearing a little more shy than usual, likely due to the foreign surroundings and having never met Dr. Nehru. "Oh, I am so sorry...Dr. Nehru, this is my daughter, Alisha. After hearing about the impact your team is making here in Mumbai, she was adamant to join us today. Frankly, I can't blame her."

A grin of excitement washed away any of the shyness as she reached out to shake hands with Dr. Nehru. "Thank you for inviting me, Dr. Nehru. I can't wait to meet some of the children."

"Fantastic. Actually, if you are willing, I would like you to help supervise some of the younger children with my daughter, Dharvana." He motioned for his daughter to join the group. "She is thrilled that you are joining us today. And, yes, our love for this area of Mumbai was influential in her receiving the name Dharvana."

Dharvana put her arm around Alisha's shoulder and said, "Come. Follow me. I will introduce you to some of the kids. They are super excited to meet an American girl!" Her excitement was palpable and contagious. I could tell that Dharvana had an amazing heart and a true love for people. Part of me wanted to follow Dharvana myself to meet the kids and watch her in action, but we had to prepare for our responsibilities as well.

Dr. Nehru watched the two girls walking together until they disappeared through a small doorway at the end of the common area. The sign on the door was written in Hindi script, but under the black, connected letters that looked like artistic scribbling to my American eyes was the English word 'Nursery.'

Dr. Nehru extended his arm towards the altar area on the temple stage. "Alright. Now that kids are in very capable hands, let's go over the schedule for the service today." He turned and pointed towards a couple of empty chairs in the middle of the courtyard before looking back in my direction. "By the way, is Trevor not joining us today? I have only known him for a few months, but he is usually not one to miss a good Indian meal."

"Without a doubt. He was bummed to say the least. He let me know that his stomach was angry and may need some time for forgiveness, but the rest of him sends his best." Dr. Nehru chuckled as he took a seat in the metal folding chair across from where I was now seated. I adjusted my chair so that I was facing Dr. Nehru more directly and continued, "He is over at the stadium making final plans for tomorrow's event. With over a hundred thousand expected at the stadium, he wants to be sure that everything is perfectly in order."

"Understood. Trevor is quite the character, but a great person."

"One of the best, Dr. Nehru. One of my closest friends on the planet. And when it comes to planning and the details, he is as buttoned up as they come."

"Dharvana and I will look forward to seeing him tomorrow. Thanks again for the tickets."

"My pleasure. Should be an amazing event."

With Dr. Nehru's notebook open on his lap, we went over the day's agenda. Once finished, Dr. Nehru waved to a beautiful, dark haired woman near the banquet tables, encouraging her to join us. As she approached, Dr. Nehru stood and introduced us. "Andrew, Nisha. Nisha, Andrew." Nisha was a diminutive, articulate, and soft spoken woman that would serve as my interpreter for the service, converting my English message into Marathi, the mother tongue of this region in India.

"Pleasure to meet you, Andrew." She bowed gently as a sign of adoration and respect. "I have heard so many good things about you and brother Trevor."

"Thank you, Nisha. Trevor was disappointed that he could not make it today but looks forward to meeting you soon."

Dr. Nehru walked over and grabbed another chair from behind the pulpit and placed it next to where we had been sitting. "Please...join us. Have a seat." He patted the seat that had been set for Nisha.

After we had all settled back into the chairs, I turned my attention back to our interpreter. "My understanding was that the common language was Hindi here in Mumbai." My comment was more question than statement.

"You may not be aware of how dramatically Mumbai has evolved over time. The city has become extremely cosmopolitan," Nisha explained, "The official language of Mumbai is Marathi and is the most widely used language in this entire state of Maharashtra. Of course, Mumbai accepts many other languages like Gujarati, Kannada, English, Telugu, Konkani, Dangii, and Varhadii, but Marathi is definitely the most widely used in this part of the city."

"How does Hindi fit in, then?" This was the first time that I had contemplated how many different languages existed in this wildly diverse country. India didn't just simply have different regional dialects, it had different languages altogether.

"Great question, my friend." Dr. Nehru retook the reins in my continued education. "There is a popular aphorism here in India. *Kos-kos par badle paani, chaar kos par baani.* In English, it means that the language spoken in India changes every few kilometers, just like the taste of the water." We all laughed at this all-too-perfect description.

The doctor turned sociology professor continued, "Hindi and English are now considered to be the mode of communication of the educated elites of the major cities in India and English is the preferred language of business throughout India. We can thank our British friends for that."

As if appearing out of thin air, two gentlemen presented the four of us with Masala Chai, each small teacup set atop a tiny china saucer with a small spoon and two sugar cubes sitting next to the cup. "Miel, no miel?" One of the Chaiwallah gentlemen asked more forcefully than I expected.

"Excuse me?" I didn't understand the question.

"Miel, no miel?"

Nisha quietly explained, "Would you like Milk with your tea?"

"Oh. Oh, yes. No thank you." I turned a shade pink with embarrassment for not understanding. It should have been fairly obvious since he was holding a small creamer as if ready to pour into my steaming cup of tea precisely when he had asked the question.

Dr. Nehru continued without missing a beat in his proper English tinged Indian accent. "Quite a good idea to stay away from dairy products that are not fully frozen, my friend. Typically, these products are not homogenized and can really wreak havoc on your insides." The always caring doctor pursed his lips just a bit, indicating that he was very serious about this warning.

A devious but playful smile replaced the more serious cautionary look. "If given the proper chance, Andrew, even the softest of bathroom tissues, when used out of a far too frequent necessity, can play the part of sandpaper, if you know what I mean."

I smiled with him at this attempt at toilet humor, but the thought made my stomach turn a small somersault as my mind wandered in this direction.

The service went off without a hitch. Over two hundred people had crammed into the small courtyard, craning their necks to see and hear the message of love, compassion, and peace being brought by the intriguing, silver tongued American preacher, a message that was translated beautifully by Nisha. Amazingly, I was neither nervous nor frightened to speak to these people. There was a warm, curious, and embracing nature in the people standing before me that eased my nerves and made me feel comfortable at home behind the lectern.

They were amazingly attentive. No, they were much more than attentive. They were laser focused on the message. No one was perusing their cell phone for incoming text messages, googling my background, or yelping for a restaurant to visit after the service. No one was carrying on a side conversation. No crying babies in the crowd. Fortunately, the young children were all being watched by our daughters. I would later find out that having a crying baby during a service was considered disrespectful to the speaker and was considerably frowned upon by the weekly attendees.

The sermon centered on love for one another and the gift of God's love for all people throughout the world. Following Dr. Nehru's advice, I intentionally spoke at a third grade level, understanding that most of the listeners had very little formal education. I was careful to contrast some of the Hindu and Muslim beliefs with the basic tenets of Christianity, hoping to plant an initial seed which might germinate in the weeks, months, or years to come through Dr. Nehru's teaching or to continue to water seeds that had already been planted in weeks or months before by other much more gifted speakers.

When Nisha would translate in the beautiful local language, I could see the nodding of heads in agreement or understanding. At some points, people would simply bow their heads in prayer. Some wept openly as Nisha recounted the promises that God makes to us even in the midst of poverty, oppression, despair, or grief. I can only imagine how that message of hope might feel to someone that lives in this environment.

In our preservice meeting, Manoj mentioned that the crowd would include individuals at varying levels of their faith journey. Since his family had started this weekly ministry over a year ago, over fifty residents had accepted Christ as their personal savior, and more than half had been formally baptized. I could see the pride and joy well up in those huge brown eyes.

Behind the continuously growing crowd of onlookers, I noticed that many of the younger children had come back into the courtyard and had started to play a game of miniaturized cricket with Alisha and Dharvana acting as referees and coaches. They darted back and forth between the wickets, some running towards the crowd in search of their mothers, Dharvana and Alisha occasionally having to leave the game to corral the escapees. At one point, I noticed my daughter glancing at me over the crowd, using the back of her sleeve to wipe the sweat from her forehead, and the uniquely daughter to father telepathic communication was abundantly clear. 'You are going long, again. The kids are getting pretty restless. Might want to start winding down, father.'

As I concluded my message, I nodded to Manoj and he hit the play button on his iPhone that was Bluetooth connected to a portable Bose speaker that he regularly carried in his backpack for this purpose. Philips Craig and Dean rang through the packed quad with a beautiful rendition of 'Shine on Us.' The simple verse was quickly picked up by the crowd and by the third stanza, most of the crowd was singing along in full voice. There was a different level of reverence, a different feel of awe that I hadn't experienced in many years. This was what real hunger for the Word of God looked like. This is exactly why we were here.

"Amen." I said softly under my breath as the song faded. "Amen."

Madness in Mumbai

"O, speak again, bright angel! For thou art as glorious to this night, being o'er my head as is a winged messenger of heaven"
— **WILLIAM SHAKESPEARE, <u>ROMEO & JULIET</u>**

"Time spent in India has an extraordinary effect on one. It acts as a barrier that makes the rest of the world seem unreal."
- TAHIR SHAH

I

MUMBAI, INDIA
7:09 P.M.
JUNE 3, 2022

O ver eighty-two thousand people from all over India filled the seats of the recently built, and the world's second largest cricket stadium prominently set in the Andheri East section of Mumbai. The attendees had started to arrive early in the morning at Kingsford Garden Stadium with a palpable sense of anticipation growing throughout the day, working towards what would be a billowing crescendo of cheering and chanting, an energy packed explosion of emotion that was to be expected at these rallies.

The monsoon season had come early this year and the rains over the last several days contributed well towards the impeccable air quality that was uncommon in early June. Typically, the forecast for Mumbai on my iPhone's Weather Channel App would include the words hazy, dangerous, or smoky, but today's skies were an almost fluorescent blue with a few clouds scattered about with no chance of bad weather that might ruin this event. Rajiv Bansal, the leader of the Global Calling Organization based out of Delhi, was making his way

3

through the tunnel below the stadium near the visiting team locker rooms, towards the large stage at the south side of the pitch. With him were three members of his team from Delhi and two strikingly large bodyguards that had been appointed to him by stadium management. Rajiv had become quite a celebrity in India over the last two years, reaching almost rock star level status, blessed with a commanding voice, a strong and confident physique and a gift for storytelling that was capturing the attention of the world. This event would mark the fourth in a row where a stadium in India was completely sold out due to excitement to hear this charismatic leader. The difference today would be the sheer size of the audience, more than double the size of the most recent event held in Udaipur.

Trevor and I were moving down the home team's tunnel, approaching the field entrance from the opposite direction that Rajiv and his team were taking, with our own group of over twenty U.S. and European leaders from our respective Global Calling regional offices. This event in India would be the largest event in our group's history and an opportunity for the leaders around the world to become even more united in the mission that was laid out before us. The excitement was intoxicating. The atmosphere was breathtaking. In my mind, I imagined that this is exactly what it must have felt like at the Billy Graham crusade meeting at Yoido Plaza in Seoul, South Korea in 1973, a gathering of over a million people, the largest audience in the history of his ministry. We could feel the rhythmic thump of the music inside the walls of the tunnel as we continued through the almost complete darkness toward the stage entrance.

The global appeal was amazing. The world seemed to be starving for a message of love, peace, generosity, charity, and acceptance that was at the core of our global vision. The recent resurgence of ISIS attacks across the world, the growing animosity between superpower nations, the persistent and depressing problem of abject poverty in third world countries, and the failures and atrocities as a result of misdirected socialism in many poorly led countries seemed to ignite a passion for change that the world had never experienced. From Singapore to Belfast, from Sao Paulo to Mumbai, people were looking for a new answer, a new world view. The political and social turmoil, the hunger for power and the obvious perversion of many different religions for the purposes of individual, government and corporate greed had grown old. In all parts of the world, hearts and minds were becoming changed for good, and the mobilization of this new ideology was starting to accelerate.

As I got closer to the entrance that led to the cricket pitch, the roar of the crowd over the pounding lead guitar and drums continued to swell in my ears and I couldn't help but feel a sense of pride and accomplishment, as Global Calling was a natural world wide extension of The Call, the organization that Trevor and I had started and helped lead for almost three years in the United States, until we were both given the opportunity to relocate to India to help Rajiv and his team manage the unprecedented growth of the organization. Trevor and I had been working out of the Goa regional office for over five months and had been fortunate to travel all over India during that time. Global Calling was not simply a rally organizer, but it demanded a local presence as well, working with local charities, churches, and other religious organizations to provide for the welfare of those living in impoverished and underserved parts of their respective geographies. Trevor and I were acting as Human Resource Directors as well as Operational Directors, hiring over one hundred regional managers in the first six months, and then providing direction and funding to support the initiatives planned for each target area.

My wife, Beth, my two children and I had been welcomed into the Goa community with open arms. The people of India are truly beautiful. They are warm, caring, generous, loving, trusting, and always willing to help when needed. On our first visit to Panjim, our driver for the day informed us that this was normal, and that Indian culture has deep roots in the belief that guests are supposed to be treated like Gods. The fully embraced level of hospitality stems from the ancient Sanskrit phrase *Atithi Devo Bhava*, which embodies this Indian Hindu-Buddhist tradition. We were blown away by the reception.

Alisha started school at the Immaculate Conception Catholic School, only a half mile away from my office and only a couple miles from our new home in Panjim. Cade, a Boerne High School class of 2021 graduate, used the move to India as a convenient excuse to take what he alone deemed to be "a well-deserved" gap year. With Rajiv's help and after a number of online interviews, Cade was offered conditional acceptance into a highly regarded Computer Science and Molecular Chemistry combination program at the prestigious Birla Institute of Technology in South Goa, often referred to as 'BITS' by the local residents of the greater Goan region, if he would agree to begin his studies in August of 2023. The class starting in 2022 had already been filled and this specific program only provided for twenty-two deserving students.

In a slightly less than successful attempt at humor, the Dean of Admissions told Cade, after providing this conditional offer of acceptance, that unfortunately, "The school would not be willing to give a 'BIT' of consideration to adding an additional student this close to the start of the school year, pun intended." The Dean let out a quick snicker of laughter at his clever joke. For Cade, with or without the joke, the mandatory year of a study sabbatical was welcomed with great enthusiasm. What better excuse could be provided for allowing him to become one with his prized new possession, the highly anticipated, recently released, must-have gaming system, the PlayStation XT6? Brilliant!

Because Goa was once a Portuguese colony, it is truly a multi-cultural showcase in India. The Portuguese ruled in Goa for as long as four hundred and fifty years, until the liberation of Goa on December 17, 1961 under the Indian Prime Minister at the time, Jawaharla Nehru. If you were to ask my kids, they would tell you that the best part of the Portuguese influence is the impact on the food. The spices used in Goan curry, for example, are much different from those that you would typically find in other areas of India and the prevalence of good seafood, from prawns to Lobster to fresh fish, makes eating in this area of the world a true pleasure. While we all like traditional Indian food, like Chicken Tikka Masala, Lamb Kabobs, Butter Chicken, Gobi Manchurian, and Samosas, the food in Goa feels more like home.

One of the benefits of living in India, as opposed to many other countries outside of the U.S. is the fact that most

Indians speak understandable and very proper, English. The British ruled India for almost two hundred years and one of the residual effects was that the English language had firmly established itself as the language of administration and trade by the mid-1700s. By the mid 1800's, universities had opened in Mumbai, Kolkata and Chennai. English was gaining popularity as the language of government, of the social elite, and of the national press in India. After living here for half the year, it was easy to understand, that because of the similar language used for communication, companies from the U.S. generally enjoyed doing business in India.

As we rounded the final portion of the dark tunnel, our group almost bumped into Rajiv and his party, meeting in the large breezeway that led to the field and lower level of the bleachers.

"Greetings, friends," Rajiv said in his very formal English/Hindi accent. "Sorry we were not able to arrive earlier. Our flight from Delhi was delayed by over three hours. Many prayers have been lifted up for this momentous occasion." The lift in his voice and his beaming grin clearly indicated his excitement for this event.

We clasped hands and gave each other a warm embrace. "Good evening, my friend." I was always glad to see Rajiv. Our greeting turned into a collective reunion as both groups gave the appropriate handshake or hug and all manners of greeting pleasantries. "Not a worry. What an exciting, moment! Have you seen the crowd?"

"Yes...wow...indeed," Rajiv was giddy with anticipation. "I was informed by my administrative assistant that the event has been fully sold out. I am telling you, my friend. This is absolutely amazing."

"I was told that there are over thirty thousand more that are immediately outside of the stadium that are simply hoping to hear the message and music. We have already asked the stage crew to make sure that the speakers are pointed slightly higher so that the sound will carry outside of the arena," Trevor added with the same level of excitement.

As a collective group, we eased toward the entrance and peered out over the stage at the remarkable crowd. The entire stadium was jam packed with thousands of people standing immediately in front of the stage jockeying for position. We could see and hear the band, Points of Light, playing on stage. We had first come upon this group of tremendous musicians at a conference that was held in Delhi during the second week of January. They had been recommended by the Director in the Delhi office due to their crossover style between Indian Classical and Contemporary Christian genres. I had come to really enjoy the mix of old and new in this creative musical expression. The four vocalists, two males and two females, had a unique and perfectly balanced harmony that reminded me of a group I had listened to during my college years named First Call. Adding the Sitar and the Tabla along with other traditional Indian instruments created an ethereal quality that I found to be very pleasing to the ear.

As per our instructions, we waited in the wings until the stage manager, standing behind the twenty four foot tall back curtain, waved at us to make our way to our place on the stage. Today, I would be sharing keynote speaker honors with Rajiv. I was excited and nervous. He was a superstar all over India.

Was I really expected to follow the "Bono" of India? I was still relatively new to this amazing country and my comfort level and confidence in public speaking, which was typically very high, had not yet reached the level I would have hoped for in a moment of this great magnitude.

As soon as I made it to the left side of the stage, and before the music had ended, I was jolted by a sound that I assumed must be the band blowing out a speaker. The stage rocked dramatically to the left, throwing me off balance. I landed hard on the steps that led down to the field, my head bouncing off the landing and up against the railing. Dazed and confused, I reached for my temple and felt the unmistakable moistness of blood. Another explosion rocked the arena. This one seemed further away from my position and the stage remained in the same position.

Disoriented, but still alert enough to assess that something was wrong, I crawled back to the floor of the stage and surveyed the situation. The crowd was scurrying in every direction, obviously looking to escape the arena. My ears were ringing but the sound of what seemed like fireworks started to get louder and louder. Pop. Pop...pop. Pop...pop...pop. There was no mistaking it. This was the sound of gunfire. There were obviously multiple shooters as the sound of rifles discharging multiple rounds per second was coming from all directions.

Looking into the crowd from my crouched position, I could see puffs of smoke rising above quick bursts of firearm discharge in many areas of the arena with people fanning out in all directions away from the gunmen. I watched in horror as many shots found their mark. From the upper deck, I could see a handful of bodies falling some fifty or so feet to the mezzanine below as terrified members of the crowd were frantically pushing people in the front rows as they looked for an escape. Those people that were able, could be seen leaping over rows of seats as they tried to flee in all directions from the gunfire.

On the opposite end of the stage, I watched as a man in a wheelchair was frantically powering the wheels of his chair in the direction of a large crowd of people that were completely bottlenecked in front of a large field level gate that led to the stadium's north concourse. As the young man in the wheelchair approached the crowd of over one hundred frightened attendees, I watched him dismount the chair and sprint towards the concession area where he must have just entered the arena. As he disappeared into the tunnel, the chair exploded with more force than I could have ever imagined. People nearest the chair were killed instantly and shrapnel from the blast must have covered a two hundred foot radius around the epicenter. At least fifty people were lying motionless in a morbid circle of humanity around the spot where the chair had been strategically positioned. I covered my face with both hands wishing with all my might that this horror show would end.

The rapid fire gun shots started up again. Immediately in front of me, I saw two of the crowd members go down, one young man with a shot to the shoulder and one in the back of a teenaged girl's head. I was paralyzed by the shock and horror of the situation. I stood motionless watching the carnage unfold in front of me. I wanted to go to them, but my feet were cemented to the ground. Where was my team? Where was Rajiv? Where was Trevor?

Out of the corner of my eye, I could see Ananth, one of Rajiv's bodyguards sprinting across the stage in my direction. He was yelling something at the top of his lungs, but I couldn't make out the words due to the ringing in my ears and the cacophony of sound in the arena. He tackled me as if he were a linebacker sacking a quarterback and rolled with me in his arms until we were behind the backstage curtain. "Are you alright, Andrew?" He stammered, completely out of breath.

With a resounding whoosh as the only warning, a flash of light lit up one of the unused entrances to the arena on the top tier of the stadium. A rocket screamed towards the stage, hitting its mark immediately below the supports that held up the right side of the stage and the catwalk that led backstage.

"What is going on?" I was still a little dazed and groggy after the initial fall, but this explosion again sent me reeling. My ears emitted only a high pitched ringing tone. I was sure that my ear drums had popped. Propping myself up on my hands and knees, I looked at the right side of backstage, which was now completely leveled. There was only smoke and a pile of splintered, black painted particle board that had been the stage floor only moments earlier. I could see that at least half a dozen stage hands had been blown to the below stage turf, one of them impaled through the thigh with a piece of the stage, most of them writhing in obvious pain and some not moving at all. One had clearly been decapitated.

"There were multiple explosions around the arena. Suicide bombers, I believe. I think that there was a bomb under the stage." His speech was frantic but concise. "Rajiv was hit in the leg, but Ananth was able to carry him back into the tunnel."

The gunshots continued all around us. Deafening cries and horrific wailing could be heard immediately in front of the stage. A bullet ripped through the thick felt curtain that provided very flimsy cover from this type of fire power, ripping a nine inch gash that was only inches from our position.

"We have to get you out of here," he shouted over the roar. "Follow me."

He sprinted off towards the tunnel entrance and I followed him as quickly as my fifty-two year old legs could take me. He was only twenty yards ahead of me when I saw the bullet explode through the side of his head. My protector was killed instantly, and his momentum carried him over the railing onto the field ten feet below the gang plank that was affixed to the stage from the entrance.

I kept my pace and made it into the tunnel, tears welling up in my eyes. Looking back, I could see this brave man in a heap, lying motionless on the field below. I was sure that the bullet that took his life was meant for me.

My heart was racing, as I limped towards the darkness that would provide me safety. I could hear the loud echoes of what sounded like a team of horses coming directly towards me from the center hallway under the stadium. I backed up into a dimly lit doorway and watched as thirty or forty armed military officers ran past my position in the direction of the stage entrance.

I slid down the wall into a sitting position and prayed for protection. I hadn't been this frightened and unsettled since my trip from Boerne to the ranch country of South Texas in the back of Niki's jeep a couple of years ago. "Not again, not again..." I remained still, ears still ringing and head pounding out the wild rhythm of my rapid heartbeats. "Why Lord? Why?" I muttered to myself as I consciously took in one deep breath after another, trying to escape the incapacitating fear that now gripped me, stronger than I could ever remember. The highlight reel of my life flipped image after image in my mind as I closed my eyes while my subconscious uncontrollably led me down the very dark path that included the possibility that I might never see my family again. I buried my sweaty forehead in my hands and rocked back and forth as I recited the Lord's Prayer.

Journey to the Subcontinent

For he shall give His angels charge over you, to keep you in all your ways. They shall bear you up in their hands, lest you dash your foot against a stone. You shall tread upon the lion and the cobra, the young lion and the serpent you shall trample underfoot.

- Psalm 91: 11-13 (New King James Version)

"Believers, look up – take courage. The angels are nearer than you think."

- BILLY GRAHAM

"We owe a lot to the Indians, who taught us how to count, without which no worthwhile scientific discovery could have been made."

- Albert Einstein

2

trevor, Harold, and I were quickly collecting our belongings after going through the ridiculously long TSA precheck line in Terminal C, the main international terminal at Newark International Airport. After placing our electronics back in our bags, putting our belts and coats back on and shoving keys, passports, and cell phones into our pockets, we started to make our way through the crowded food court area towards the United Airlines International Club. This is where we would spend the next couple of hours before boarding flight UA600, bound for Delhi, the first leg of our thirty-six hour journey to Goa, India. In typical form, Trevor's slightly overdeveloped anxiety over the possibility of missing a flight had demanded that we arrive at the airport more than three hours before our scheduled departure. Harold and I had learned to accept this quirky trait, having traveled with Trevor at least ten to twelve times over the last nine months as 'The Call' had gone global. In fact, it had turned into an always predictable, yet always

17

good natured opportunity, to poke fun at his "gotta get there early" neurosis.

Harold Jaworski, or Hayward, the nickname Trevor and I typically used for him, had proved to be a very relaxed traveler. Completely in line with his general disposition and personality, nothing seemed to bother Hayward; delays, luggage fees, tiny seats for his six-foot seven-inch frame, rude airline personnel, bad airline food... nothing phased him. His carefree and always joking nature tended to diffuse much of the anxiety and frustration that one might typically expect when taking a trip to India. He earned the nickname Hayward on the basketball court in high school and college due to his bombastic obsession regarding one of the main characters in a relatively obscure sitcom from the late 1970s named "The White Shadow." When playing pick-up basketball, one of our favorite work avoidance techniques while traveling together, Hayward would often refer to Trevor and me as Salami and Coolidge, two other larger than life characters from the same show. Fortunately for both of us, neither one of these stuck to us quite like Hayward stuck to our deserving friend Harold.

Before making the turn towards the escalators that led to the United Airlines lounge, we made a quick pit stop at the Hudson News store to load up for our trip to India. During our briefings earlier in the week, a couple of our Indian counterparts in the organization provided us with tips that would later prove to be some of the best advice American travelers to the sub-continent could ever receive. I picked up two bags of my favorite candy, paydays and Haribo gummy bears, two bags of salted cashews, a handful of protein bars and a box of extra-large Slim Jim beef jerky sticks. According to our trusted friends and now India travel advisors, these items would come in handy during our trip, depending on where we were traveling and what we were eating.

After paying for the required rookie traveler pack items, I remembered one of the most important pieces of advice that I had received regarding travel in India. I had been instructed to purchase as many disposable wipes as we could carry. For appropriate backside protection, I circled back and picked up three packs of cotton flushable wipes and placed them in my carryon bag. As I would find out over the next few weeks, the quality of toilet paper can become a major concern during long trips in India. For first time visitors, there are days that you go through toilet paper like a chain smoker goes through cigarettes. Before my trips to India, I didn't have a great deal of appreciation for Tuck's pads or Boudreaux's Butt Paste. All of that, to my utter disappointment, is forever changed. I now have a profound appreciation for these remedies, both having become trusted travel companions for all of my trips throughout India.

The opportunity to spend the next two years in India to assist in the development of the 'Global Calling' movement was a blessing and a privilege. Although Beth and I had always wanted to make a trip to India and Southeast Asia at some time a little further into the future, this would allow us to immerse ourselves and our children in the culture for a prescribed period of time and would be fully funded by the burgeoning new ministry. We felt that this was an opportunity that we simply couldn't pass up. Having Trevor and Harold decide to join us for this period was a bonus.

The United International Club lounge was buzzing with activity on this Friday night. The lounge attendant informed us that this was typically one of the busiest days of the week for international travel out of Newark. The line for homemade guacamole was at least fifteen deep, but Trevor was insistent that we try the New Jersey version of this typical southwestern specialty. He placed his bags next to mine and jumped in line. As he waited, I went through the listings of houses that Beth and I had placed in three buckets, those that were 'of interest,' 'a possibility,' and 'fantastic, but a stretch.' I tried to arrange them in order of priority and geographic location in an attempt to make our house hunting as efficient as possible during our three search days in Goa.

As Trevor settled into the long line of travelers that were waiting for their turn to direct the making of their preferred guacamole mixture, Hayward jumped out of his seat and grabbed Trevor's carry-on bag that had been placed under the table for safe keeping when we had first arrived in the lounge. Like a stealthy cat, he slipped behind a wall divider and almost sprinted across the room before placing the bag behind a large potted plant that decorated one of the common areas. Two young kids were sitting in the seats next to the plant. Hayward raised his finger to his lips in the 'please keep this a secret' kid language. Hayward rushed back to his seat and grabbed one of the complimentary copies of USA today from one of the cubbies built into the side table next to him.

Trevor arrived back at the table with a heaping paper plate of guacamole and tortilla chips. To our amazement, it was shockingly delicious. The three of us polished it off in a matter of minutes as we discussed our excitement about the trip.

"Hey, where did my carry-on luggage go?" Trevor stood up still holding the now empty plate of chips and guacamole.

Without missing a beat, Hayward peered over the top of his copy of USA Today. "I didn't see it, brother. Could you have left it down in customs?"

"No. I don't think so. No way.... I could have sworn it was right here." Trevor frantically looked around the small seating area that we had chosen. Obviously confused, he walked around the chairs, looked under the coffee table, and stepped back into the aisle to take a wider look around the entire lounge. You could see the anxiety level increasing by the second as he started to pace back and forth and then widened the search area to include the guacamole cart location, the beverage station, the lounge's front desk area and the restrooms. I was struggling to keep from busting out in uncontrollable laughter as he slowly made his way back to where we were sitting.

The search had already gone on for an uncomfortable five minutes when Trevor blurted out, "Dude, seriously. I must have left it somewhere. I have no idea." Sweat was starting to bead on his forehead as he clumsily stomped around our seating area searching every nook and cranny. "I guess I will head back to the custom's area, or maybe I left it in the baggage check line."

"It was me," the almost inaudible comment came from behind the sports page of the USA Today.

"What? What did you say, Howard?" Trevor stepped closer to the chair where Hayward was still seated reading his paper.

With no change in facial expression, Hayward folded down the paper and pointed across the room. "I think you might have left it over behind that large plant across the way."

"Dude, what is wrong with you. You let me wander around like a moron for ten minutes? I questioned half of the people in the lounge. Seriously. Really not cool!" Trevor stomped across the room to retrieve his luggage. I just shook my head. This was simply another prank by our resident master prankster. You could never let your guard down when Hayward was around.

Although gullible at times, as evidenced in the case of the disappearing luggage, Trevor Haas was a true man of God. He had proved to be one of my closest friends on countless occasions. Our time together in Colorado, combined with the two years of continued work together since Nicolai was apprehended and my family was rescued, had brought us closer together than we ever dreamt possible. Trevor had truly become part of the family. The decision to answer the call to go to India would have been much more difficult if Trevor had chosen to stay in the U.S. This trip would provide us with a face to face introduction to the international teams, an opportunity to better understand the global strategy of the organization, a couple of days of sightseeing and enough time for house hunting in our adopted city of Goa. All in all, we would be in India for the next twelve days. The actual relocation was planned for early March.

After we finished going over the twelve day itinerary for the third time, tweaking it slightly according to our personal desires for different sightseeing opportunities and restaurants that had been recommended, the loudspeaker came to life alerting passengers on flight 600 to Delhi that the boarding process would begin in the next fifteen minutes at gate C55. Fortunately, the attendant continued, this would be an on-time departure.

We gathered our belongings, including our large bags of American made food provisions, and headed for the gate.

3

DELHI, INDIA
11:31PM
JANUARY 8, 2022

As we descended through five thousand feet on our approach into Indira Gandhi International Airport in Delhi, India, an intense smell that was incredibly foul and as thick as a dense fog enveloped the entire cabin, instantly making my stomach turn in a way that reminded me of my first visit to the city dump with my father as a teenager. I wondered if a fire had broken out on board or if there was some backed up plumbing that might need attention once we landed. I took off my headphones still searching for an answer when an Indian businessman sitting in the adjoining pod next to me said, "Welcome to Delhi." in a strong yet somehow calming Indian accent.

We had not spoken to each other for the entire sixteen and a half hour flight from Newark. In this age of noise cancelling headphones and full privacy first-class cubicles, the conversation void was not a surprise, but at this point in the journey, I am sure he could see in my face that I was on my first flight to India. He smiled broadly and continued, "Don't worry, my friend, it has not rained for a few weeks. After a couple of hours, you will get used to the smell."

"Was he serious", I thought to myself. "Would I have to endure this stench for my entire stay? What in the world could cause the entire atmosphere around Delhi to smell like a rotten combination of smoke, raw sewage and stinking garbage?" I could feel my stomach turning in knots as the rancid smell intensified. As the wheels touched down, I could taste the thickness of the smell and felt completely nauseous.

Lines from the 80s movie 'Throw Momma from the Train' flashed through my mind for some reason, bringing a wry smile to my face. I could hear Billy Crystal, who played the character of Larry Donner mutter to himself, "The night was hot, wait no, the night, the night was humid. The night was humid, no wait, hot, hot. The night was hot. The night was wet and hot, hot and wet, wet and hot; that's humid. The night was humid." In my case, it was more like, "The night was smoky, wait no, the night, the night was smelly. The night was smoky and smelly, smelly, and smoky, that's just disgusting. The night was disgusting." Amused by this, I laughed quietly as we continued to taxi down the runway towards the terminal.

Smoggy air had somehow taken over the cabin in only a matter of seconds, causing my eyes to water violently, as if a cloud of cedar pollen had flown directly into my face. My nose began to run as well, another sign that my America-accustomed body was throwing out every defense available to guard against this airborne assault of the senses.

Squinting through the slits that were normal eyes just minutes earlier, I made my way across the aisle to where my luggage was stored. Having been warned about the perils of checked baggage loss or delay in India, I had checked my large bag and I carried on a small hang-up bag and my computer briefcase. I retrieved them from the overhead compartment and started towards the great unknown that was India.

In the jet way, a well-worn tube that allowed passage from the United 777 plane into the airport, over twenty Indian workers lined each side of our path, their clothes dirty and tattered, some wreaking of body odor in the forty plus degrees Celsius temperature inside the enclosed space. Their curious eyes studied every move we made, looking the world travelers up and down, while being very careful not to make actual eye contact. To me, this seemed to be a residual effect of an outdated and prejudicial caste system that I generally understood but that, to this very day, still makes me extremely uncomfortable.

I have always believed that all people are created equal, but the walk down that jet way proved definitively that while this statement may be accurate, the opportunities afforded to people are quite the opposite of equal. This realization would receive further confirmation as my first trip to India continued. My excited curiosity was being replaced by a welling up of profound sadness, as I continued to make my way down the long concourse towards the required Customs Service pass-port checking station.

As we entered the massive airport complex through the arrival gate doors, the foul smell that we had experienced on the plane and in the jetway was replaced by a pleasant combination of floral incense. I deeply breathed in the fragrant conditioned air, thankful for the immediate relief to both my nose and stomach.

Triskal, Umbria, and Maritius were hovering high above runway 4B, as they watched the Boeing 777 touch down with their reports on board. Their powerful, glowing wings fluttered in perfect synchronization as the plane's rear wheels bounced gently on the tarmac just once, creating puffs of white smoke as the plane settled into the landing and allowing the front wheels to gently make contact with the runway.

They had been given a great responsibility by the Heavenly Father, and all three of these mighty members of the heavenly host were eager to protect the three souls on board that would make an indelible imprint on the world, and India in particular.

They watched the plane taxi past two of the airport personnel that were using flashlights to signal the pilot to move towards the designated jetway on the west wing of the international terminal. Once the huge jet was parked safely, the three glided gently over the plane and through the walls of the airport, materializing in human form without being noticed, before joining the large crowd that had just deplaned from another flight at the gate immediately adjacent to gate 47 where these three Godly men would soon be exiting. They watched as the passengers from flight 600 started to deplane. After only a few minutes they saw Trevor, Andrew, and Harold exit the jetway. They passed the ticket counter, stopped for a moment to secure their belongings, and then continued unknowingly past the angel's position, heading towards the baggage claim area.

Although the three men appeared exhausted and a bit disheveled, the Angels were thrilled to see them in person and glad to oversee their protection from the evil that they knew was waiting for them.

The angels, now looking exactly like any normal passenger coming off the flight, with the exception of having no hand baggage with them, followed Trevor, Andrew, and Harold through the long corridor that led to the immigration check-point. Immediately before reaching the line, Triskal, Umbria, and Maritius stepped behind a large advertising billboard for Skoda automobiles, giving them plenty of coverage so that they could revert to spirit form. They floated back through the hallway and over the immigration agent's booths, through the 'Duty Free' shopping area until they reached the large Baggage Claim area. From their position high above the belt that had been assigned to the flight from Newark, they waited until the three men had cleared immigration, gathered their large suit-cases, and made it safely through the customs line.

In the opposite corner of the large room, Triskal saw a flash of glowing orange light. They had arrived. Malik and Harut flew a direct pattern towards Trevor, Andrew, and Harold. In the language reserved for the angels, Triskal gave Umbria and Maritius the command to defend.

Instantly, Triskal, Umbria, and Maritius screamed across the room, bright white fire from their wings leaving a mini jet stream in their wake. Malik and Harut, broad swords in hand screeched to a halt before flying directly into the wall of three angels that now separated them from their prey.

Malik, with his yellowish eyes glowing with anger, almost hissed with pleasure. Other than the color of his eyes, his overall appearance was not much different than any of the angels now standing directly in front of him. "Triskal, what a pleasant sur-prise." The sarcasm was dripping from his demonic tongue. "Someone must be praying for these three." The demons were almost indistinguishable from the angels in appearance. Their bodies draped in regal attire and brandishing swords as an arrogant display of power only, knowing full well that swords were useless against those of the heavenly host. The more powerful the demon, the larger and more adorned the sword, a gaudy display of vanity more than a trusted weapon. These were the fallen, now working to create division, confusion, hatred, selfishness, deception, covetousness, and distrust on Earth in a concerted attempt to encourage evil. Their ultimate goal was to earn the souls of those that could be tempted and persuaded to play out their desires on Earth, souls that would choose to turn their back on the Creator.

"Away with all of you, Malik! You have no dominion over those that are God's chosen," Triskal spoke with confidence and obvious power beyond these two impish fools.

"No worries, my good friend. Only time will tell how we will defeat you here. Just wanted to assess our competition. That is all. Remember, power comes from prayer, right Triskal? This is what we have been told before by your heavenly host associates. Over and over. Well, you aren't in Kansas anymore, Triskal. You might find a little less prayer power in this part of the world."

Without hesitation, and without the need for verbal communication, Umbria and Maritius swung their mighty swords, flinging the swords of Malik and Harut through the walls of the building in an arc of smoke and fire only visible to spirit eyes.

"Do not forget your place, Malik." Triskal continued, his powerful voice making Harut quiver in fear. "Your interference in God's plan is merely an illusion of the deceiver. God's will is perfect and will be done."

A large gash in the space around Harut and Malik suddenly opened up like a zipper. In a rush of wind and steam, a massive evil spirit soared out of pure blackness into the room. His immense size dwarfed the other two demons. In his large, powerful, hands he held the two swords that had been flung outside of the building. "Please forgive us, our lord!" Malik bowed sheepishly, waiting for a blow that never came.

Baal Azazel did not address his two minions, but instead focused his attention on Triskal. The handle of his sword was a gross display of precious stones inlayed in thick gold. He pointed the blade in Triskal's direction as he shouted, "I should have known to expect you! You will not be able to contain the evil that is in store for your precious chosen ones."

Azazel swung around and grabbed both Harut and Malik by their comparably tiny necks and flung them headlong across the room. He turned back and threw both swords into the abyss that he had created as an entrance to this world. "These two won't be needing swords again," he smiled with a menacing grin. A guttural growl came from deep in his throat as he watched the swords slowly disappear.

He looked back at Triskal for a moment, his reddish black eyes glowing wildly and then rose with his now burning sword still pointing directly at Triskal before disappearing back into the blackness from where he had come. The hole in space disappeared as quickly as it had opened.

Triskal bowed his head in a short prayer for the people that they would need to protect from these powerful demonic entities. Umbria and Maritius joined him in this solemn act of submission, each of them knowing that the days ahead would be challenging, and that the Heavenly Father's wisdom and power would be absolutely necessary in order to protect the chosen. God's will would be done, as always, but sometimes the acts of the wicked made for a messier path than they would prefer.

Triskal opened his eyes and grabbed the hands of the two mighty members of the Heavenly Host standing before him. "Brothers, the victory has already been won for many of those that believe. The overwhelming prayer support for this special event continues to give us great power over darkness." Triskal's confidence indicated that he was clearly unphased by the entrance and antics of Azazel. "But we have tremendous work to do to bring those that are lost to a meaningful relationship with our Lord and Savior, Jesus Christ. These are the very souls that we have been sent to protect. We have been given the distinct privilege of introducing the word of God, so that they may also be given eternal life with Him in Heaven. The evil one continues to infect this world with complacency, distrust, jealousy, dissatisfaction, covetousness, animosity, anger, and bitterness. God has trusted all of us with this great responsibility to fight in this battle for His children. We must complete the race that lies before us. Lives will be changed, and the world will know the power of the one true God."

4

The airport in Delhi was state of the art, a flashy, modern, artistically crafted international flight hub with polished steel ceiling tiles, ornate white marble columns and creative Indian artwork everywhere we turned. I am not sure what I had expected, but the facilities at the airport certainly exceeded these expectations dramatically.

The immigration line was a complete jumble of humanity. Although many Indians might argue that they set the standard for organization, the complete lack of planning and direction with respect to managing this queue led to a seventy two minute snail walk through visibly haphazard rope lines that ended at one of the four immigration counters manned by an officer that was obviously in no real hurry to move the line along. "What is your Nationality." American. "What brings you to India." Work. "What type of Work?" An organization called 'Global Calling.' "Where will you be staying in Delhi?" At the Radisson Blu Hotel, Noida. "Who will be hosting you in India?"

The grand Indian inquisition would continue for at least five to six more minutes until I was finally allowed to pass. Looking back at the hundreds of people that had now joined the queue, I found myself surprisingly grateful that it only took us a little more than one hour.

I waited patiently for Harry and Trevor to finish their interrogation from their assigned immigration officer. After another ten minutes, the three American amigos had been reunited and headed toward the airport's main annex.

Strategically, not unlike many International Airports, whether U.S. or not, all passengers were forced to pass through the gargantuan 'Duty Free' area that covered one third of the International Arrivals Terminal. One after the other, I was accosted by salespeople trying to sell me something, in a very abrupt and forcible manner, before I could reach the safe zone of Baggage Claim, spraying me with the latest cologne, physically placing candies in my hand, forcing me to feel the fabric of a sari, asking me to try on a new Fossil watch. The short walk seemed like an eternity. As I stepped beyond the threshold that separated Duty Free from Baggage Claim, I glanced back to see the wake of Indian salespeople that I left behind quickly falling back into place, lying in wait for the next worthy target.

The three of us made our way to baggage claim carousel H, grabbed our luggage, which had arrived with no issue, and headed to the exit doors that were marked 'Green Lane – Nothing to Declare.' I handed my exit ticket to the armed guard protecting any unauthorized exit and walked through the sliding glass door into what can only be described as a mob scene of mass proportions. Drivers with crude signs lined the entire walkway that led to the parking lot. Indian residents that were waiting for family members were stacked ten to fifteen deep behind the drivers and a steel barrier separated the drivers from the exiting travelers. As I walked into the oppressive heat of the Delhi night, and keeping in mind that we had arrived at close to midnight and there are still thousands of people in congregation outside the airport, the rancid smell slapped me across the face once again. "Wow!" I had never been in a position where the smog conditions were so bad as to make it very difficult to catch a breath.

After over ten minutes of searching for our hand scribbled names on one of the thousands of dirty, worn-out placards, I noticed a sign that might possibly be designed for us, our names roughly drawn in black Sharpie ink on a small whiteboard and creatively spelled in a way that caused what I thought were very typical last names to appear more Russian or Greek. As I approached the very diminutive middle-aged man, he started chanting our names as only he could pronounce them. It was obvious that he was the artist behind the sign creation.

I spoke my name as I would typically say it and the man nodded vigorously, pointing to the name on the sign. "Oh, yes…. oh, yes…. pleased to be driving you, sir. Oh, yes…. oh, yes…. please come…. please come…." Three other, small, very unkempt young protégés of the leader started to grab for my bags. I politely said, "No, thank you." This was not my way of being nice. This was an attempt to keep the filthy outstretched hands off my bags. The dirty hands closest to my bag were attached to filthy arms that were only partially covered by a wrinkled, tattered, and soiled button down shirt that was at least two sizes too small. The smell of intense body odor filled my sinuses as the small man moved closer. My senses were overloaded! The sights, the smells, the sounds of car horns beeping like a massive horn symphony. I had the overwhelming urge to flee back into the airport and wait for the next flight back to the United States.

The leader, who evidently would be my assigned driver for the week, coaxed me into following him towards the parking lot across from the airport exit. I use the words "parking lot" here very loosely. It was like nothing I had ever seen before. They had created an Indian taxicab version of car Tetris. As drivers would arrive at their cars with their precious new passenger cargo, cars would zig and zag, moving left, then right, forward, then backward, until passage was given to the car that was ready to leave the airport. Miraculously, this process that looked completely impossible and in complete disarray to an observer from a first world country actually worked fairly well, delaying us for only five or six more minutes before we were loaded and ready to head for the hotel. Remarkably, there seemed to be a crude organizational process and coordination strategy that was somehow understood by the competing drivers.

The door to the Suzuki Maruti was opened for me and, even with my consistent persistence regarding the "no touch policy" for my baggage, grimy hands had found their way to the handles and the bags were being loaded in the back. Almost immediately, the sweaty, filthy hands were back in front of me outside of the open Maruti door. Fortunately, I caught myself being a spoiled and judgmental American. Who did I think I was? These people, far less privileged than the three of us, were bending over backwards to try and provide five star service. Anger at myself welled up inside of me as I grabbed my wallet and gave the young man an American five dollar bill, having had no opportunity to exchange dollars for Rupees in the airport, which had been my naïve plan from the start. He backed slowly away bowing at every step with hands pressed together in front of his chest in the typical 'Namaste' position, the bill wedged in between his palms.

Looking back over my headrest from my front passenger seat vantage point towards the captain's chairs that made up the second row of our car, I could see the same sense of self-realization on the faces of both Trevor and Hayward.

"Wow," I said with genuine amazement.

Hayward and Trevor both answered the non-question in unison, "Wow."

Our driver got into the right driver side seat and turned to look in our direction. "Pleased to be driving you today evening, sirs. I am Suresh Singh. Please to be knowing that there is water in back." Although his accent was thick, he spoke slowly enough to be easily understood. Quite possibly, he had received valuable instruction on the benefits of speaking slowly when driving around foreign passengers.

"Thank you, Suresh," Harold said as he reached over the back of the seat to grab a bottled water. "How long until we get to the hotel?"

"I am saying forty minutes, sirs. Traffic is heavy at this hour of night." Suresh started the car and headed towards the main gate that served as the gateway of entry and exit for the hundreds of drivers that were taxed with picking up their respective assignments.

As we exited the airport grounds through the maze of eight to ten foot tall concrete barricades, I caught sight of the broken down slums that outlined the entire property, a make-shift camp of lean-tos and crude huts, housing the very poorest of India. My heart sank as the abject poverty overwhelmed us on all sides of the car. Pigs on one side of the road were foraging for food atop a heap of trash that must have been waist deep on the bank of a putrid smelling waterway that dissected this particular slum. Trash covered the water's surface to such an extent that, in the moonlight, it was difficult to make out where the bank ended, and the stream began.

As we entered the main thoroughfare that would take us across Delhi towards Noida, we joined the bumper to bumper traffic that I would find to be the norm during all my travels in Delhi. We darted in and out of tight spaces, like a vehicular game of Frogger, our driver working to make any progress possible when the opportunity presented itself. Evidently, in India, traffic lanes are merely a suggestion, not a requirement. As I looked to my left and right as we sat in the middle of a three lane highway, I counted four sedans, our SUV, one motorcycle, and a huge Hata truck that sat side by side in these three lanes. Less than nine inches separated us from any vehicle in front, back or to the side. Not only was I sweating due to the lack of air conditioning in this moveable oven called a Maruti, but because of the sheer nervousness that comes with your first driving experience in India.

After an hour and twenty minutes, we turned onto the "Noida Flyway," where the traffic was much less congested, but where the stench of smoke, sewage and trash became almost unbearable. I asked my driver what the cause of this horrible smell might be. "The river, my friend. Very bad. In hot season, much too bad," came the response that I had expected, a little difficult to understand due to his thick Hindi accented and broken English. That might have been the understatement of the trip thus far. I had to focus my energy on not having to vomit. I sat in disbelief, staring out into the darkness over a nondescript field to my left that separated us from our hotel in Noida, a building that our driver kindly pointed out as we reached the top of the bridge.

The kindness of our driver (and all drivers that I would have the pleasure of meeting during my many trips in India) was both heartwarming and completely genuine. I guess that our faces showed a tremendous amount of anxiety and concern, as he began to suggest places that we "must visit" while in India. His proud and beautiful descriptions of the Red Fort, India Gate, the Taj Mahal, Connaught Place, along with various temples throughout his country instilled in me a hope that beyond the poverty and disarray that had, for the last several hours, tainted my arrival in India, a beauty would emerge that might be mesmerizing if not overwhelming. Many of our friends and fellow Global Calling leaders gushed of their wonderful experiences in this country, and yet I was feeling lost in a foreign landscape filled with poverty, filth and the complete unknown.

My ears were ringing as we reached the front gate that allowed entry to the Radisson Blu's drive through entrance. Fortunately, the cacophony of horns was now replaced by the hum of the Suzuki motor and light Indian music inside our vehicle, as two armed gentlemen carefully inspected the Maruti. A rolling mirror was used to look under the car for explosives. The trunk was opened, and our bags were visually inspected. The driver popped the hood for a closer look at the engine compartment. Once the thorough vehicle check was complete, the large steel gate was swung open and we were directed to drive to the front entrance. With so many terrorist attacks throughout the world, including India, with the Oberoi Trident and Taj Mahal Palace hotel attacks in September of 2008, the extra security measures were a welcome site for this American.

The beautiful entry doors had been fashioned into a TSA looking metal detector, baggage scanning station. As my luggage was loaded onto the belt by the bellman, a Sikh gentleman clothed in traditional Indian garb used a wand to check for any metal in my pockets and then patted me down gently until he came across my wallet. He asked me politely to remove the wallet and hand it to him for inspection. After he was satisfied with its contents, and trust me, he looked at everything in the wallet, he handed it back to me, bowed slightly with hands pressed together in front of his chest, and gestured towards the lobby through the front door.

Before I made it to the front desk, I was greeted by a well-dressed young man with a grand smile. "Welcome, Mr. Morrison. It will be a pleasure to have you here at the Radisson Blu Noida Hotel. I am Santosh and I will accompany you to your room. We will be needing your business card and your passport."

"Don't I need to check in first?" I asked.

"No, it is my pleasure to check you in when we get to the room." Santosh was already walking towards the bank of elevators.

Having traveled all over the world, this was a first for me. As we walked towards what Santosh referred to as the 'lift'

(Elevator for us Americans – the British influence was obviously still alive and well in India), a sweet and strong floral scent was a pleasant change from the acrid smoky air outside the hotel. In most cases, I don't think that I would have been so tuned into the smell of a hotel lobby, but the smells of India, both good and bad, constantly remind you of how powerful the sense of smell can truly be.

The hotel was very well appointed with flowers adorning every nook and cranny. The restaurants that flanked the lobby would fit well within any upscale American hotel. It was as if I had found an oasis in the desert. For the first time since arriving in this country, as my heartrate began to slow, I consciously drew in a healthy breath and exhaled heavily. "Relax, Andrew," I whispered to myself.

It was close to 1:45am and I was anxiously looking forward to a warm shower and a couple hours in a real bed. As we headed for my room, I waved to Trevor and Harold who were now sitting on a bench in the middle of the lobby next to their luggage. "Still waiting for our personal check-in concierge, Mr. important!" Jaworski's loud taunt echoed throughout the large lobby. "Don't worry about us. We will mind our business here in the lobby while you get some beauty sleep." If nothing else during our travels, we could always count on our often inappropriate but always good-humored comedian.

I shook my head and smiled, "See you guys at nine in the morning for breakfast. Sleep well." Trevor waved back and Harold shrugged his shoulders in the all too familiar, "Whatever," response as I turned toward the bay of elevators.

As we got off the elevator at my floor, a different smell hung in the air. It was the smell of coriander and turmeric, a smell that I would find in most hotels in India over the next several months. Not overwhelming, but unmistakable, usually stronger in the morning than in the evening.

It was now a little after 2:00AM in the morning and I wanted more than anything to find the bed, but Santosh was unwavering in his commitment to following the hotel's formal procedure for guest check-in. He walked me through the room, carefully pointing out everything the room had to offer. I had never received such a thorough tour of a fairly standard hotel room. By Indian standards, this was a four-star hotel. By American standards, I would give it a solid two-star rating. I would equate its look and feel to a clean, yet slightly outdated boutique hotel, similar to many hotels that I have stayed in while visiting New York or San Francisco.

Santosh went as far as teaching me how to use the remote controls, not only for the two televisions in the room but also for the opening and closing of the blinds and shades. He explained that the room key must be inserted into the slot as you enter the room for the electricity to be turned on in the room and provided a demonstration on how this worked. He then provided additional instruction regarding all light switches in the main hallway, the bedroom, the vanity area, shower, and toilet room. Evidently, there was a remote for this as well.

He seemed well versed in the types of soaps and shampoos that were made available to all guests, as well as the type of bottled water on the bedside table, water that was purportedly taken from glaciers in the Himalayas, and according to Santosh, "Without question, the purest water in the world."

He was not only a good concierge for the hotel, but a fantastic representative for all products found in the room. I was made aware of the iron and ironing board location, the presence of a blow dryer in one of the sock drawers under the hanging section of the wardrobe, the location of the vanity kit on the sink counter and the men's grooming kit in the silver jar next to the mirror. The last demonstration that I would be willing to endure this evening involved the programming of the safe, which I was encouraged to use at all times as a precautionary measure for the protection of any valuables, including jewelry and passports, during my stay at the Radisson.

As he moved to the Bidet portion of the tour, I let him know that this particular part of his routine could be passed over. I am simply not the bidet kind of traveler, I guess. I would stick to the toilet paper method of clean up, thank you.

With the twenty minute room tour complete, Santosh pulled a seat out from behind the desk and asked me to have a seat. He asked me to produce my business card and passport (I guess that the passport just doesn't quite cut it when you are confirming identity. A business card would certainly provide the needed assurance, right?)

"Hmmmm. Alright, any chance we can move this along more quickly?" I was starting to feel a bit edgy. I simply wanted to fulfill the requirements that would lead to Santosh handing over the keys to the room. I stood up and stretched before walking to the shower to turn it on as a sign that it was time to end the tour.

Cluing into my obvious desire to be left alone in the room, Santosh closed his binder, having gained the required signatures next to the room rate and dates of the stay, handed me the remaining keys and thanked me for my time. Grateful that we had come to the end, and without the opportunity to exchange dollars for rupees, I tipped him twenty U.S. dollars and showed him to the door. "Thank you, Santosh."

"Thank you, sir. Enjoy your stay, and please call if you need anything additional." With that, I closed the door and headed back to the bedroom. Sensory overload had subsided, and my eyes began to gain a jetlagged heaviness. I opted to skip the shower and walked into the bathroom and turned it off. I quickly discarded my clothes in a heap on the floor next to my luggage and sat down on the king size bed. I grabbed the Indian travel adapter plug out of my laptop bag, plugged in my iPhone, turned on the sound soother and set the alarm for 8:00AM. With the remote control that Santosh had pointed out during the guided tour of my room, I closed every shade until the room was completely dark, except for the dim blue night light on the floor in the bathroom. I pulled back the blankets and slid into the firm, yet comfortable bed, and flicked off the lights with the separate remote control unit, as instructed by Rajiv before quickly drifting off to sleep.

5

After a huge breakfast of Masala Dosa, which would become a morning staple for me during my time in India, fried eggs, toast with jam, and miso soup, a surprising but delicious breakfast staple in many Indian hotels that I believe is included due to the number of Chinese travelers to the hotel, we made our way to the lobby where the three of us would meet our driver.

Suresh greeted us as we approached the front lobby doors, "Pleased to be seeing you, sirs. Your car awaits." In Hindi, he instructed one of the hotel bellmen to grab our luggage and place it in the back of the same Suzuki Maruti that we had used the night before. In typical American fashion, the three of us resisted help with our luggage, but this was deemed completely unacceptable to our new Indian service providers. They would have none of it.

After the three of us, along with our luggage, were fully loaded and buckled in, we set out to meet with Rajiv Bansal, the charismatic leader of the Global Calling, India Division.

Although his primary personal residence was in Mumbai, he had called a meeting of all regional leaders to Agra for a chance to welcome us to their country. The Agra regional office was only ten minutes from the historic Taj Mahal and had a conference room that could comfortably accommodate the twenty four individuals that would be attending the meeting.

Our agenda for the day would start with a three hour drive straight to the Maharashtra Restaurant, only a five minute walk from the iconic Taj, where we would have a light buffet lunch and a short tour of the majestic, ivory-white, marble mausoleum that had been built by Mughal emperor Shah Jahan to house the remains of his wife, Mumtaz Mahal in the mid-1600s. At 2:00 p.m., we would meet at the office with the ministers and leaders from all over India, Pakistan, Nepal, and Sri Lanka. After the meeting, which was scheduled to end by 7:00 p.m., we would be dropped off at the airport in Agra for our 9:15 p.m. flight to Goa.

The lunch consisted of lentils and Naan bread, with Tandoori Chicken and Lamb. We ate quickly, due to our cramped schedule and then made our way across the stunningly crowded street towards the promise of this awe-inspiring monument. Although the air quality had obviously stained the white marble to a noticeable extent, the size and beauty was substantial, yet not overwhelming. According to our well informed, and uncharacteristically well-spoken tour guide, over twenty thousand workers and over one thousand elephants were brought in to construct the two hundred forty foot tall mausoleum. The tallest, main dome chamber was flanked by four smaller domes or minarets. In accordance with Islamic tradition, verses from the Quran were inscribed in calligraphy on the arched entrances to the mausoleum in addition to numerous other sections of the complex.

The mausoleum housed an octagonal marble chamber adorned with ornate carvings and semi-precious stones. This chamber was described as the cenotaph, otherwise known as the false tomb, of Mumtaz Mahal. The actual sarcophagus containing her remains was evidently below this room, at the garden level.

The rest of the Taj Mahal property included a main gateway of red sandstone and a square garden which was divided into quarters by long pools of water, as well as a red sandstone mosque and an identical building called a jawab, which Rajiv translated as meaning reflection or answer, directly across from the mosque.

Although the history was mesmerizing and the beauty was unmistakable, the actual structure was somewhat underwhelming. Like so many monuments that I had built up in my mind through the years, this one did not live up to my expectations. It reminded me of my first visit to the Alamo in San Antonio as a teenager. I had expected to see a mighty fortress but was met with a tiny fort. That said, I was extremely pleased to have been given the opportunity to visit this historical place.

We made the short drive to the office where we were greeted outside of the building, in the small courtyard, by half a dozen of our colleagues that had been informed of our impending arrival. Although we had never met any of these people in person, the warm embraces and genuine smiles of excitement made the initial introductions very comfortable.

"Good afternoon, gentlemen." Rajiv's warm and rich voice greeted us as he walked out of the glass double doors that led to the office reception area. "Welcome to India."

"Hello, Rajiv," Harold was nearest Rajiv and shook his hand vigorously.

I accepted Rajiv's next handshake and greeted him as well. "Great to see you in person, Rajiv. What a beautiful city! Glad to be here."

We were escorted through the marble and glass entryway into an exquisite reception area. The marble was a rich ivory color with specks of black onyx and crystal that, because of the amount of sunlight that flooded through the ceiling height windows, created a brilliant shimmer effect.

The receptionist, named Vyanjana, as her nametag pointed out, placed her palms together in Namaste position, bowed gracefully and offered to show us to the reserved meeting room. In single file, we followed her through the double doors behind the desk down a long corridor that was flanked by small offices and meeting rooms, until we reached the large executive style conference room.

After choosing our seats around the rich mahogany table, two Chaiwallahs dressed in all white took our orders for tea and coffee. This traditional custom in India, although unexpected and a tad bit uncomfortable for new visitors to India, turns out to be a very nice and convenient office perk. Rajiv would explain later that this provides great pride and a very livable wage for many underprivileged inhabitants of the area.

"Gentlemen, welcome," Rajiv greeted everyone in the room with a warm and infectious smile. He turned on his laptop and the overhead projector as he continued, "We are quite thrilled to have such an amazing team joining us here in Agra. So much exciting news to convey to the group. So much yet to be planned. God has truly blessed all of us gathered here today and has now provided us with the great opportunity and responsibility to share this blessing with all of India and the rest of the world."

"The progress, year to date, has been unprecedented and far beyond our wildest imagination. We continue to penetrate more and more of the major cities in India and are reaching the hearts and souls of many people that are hungry for the promise of a personal relationship with God." Rajiv turned to the next page in his notes. "It was Canon Holmes of India, almost a century ago now, that called attention to the 'inferential character of the average man's faith in God.' God is simply a deduction from evidence that people are satisfied with, but with respect to the opportunity for personal relationship, this is usually not contemplated, or believed to be somehow out of reach. Many people see God as just an ideal, possibly another name for goodness, peace, beauty, or truth. Or maybe, they view him as law, or life or creative impulse that is simply part of our existence. Tozer outlined this beautifully in his work called 'The Pursuit of God.' I believe that these truths are still relevant today." Rajiv paused and took a sip of water. "Although there are many visions of 'What God is', the question 'Who God is' is often lost or never even contemplated. While many would acknowledge the existence of God, they simply don't think of Him as knowable."

"But today, I stand here humbled before you at the powerful work being done here in India. Because of God's will that all might hear His Word and see him for who He is and what He is, and because of the important work being done by every one of you, along with everyone that has joined us in this ministry, we have seen countless thousands come to develop a personal relationship with Jesus Christ, a personal connection with God. In fact, many of them have taken on evangelistic roles in their community to further God's message to all people that are able and willing to hear the Word of God. We have started over two hundred and thirty churches all over India. Over six hundred and fifty have joined the Global Calling Ministry team in the last eighteen months. God is truly amazing!" Many in the crowd yelled out 'amens' and 'praise the Lords' in an offer of affirmation.

Rajiv looked down at his notes and continued, "Goa has been our most recently targeted geographic area and we have seen an amazing response to the ministry in this region. For that reason, we will be sending these outstanding leaders, Harold, Trevor, and Andrew to the regional office in Goa to help us continue our strategy development that will not only impact India, but the entire world."

Rajiv paused and looked around the room at the amazing team that was gathered. "Our mission here in India is clear. We must continue to spread the message, God's word, the good news of our Lord and Savior and his love for all people. It is a message that deserves to be heard by all that live here. It is a message that has been shared with many, but many still have not had the benefit of hearing the amazing promises of grace, hope, love, redemption, forgiveness, and everlasting life that only comes from God. What an amazing, and quite possibly at times, a daunting responsibility. I stand with all of you, ready and eager for this challenge."

The entire group stood and cheered in a clear show of mutual commitment to this global calling before Rajiv continued to lay out the strategy for the coming year.

The Recruitment

He cast on them the fierceness of His anger, wrath, indignation, and trouble, by sending angels of destruction among them.

- PSALM 78: 49 (NEW KING JAMES VERSION)

All the difference between men and angels is, men are passing through the day of trial that angels have already passed through.

- BRIGHAM YOUNG, *JOURNAL OF DISCOURSES*

"And thus I clothe my naked villainy
With odd old ends stol'n out of holy writ;
And seem a saint, when most I play the devil."

- WILLIAM SHAKESPEARE, *RICHARD III*

6

MUMBAI, INDIA
8:37 A.M.
FEBRUARY 20, 2022

Rahul Prasanna crouched behind a stack of old tires next to a condemned and abandoned apartment building as he watched his target cross the street towards his place of work, the Kingsford Garden Stadium in the Andheri section of Mumbai. Rahul knew this neighborhood like the back of his hand. He had lived with his grandmother only a few blocks away from the time he started primary school as a five-year-old, until he graduated from secondary school, the equivalent of American high school, at the age of seventeen.

Rahul was a model child until he reached the age of fifteen. On the poor end of the economic spectrum, food was scarce and clothing even scarcer. But Rahul was clever and could run like lightning. His move to the dark side of adolescence started slowly. He might steal a piece of fruit from a street cart while the vendor was setting up and not paying careful enough attention. He might snatch a bag of chips or nuts hanging from a clip in a storefront window and sprint across the street, disappearing in mere seconds into one of the slum's complicated and tiny alleyways. The game of theft gained more and more momentum over approximately two years, until he made the mistake of biting off more than he could chew.

On a chilly December morning two years ago, he had set his sights on the biggest theft yet. Rahul had been working out regularly with a group of boys from the neighborhood, gaining significant upper body strength and a ton of additional confidence. He planned to grab a 50" Toshiba television that was displayed daily on a small table outside of Aggrawal's Audio and Video superstore. The use of 'superstore' was questionable at best, since the entire store was confined to no more than two hundred square feet of the Adwhari mini-mall's bottom floor.

Rahul had carefully planned his grab and go escape route, choosing to grab the television on the run and take the first right around the side of the building that headed in the direction of his grandmothers small, one bedroom flat. He would need to run less than a quarter of a mile to get to the safety of her place. He would make sure that he chose the timing of the heist to coincide with her daily ritual of walking to the temple for morning prayers, which usually took approximately an hour and a half.

He had dreamed of owning his own television for years, having always been forced to stand outside of a market or café to watch the screen, without actually hearing the sound. Often, he would stealthily move from window to window, straining to see inside the houses of more fortunate slum dwellers to catch bits and pieces of a cricket match or Bollywood movie. It just wasn't fair, and Aggrawal could certainly survive without one of his precious television sets.

He had rehearsed the explanation that he would give to his grandmother over and over again in front of the one mirror in the house. "Dadima, I got you a present. I have been saving my money for many months from collecting the old electronics and selling them to Mr. Jagesh at the flea market. I finally had enough to get a TV. Aren't you proud, Dadima?" He would tweak the message each time he went over it, but the core stayed the same. She simply could not find out that it was stolen.

The time had come. After his grandmother left for the temple, Rahul sprinted towards Aggrawal's amazing promise of connectivity to the world. He arrived at the small outdoor shopping center and pretended to browse through merchandise at a couple of the small clothing shops that were adjacent to Aggrawal's Audio and Video store. After being shooed off by two of the merchants that knew full well that Rahul had no real interest in purchasing their merchandise, he exited the mall area and squatted down in one of the small alleyways on the side of the building, behind a row of Vetiver grass. The grass hedge, the only greenery on the property, was planted next to a small parking lot that was only able to fit a handful of small cars or motorbikes.

Rahul watched as the successful businessman, Mr. Manoj Aggrawal, carefully placed items outside of his store as a ploy to grab the attention of the passersby on the street in front of the mini mall. There was a mobile phone display that held the latest Apple and Samsung units, a wireless headphones poster advertising the latest in noise cancelling quality, and a couple of laptop computers that were opened and flashing bright screensaver pictures. Then, out it came in the arms of

Mr. Aggrawal – the magnificent object of Rahul's affection, the Samsung 50″ 4K high-definition smart television.

Rahul's pulse quickened as he watched the shop owner carefully take the TV out of its' packing material. After plugging it in, the screen came to life with the huge Samsung logo screaming high quality definition to the world that might be watching. The typical Netflix, Hulu, Amazon, Apple, and other various widgets popped up on what looked like an MSNBC stock ticker ribbon located at the very bottom of the screen.

He checked his cheap, but relatively fashionable, purple Swatch watch for the time. He had already been away from the house for over forty two minutes. Why did it take so long for Mr. Aggrawal to get the television turned on? He had been working on it for over five minutes and from Rahul's vantage point, the TV seemed to be fully operational, but the logo was still plastered across the center of the screen. In a matter of seconds, CNN of India took over where the Samsung logo had been, and a world market stock ticker took the place of the band of widgets. The mostly green stock prices that scrolled from right to left indicated that the Mumbai exchange expected a strong open for the day.

"Whew! We might still have time," Rahul nervously patted his thighs. He had come this far. He would remain still and wait for the right opportunity. Aggrawal moved to the front of the TV, watched the CNN 'Opening Bell' report for a couple of minutes, and then headed back into the store.

This was it. It was time to move. Rahul leaped over the Vetiver grass and sprinted towards the shop. He slowed just enough to get both hands firmly under the display and continued towards his escape path. The TV moved only a couple of feet before the power cord attached to the wall held tight. His sweaty hands slipped off the television and his feet flew out in front of him, causing him to land flat on his back, knocking the breath out of him. His head slammed against the concrete pavement, causing the world to go foggy for a minute or two. The sound of glass shattering behind him was the last thing Rahul heard before his world went black.

Mr. Aggrawal was standing over him when he woke up, with a combined look of both puzzlement and anger painted on his usually friendly face. One of the ladies from the booth next door stepped around Mr. Aggrawal and started asking what had happened.

"This boy is a thief," Manoj Aggrawal yelled at the top of his lungs. "A common criminal. He tried to steal this television and has totally destroyed it. I must be calling the police." Manoj went back into the store.

By the time Rahul was able to stand, a police officer, who had obviously been near the scene grabbed Rahul by the wrist and put handcuffs on him. "Sit down, son." The officer was brisk but polite, "A car has been called and we will need to bring you to the station."

Rahul's eyes dropped to the ground. His dreams, along with the TV, had both been shattered. "Yes, sir," Rahul moaned in quiet submission.

Across the street from the mini mall, as the attempted heist took place, a shadowy and well-known figure in the neighborhood had watched the situation unfold. Aakesh Sharma was more thug than anything else, having spent time as a drug dealer, gang enforcer, and thief himself. He seemed to always find more than his fair share of trouble and was connected to some of the worst criminals in Mumbai. Aakesh was a typical slum kid with a Hindu mother and Muslim father, raised in arguably one of the toughest and poorest slums in Mumbai. He had developed a keen interest in radical Islam by the age of fifteen and had a pronounced hatred for the West. His father had been killed in some form of slum violence when he was only six years old, and although his mother refused to discuss what happened, it had been obvious to Aakesh that the authorities had no interest in their situation or finding whoever was responsible for his father's death. His hatred for public officials, politicians, Christians, Jews, and anyone in law enforcement continued to grow as he got older. He characterized all these groups as 'the sworn enemy.'

While spending two years in jail for armed robbery, Aakesh had cultivated a relationship with his cell mate, Fahad Omar, who was serving four years in jail for involuntary manslaughter of an American college student that had been studying abroad in India. Fahad was heavily involved with an organization based in the northernmost part of the Punjab province that was focused on the eradication of Judaism and Christianity. They were becoming well known throughout India and abroad as IBAWIF, the Islamic Brotherhood Against Western Infidel Factions. They tended to target the poor, especially if there was a Muslim connection, and their numbers were growing at an alarming pace. In the first three months of the year, IBAWIF had taken responsibility for thirteen brutal attacks, accounting for over two hundred and forty deaths. Aakesh was easily brainwashed by Fahad over the two year period of incarceration, quickly becoming a disciple of Omar, vowing to join the cause immediately upon his release. Fahad promised power and riches beyond Aakesh's imagination, preying on Aakesh's obvious covetousness of the 'Richey Richies' outside the boundaries of the Indian slums.

As promised in the prison cell, Aakesh was contacted by one of Fahad Omar's proteges the day after his release. He was given a train ticket to Roorkee and instructions on where a team would be meeting him for transportation to the camp. Because of his relationship with Fahad Omar, and his obvious commitment to the cause, Aakesh was not required to go through the typical arduous and inhumane induction program, but instead was given special communication and management training before being quickly thrust into the critically important position of key personnel recruiter based back in Mumbai.

His first recruit would be Rahul, the now semi famous Aggarwal Electronics thief and one of the kids from his neighborhood with just the right profile and a shared motivation. Beyond the games of cricket in the park and Kabaddi in the street outside of the slum, Aakesh had spent many nights with Rahul sitting together on a rock outcropping that overlooked runway four of the Chhatrapati Shivaji Maharaj International Airport discussing the greed, immorality, hubris, and evil of the West.

After watching Rahul's failed attempt at stealing Mr. Aggrawal's big screen television, Aakesh had disappeared into the maze of the slum, planning to visit with Rahul in the morning after the dust had settled. He knew that this failed attempt would do nothing more than send Rahul back to his mother's house with the firm, but hollow warning from law enforcement that 'if it happened again, he would be hauled off to the judge and most likely would spend time in jail.'

As Aakesh had expected, Rahul had turned out to be a perfect target and accepted the invitation readily, having always wanted to find a way to become more powerful, and even more importantly, to find a way out of the Mumbai slums for good. Aakesh had given him a train ticket, one hundred rupees for food and drink and instructions for his pick-up at the train station outside of Roorkee, India. Rahul would spend the next six months in intense paramilitary training and terrorist tactical management.

Today, months after the completion of that training, Rahul was now the recruiter. Today would be no different than any of the other days when he was surveilling a potential recruit. Once again, this would not be the best day to approach his target, Sanjay Swaminathan. In keeping with what Rahul had observed in his last four attempts, Sanjay could be seen walking down the sidewalk adjacent to the stadium with the same group of young men that shared the same employer.

Rahul needed to find the right opportunity to bump into his old friend when he was alone. Otherwise, he could not provide an effective sales pitch. After watching the four Kingsford Stadium employees scan their cards and enter the main gate, Rahul left his hiding spot and headed back towards his moped that was parked about a quarter mile away.

7

MUMBAI, INDIA
8:37 A.M.
MARCH 2, 2022

For many months since completing his own training, Rahul had tried to block out the memories of his horrible treatment under Commander Singha at the Roorkee compound, the beatings, the forced starvation, the solitary confinement, the unbearable heat, the squalor, and the threats. All in all, he had compartmentalized these experiences into an irretrievable file in his brain that was avoided in the same way he tried to ignore nightmares and memories of abuse by his father and grandfather during his childhood.

All of this was in the past. For today, Rahul's orders were clear. He was now the recruiter. He had been sent on a mission to bring someone onboard that worked at the stadium and that could provide details regarding the upcoming 'Christian rally' that was scheduled for June 3, and he was running out of time. He had been given strict parameters. This person must be at the manager level or above at the stadium and must be a male. He would need to start training no later than April 5.

Today was his lucky day. Sanjay was obviously late to work and walking to the stadium alone. Leaving his hiding place behind the discarded steel drums that had once been filled with heating oil, Rahul bolted across the street, zig zagging through a bustling crowd of people that were headed to the stadium entrance, until he reached the sidewalk directly in front of the cricket stadium. He slowed his pace to a comfortable walk to avoid unnecessary attention as he made his way towards Sanjay. He wanted his first interaction to be perceived as a chance meeting. Today had to be the day.

Rahul had spent countless hours playing in the streets with Sanjay. Their small shanty like homes, where each boy lived with a mother, no father, and two siblings were only thirty yards apart. They were aggressive rivals in anything that they did or said. They were the same age and had the same body type-tall, lean, extremely fast, and with great hand-eye coordination. Both were confident and considered very cocky by their peers and most of the adults in the community. Invariably, they were noticeably the two best athletes in whatever sport or game they might be playing.

Once Rahul and Sanjay were about twenty yards apart, Rahul waved his arm and yelled out, "Sanjay.... Sanjay. How are you, old friend?"

"Wow. Rahul? How long has it been? Two...three...four years?" Sanjay gave a wry, contorted, 'my less than favorite old nemesis' grin, as he continued, "What brings you around these parts today? I thought you were in jail."

The words stung Rahul, but he was undeterred. "Ah, just a little misunderstanding. Wrong place, wrong time, buddy.

Actually, I have been back in the neighborhood for a couple of years. You want to grab a coffee at Dunkin? Glad to fill you in."

"Nah…. but thanks. Gotta get to work. Already late today." Sanjay was clearly frustrated and in a hurry. The faster he could get to the time clock, the lesser the scolding from his boss, Hetal Patel.

"Yeah. I get you. How about after work? My treat." Rahul was not going to back down until a face to face meeting was scheduled.

"Well…alright…maybe around 5:30PM for a quick coffee. Have to be home by 6:30 for dinner."

"Great!" Rahul blurted out. "No, really. That will be fantastic. Look forward to catching up. Can we meet right here at 5:30? We can walk over together." Rahul was thrilled. The setup had been much easier than expected.

"Sure, Rahul. Wow! Good to see you. I have to run but will catch you later." Sanjay shook hands with Rahul and continued toward the employee entrance directly adjacent to the East Gate.

8

"Rahul!" Sanjay yelled from across the street. Sanjay gave a quick wave and started towards his old friend.

"This way." Rahul motioned. "Great to see you."

The walk to the Dunkin Donuts only took a few minutes. Once inside, they both ordered a Masala Chai Tea, paid the clerk, and picked up the two cups at the end of the bar before heading to a table for two in the back of the small seating area.

Rahul sat down first in one of the two folding chairs that faced each other at a table in the very back of the restaurant. No one was within twenty feet of where they were seated, giving Rahul the privacy needed as he pitched his prospective recruit.

"Sanjay, how is your new job with the stadium?" He started slowly, wanting to make sure that his target had been vetted appropriately and would be able to carry out one of the most important tasks of their mission.

"Good, man. I don't know. Pays the bills, I guess." Sanjay shrugged his shoulders. Rahul could sense that Sanjay was either not exactly thrilled with his job, or he was not in the mood for this line of questioning.

"I hear that this big group, the Global Call or something like that, is going to be having a huge show in June at the new stadium. Is that right?" Rahul spoke quickly with a tinge of obvious nervousness. There was no question that Sanjay was his guy. With the event date quickly approaching, he could not afford to let this opportunity slip out of his hands.

"Uh. Yeah. I guess," Sanjay said with another shrug of the shoulders and the characteristic agreeable bobbing of the head. "Big wigs trying to 'save' the country and all that jazz. More like trying to get a lot of money out of Hindus and Muslims, in my opinion."

Rahul raised his eyebrows in giddy schoolboy-like excitement. The fish was definitely interested in the bait on the hook. "Yeah, dude. No doubt. Always trying to take advantage of stupid Indian people, right? We can't be taking this garbage anymore. That is why I'm here." Rahul slid his chair closer to his new recruit's side of the table and whispered the final portion of his sales pitch. "What would you say if I told you that my organization could make you rich and powerful in less than four months, if you join our ranks to fight against these greedy infidels from the West?"

Sanjay measured his friend. "How rich and powerful?" Sanjay was intrigued but skeptical.

"My friend...my good friend..." Rahul thought carefully about his words. The unscripted part of the meeting would prove more difficult than he had first thought. "You would make more Rupees in the next four months than you could possibly make at your job in the next four years. That rich!"

Rahul smiled in his characteristic 'cat got the canary' style that Sanjay recognized from their days together on the playground.

"Ok. You definitely have me thinking." Sanjay sat in silence for a few seconds. "What would I need to do?" He shifted his weight in his chair in an obvious sign of skepticism.

"Simple, my friend. You would need to take a short vacation from work." He broke off his train of thought suddenly and stammered. "You *do* have vacation at your job, right?"

"Yeah," Sanjay answered with a touch of incredulity, "Of course! I have plenty vacation! Supervisors get three weeks a year, bro. Paid." He settled back into his chair.

Rahul continued with a more relaxed cadence. "Good. Good. That is great." He gently tugged on his chin. "How much notice must you provide before taking a two week leave?"

"Two weeks." Sanjay answered matter-of-factly.

Rahul sat in silence as he contemplated Sanjay's answer. Two weeks would allow him to meet the 'start of training' deadline, while getting him back to his job with weeks to spare before the big event. "Fantastic!" The fact that the timing worked out so well would certainly help convince Aakesh that Sanjay was the right man. "You will need to go to a training camp in Roorkee to get prepared. No cost to you, Sanjay. In fact, we will pay you extra on top of your travel expenses." Rahul couldn't help but smile. The hook was now firmly set in his trophy fish.

"How much?" Sanjay asked, the skepticism rearing its ugly head once again.

"How much, what?" Rahul said coyly.

"How much would I be paid for those two weeks?"

Rahul scooted his chair closer to Sanjay, more as a delaying tactic than for additional privacy. He had yet to solidify any additional payment terms with Aakesh or Commander Singha. He would have to bluff his way through this portion of the interview. "Ummm...." Rahul stumbled ahead. "Um, you would be paid twice your current salary for both weeks. We can discuss the particulars a little later."

Two middle aged men approached where Rahul and Sanjay were sitting and took the booth immediately adjacent to their position. 'Perfect Timing.' Rahul thought. This gave him a perfect excuse to move the conversation in a different direction.

"You worry too much, as always, Sanjay. You were always the nervous type." Rahul had become much more emboldened. Sanjay was obviously going to accept the invitation.

"What would I be asked to do and what organization would I be working with?" Sanjay's voice lifted at the end of the sentence, indicating his keen curiosity.

"I would rather not discuss the particulars, here." Rahul pointed to the men that had taken seats well within earshot.

"Gotcha." Sanjay was agreeable.

Rahul whispered softly as they moved closer together across the table, "You will get your orders in Roorkee. We need information about the Global Call concert and the floor plans for the new stadium. You are the only person that can get it. You have been handpicked by very important people that I am not at liberty to mention at this time. You will know them very soon."

Sanjay leaned his chair back on the rear legs and crossed his arms. "No problem. I can get you whatever you need." His arrogant swagger was obviously exaggerated, but Rahul was not phased. Quite the opposite, in fact. The meeting was a complete success. All additional details would be sorted out at the next meeting.

9

triskal, Orion, and Maritius, each measuring well over six and a half feet tall, stood in the middle of the bustling crowd in the large public square just outside of the Dharavi slum. Explosions of color powdered the air in all directions. Thousands upon thousands of Mumbai residents danced and sang as they played Holi. The children were the most spirited of the festival goers, some with backpacks full of colored water that were attached to high powered water guns. Others were targeting friends with water balloons filled with color. Many of the more docile, and likely more senior participants, were content with the application of bright colored powders and paints to the faces of friends and family in a more ritualistic fashion. What was humorously obvious to the angels was that the clothing being worn today in the square was likely being worn for the last time.

The three members of the heavenly host smiled as they watched Trevor, Andrew and Harold follow Amit, Nailini, and their two daughters into the crowd of revelers. No threatening evil entities seemed to be lurking in or around the crowd.

"Wow. This is incredible!" Andrew jumped to his left to avoid an incoming water balloon projectile. The balloon filled with dark purple colored water exploded into Harold's chest, leaving a tie-dye looking design across what had been, seconds before, a perfectly white polo shirt. The launcher of the balloon, a teenaged boy that was using a parked moped for cover, darted away to join his friends after seeing the magic of his "explosion of color" handiwork.

Harold threw his hands in the air, "I guess I picked the wrong day to quit wearing t-shirts?"

Everyone laughed as they continued into the pulsing crowd of Holi players. A young girl approached Trevor with her outstretched hands holding a small plastic container filled with colorful powder. "Here you go, sir. My mother said that I should give you some of my color so that you can play Holi the right way."

Trevor bent down and gently picked up the offering. "Why, thank you. That is awfully nice." Her mother, standing only a few feet behind her daughter, bowed gracefully before taking her daughter by the hand and disappearing into the crowd.

"I had no idea. This is quite a celebration, Amit. Thank you for the invitation to join you and your family today," Trevor was beaming. The crowd's excitement and pure joy was electric and very contagious.

"I realize that this is not a typical Christian holiday, gentlemen, but it is truly something special here in India." Amit handed both of his daughters what looked like a weekly prescription pill box container with seven individual small holding areas, each filled with a different bright colored powder. "Go on, you two. You can join your friends, but please be careful with the color. Try to avoid the chemical colors that can burn your skin."

"What are they celebrating, exactly? What is Holi?" Another balloon caught Harold in the back just as he asked the question. This time, the large blob of color was neon green.

"It is a Hindu spring festival. Signifies the changing of the seasons but has really become more about the throwing of colored water and powder for most. Definitely the favorite holiday for anyone under the age of twenty. I find it quite enjoyable myself."

"Is there a religious significance?" Trevor hopped to his left but was unable to avoid a large puff of orange dust as a large powder packet exploded across the front of his grey jeans.

"Yes. Cultural, biological, religious, and mythological significance. Remind me to fill you in on the legend of Radha and Krishna when we get back home. We will have plenty of time to discuss as we try to scrub our arms when we get back to the house. I guess the most important cultural significance would be that Holi highlights the power of good over evil."

"Good enough for me." With his quick reflexes, Harold caught another incoming balloon without letting it explode across his wardrobe. With the throwing culprit only a few feet away, Harold returned the throw, adding bright yellow color to the boy's already technicolor shirt. "Got ya. Love this 'playing Holi' thing." The kid looked up and smiled with admiration at the completely out of the ordinary and fairly old, white American's remarkable abilities.

Amit chuckled and continued. "Two of my favorite traditions during the Holi festival are that enemies become friends on Holi, and that rich and poor celebrate together. This tends to break down class walls that typically divide us rather than bring us together."

"Very cool, Amit. So glad to be a part of this. Thank you." I wished my family could be here with me to play Holi.

"You should know this by now, Andrew. Indians are a very celebratory people. From Diwali to Holi, from Shiva Ratri to Krishna Jayanti, Indians make the most out of every holiday and they prefer to share the joy of these celebrations with everyone. With our congregation, wait until you witness our Easter celebration. You will be thrilled and amazed."

"I can't wait to celebrate with you. No question about it."

As we headed back to our hotel, we noticed many people wandering aimlessly across the crowded highways, some running into the concrete medians, as if they had lost their eyesight. This curiosity continued for a couple of miles before I finally asked the driver, who seemed completely oblivious to this activity. "What is going on with these people?" I asked him. "They look like they are drunk?"

"Oh, yes, Mr. Andrew." Our driver wore a smile from ear to ear and answered with what seemed like a strange mixture of pride and adoration. "They have been taking the bhang all day, my friend."

Unfortunately, my western understanding of inebriation opportunities caused me to think he was referring to a Bong either for smoking marijuana or chugging beer. "Oh, would this bong be for smoking or drinking?" I asked with great intrigue, never once guessing that this particularly conservative country could sport a tradition of this nature.

"Oh, no……not smoking, Mr. Andrew. They would be drinking bhang or eating golees."

Alright, I was now fully hooked. This obviously demanded much deeper investigation. "So, they drink tons of beer? Through a large funnel?"

"No. No. Not beer. They drink the bhang."

"What do you mean by 'drinking bhang'?" I continued my interrogation into this fascinating and heretofore unknown Indian custom. "And what is a golee?" In the front seat, I could hear Amit chuckling to himself.

"What are you laughing at, Amit?" I punched him lightly on the upper part of his shoulder.

"I am just enjoying the bhang conversation. So funny to see someone learning about it for the first time."

"Well, you have to admit that watching people walking into bushes or wandering aimlessly across busy streets is pretty interesting." I opened my palms and shrugged my shoulders indicating that this was a legitimate question.

"Alright. Alright. I guess you're right. Bhang was originally associated with Lord Shiva and has become synonymous with Holi. In fact, Bhang has now been designated as the official drink of Holi." Amit turned to face the three of us sitting in the back seat before he continued, "The tradition of drinking bhang is particularly rampant in Northern India, in and around greater New Delhi. This is the area of India where Holi is celebrated with the most exuberance and gusto." Amit pointed to a man that was attempting to climb the street divider with little success. "As you can obviously see with your own eyes."

We all laughed as we watched the inebriated man climb the concrete divider, falling backwards several times, before ungracefully flopping over onto his back on the other side of the four-foot-tall barrier.

Amit continued with his lesson on the art of 'taking Bhang.' "Bhang actually originated in areas like Veranasi and Banaras, where the worship of the Hindu God, Shiva, is prevalent. Men can be seen near the world famous ghats, using mortar and pestle to crush the cannabis blooms and leaves into a green paste which is used as the base for bhang. To this mixture, milk, ghee, and many spices are added."

"What is ghee?" Trevor interrupted.

"Ghee is basically clarified butter, I think." Amit paused and then pushed on. "This crazy intoxicating concoction is then used to make a nutritious and refreshing drink called a Thandai, viewed by many as a 'healthy alternative' to alcohol." Amit made air quotes with both hands.

"Sounds pretty unhealthy to me, my friend. On all fronts. Clarified butter and some cannabis. Kind of a slappy, happy butter sauce. Have you ever tried it with lobster or crab legs?" Amit smiled at Hayward's unique, yet often twisted sense of humor.

"No, Harold. I doubt you will find it on any seafood menus here in India." Amit laughed at the ridiculous, but funny suggestion. "In the Christian community here in India, Bhang is openly frowned upon."

"What about the golees?" I searched for a way to avoid further bhang discussion.

"Oh, yes. Evidently, bhang can also be mixed with ghee and sugar to make peppery, chewy balls called 'golees.'" My attempt to move the conversation from Bhang had backfired. "Some people swear by them. Wild and wacky candies, I guess. Thought I would beat you to the punch, Harold." With this, we all lost it. Even the driver laughed with great appreciation of Amit's jab at Harold.

As we neared Amit's condo, we weaved our way through this high-rent residential section of the city. We witnessed one man after another wandering aimlessly in the streets and parking lots, often tripping clumsily over their own feet. We noticed many that had literally passed out on the side-walk pavement, in the grass, or in the street itself. The Bhang induced after party carnage had taken its toll on many and almost all of them seemed to be middle aged men. It reminded me of walking through a fraternity house early in the morning after a raging party the night before, with over served eighteen to twenty somethings passed out everywhere you looked. The difference here was that the entire city seemed to have become a veritable fraternity house.

After an hour of driving, we finally arrived at Amit's condominium complex in Gurgaon. He and his wife had graciously invited the three of us to use his oversize shower to wash off the color and put on clean clothes. With our clothes completely covered in different wet and dry color, the mixture was an almost black, dark purple. I could easily pass for Barney, the purple dinosaur, if we were dressing up for Halloween.

When we turned into the complex that housed hundreds of families in this suburb of Delhi, the faces of every man, woman and child were marked with vivid color. Smiles and laughter were abundant as the celebration was quite visibly in full swing. Our driver parked the car in front of the breezeway that led to the center part of the five-story building where Amit and his family had lived for the last several years.

As Trevor, Harold, and I started through the virtual tunnel that separated the two main wings of the complex, we were ambushed by children from all directions, some with water balloons, others with elaborate water guns that were attached to backpacks that had been filled with brightly colored liquid. We dodged back and forth trying to avoid a direct hit, but to no avail. They were everywhere, each one with some form of water weaponry, laughing and screaming at the top of their lungs, as they playfully attacked the new arrivals. Obviously, they had been alerted by Amit and his son, Adit, to the fact that three, much taller than the average Indian, Americans would be joining in the Holi fun today and that they would be perfect targets for a guerilla style attack as they walked through the breezeway.

Thinking that the assault had ended, and wiping the colored water from our eyes, we continued down the corridor only to be blasted from above, this time with buckets of colored water and more water balloons from third and fourth story balconies. We were now completely drenched, and our jeans and polo shirts were beyond saving for future wear. The kids reveled in their successful exploits, high fiving in the parking garage under the back half of the building.

Harold and I looked like Nickelodeon poster children, colored from head to toe in primary colors as if we had been the subjects of a full-frontal tie-dye experiment gone horribly wrong. Somehow, Trevor had managed to avoid most of the color barrage, his clothes only baring a couple of bright streaks and spots.

The squish of my now technicolor loafers echoed throughout the garage as we took our last steps toward the open door of apartment #205 where a hysterically giggling Amit stood taking our dripping wet, color filled appearance as a sign of his successful coaching of the neighborhood kids.

Once inside, Amit ushered us into the large shower area in his apartment and provided us with towels so that we could attempt to remove as much color as possible from our skin, hair, and garments. "You guys are amazing! You get high marks for a well-played Holi."

Fortunately, Amit was kind enough to warn us that we might want to bring an extra pair of clothes which he had retrieved from our car. After toweling off and putting on clean, dry shirts, pants, socks, and underwear, we were offered a seat around their living room's sofa table and treated to many Indian treats that were made by his wife, Nailini. I didn't recognize any of the items that were served, but every bite that was served by Nailini and her housekeeper was absolutely delicious.

After catching up with Amit and his precious family, we were invited to follow them to the back of the complex where the entire development would be congregating for the continuing celebration of Holi and a more formal ceremony for the application of colors. This ceremony was a much more somber ritual with far more reverence and respect. Young and old, Indians and Americans, males and females, all participated in this very special part of Holi. Gently and carefully, we would take turns dipping our fingers into the powdered color while painting the face of the person standing in front of you, adding a stripe of vibrant color to the cheek, forehead, nose, and neck or wherever color had not already been applied. The act was much more intimate than celebratory and was truly the highlight of the day for all of us.

We were warned not to eat or drink any of the foods or beverages that had been catered for the event, due to the preparation techniques and water used. It was now obvious why Amit and Nalini had gone out of their way to feed us prior to our joining the festivities. Fabulous hosts, indeed!

After an hour or more of getting to know Amit's neighbors, friends and family who had showed up for the event, we said our goodbyes and headed back to the Radisson hotel.

My Barney the Dinosaur arms did not appear human. Amit apologetically described why the purple refused to come out in the shower at his apartment. "There are two types of powdered colors used during Holi, natural and chemical. Chemical powders are typically less expensive and unfortunately are more like intense dyes. They penetrate and sometimes burn the skin and are very difficult to remove." Without knowing the difference, we were the unwary victims of chemical based colors, although very fortunate to have chemical colors applied only to our arms and not thrown in our faces.

Rarely do I take a bath in a hotel, and rarer still in an Indian hotel, but on this occasion, scrub-a-dub-dub was definitely in order. Today, I found myself more worried about the tattooing effect of the color than the quality of the reverse osmosis water filtration at the hotel. I grabbed the loofa off the sink counter, climbed into the warm bath water, applied copious amounts of soap to the purple streaks and started scrubbing my arms for what seemed like an eternity. After a while, it felt like I was trying to remove a tattoo with sandpaper. Although some of the color did fade, the intended temporary body art was far more permanent than I would have preferred. Although most of my chemical tattoo could be hidden under a long-sleeved button-down shirt, the back of my right hand would clearly signal my exposure to the traditions of Holi during our upcoming strategy meeting tonight in the hotel.

After giving up on body paint removal, I dried off and dialed Hayward's room. "Any luck removing the paint job, Sparky?"

"Yeah, right! This is unbelievable, man. I can't get it off of my arms." The splashing of water on Harold's side of the line sounded frantic. Harold started singing the Sesame Street "Rubber Ducky" song, a children's classic from the famed Bert and Ernie episodes. We both started laughing. Holi turned out to be an unexpected gem of an experience that we would not soon forget.

"Keep scrubbing, bud. Let's head down to the restaurant to join the others. We are scheduled to meet the rest of the Global Calling team in half an hour."

"Perfect. Give me five minutes." He hung up the phone.

Training Camp

While we do not look at the things which are seen, but at the things which are not seen. For the things which are seen are temporary, but the things which are not seen are eternal.

- 2 Corinthians 4:18 (New King James Version)

For bodily exercise profits a little, but godliness is profitable for all things, having promise of the life that now is and of that which is to come.

- 1 Timothy 4:8 (New King James Version)

10

anjay woke in a full sweat. The temperature outside of his tiny enclosure felt as though it must already be approaching twenty-seven degrees Celsius, over eighty degrees on the Fahrenheit scale. Lieutenant Giridhar Krishnan, who was charged with his training, had informed him yesterday that the heat would likely set a new March record of thirty seven degrees Celsius. With a twisted and demented smirk on his highly wind burned face, Lieutenant Giri, as he was addressed by his direct reports, reminded Sanjay that his final test before graduating from his abbreviated training program would take place tomorrow in the blistering heat and that, if it did not kill him, he would be given an important assignment.

He stood up as best he could in the thatched roof hut with walls fashioned out of hardened clay and dung. He could only manage to straighten up to three quarters of his actual height before hitting the wood slats that formed the foundation of the roof. Peering out through the door slats, he could make out movement near the command center some two hundred yards away from his position. He could hear the shuffling of other recruits in the nearby cells. His body, like the other thirteen recruits, had now established an internal alarm system that woke him up before the abusive training sessions would begin. There were no Roosters in the area, but none were needed.

Sanjay's tattered grey t-shirt and camp issued, dirt stained pants, looking more like off-white pajamas to him than actual pants, were soaked to his skin. Using the sleeve of his shirt to wipe the sweat from his forehead served only to move the dirty moisture around. He could sense his own body odor and could only imagine how bad the stench must be to anyone else after ten days without a legitimate shower or bath. Combine this with the smell of his own urine and feces coming from the back of his stall, it was a truly nightmarish condition. The trainees were forced to their cabins, as they were referred to by the sadistic trainers and coordinators, by no earlier than midnight after a grueling seventeen or eighteen hour day of drills, calisthenics, obstacle course work, weightlifting, rifle shooting, crude bomb making, or whatever other terrorist related education that was deemed a requirement on a given day.

All the willing, but now mostly regretful participants in the terrorist initiation camp were confined to their cells until the locks were opened in the morning. Any need to relieve oneself while in confinement had to be carefully orchestrated, due to each individual chamber only being six feet long by three feet wide. Sanjay required about two thirds of the small space for sleep or sitting and reserved one third as a makeshift restroom. The hard pan of dirt that made up the floor of each cell had become like solid rock over time, making any bare-handed attempt to bury or cover the human waste virtually impossible.

The smell was certainly unbearable at first, but Sanjay was amazed at how the body, particularly his nose, could adapt so quickly as to make the wretched stench somehow bearable. Each morning, the recruits had approximately ten minutes to clean their own stall, use the restroom in one of the two beat up port-a-johns next to the dilapidated huts and wash their hands, face or whatever else they chose to wash in a large communal tin bucket that was placed in the center of the courtyard in front of the crude barracks. Washing actual clothes only happened after all of the residents had a chance to wash their body parts with the initially, and only relatively, clean water. Once a nonverbal agreement had been reached, indicating that the time had come for laundry, the fully naked community of bathers would submerge all pieces of clothing at once, wring them out, submerge once again, ring them out, and get dressed in the much cooler, but now moistened and uncomfortable camp attire.

Since there was no hard and fast schedule, Sanjay felt confident that this was a make it up as you go type of training camp, catering more to the whims of those that run the camp and their drunkenness over their newfound power positions.

"How in the world did Rahul convince him to leave his cushy job in Mumbai to be trained by these barbarians?" Sanjay thought to himself while finishing his crude group bathing ritual. His eyes burned from the soap, giving him an excuse to cry without being noticed. His beaten and bruised ego was almost enough to cause him to give up, but his burning intention to set the record straight with Rahul upon his return to Mumbai provided him with the energy and drive needed to get to the end of the training.

As Sanjay dried himself with the well-worn and completely filthy towel that had been handed to him by one of the aggressive and insensitive bath area chaperones, one of Commander Singha's trusted lieutenants named Arpit grabbed his arm and escorted him roughly towards his hut. As they neared the worn out gate-like door that served as the entrance, Arpit pushed Sanjay onto the dirt and kicked dust in his direction. "Get dressed, pig! Boss wants to see you now. Hurry it up!"

Sanjay crawled on all fours to the door and slithered his way through the small opening into his cramped area of confinement. On the floor to his left, he noticed that a new pair of pants and a cleanly washed shirt had been placed next to the rock that he had used as a pillow for the last few weeks. He picked up the shirt and took in the smell of laundry detergent. His eyes filled with tears as he continued to breathe in the fragrant smell of lemon zest mixed with what might be vanilla. He was overwhelmed by this simple pleasure. What did this mean? His mind froze briefly. Were these to be the garments that he would wear to his execution? Was this pleasant surprise soon to be followed by unexpected torture or even worse?

Arpit cried out from his position next to the adjacent hut. "Move it, you disgusting rodent. Singha waits for no person. We must move."

"Coming," Sanjay answered the command in a sheepish whisper, "I am almost dressed."

Sanjay moved more quickly, slipping on the new pants and shirt as he continued to contemplate the possibility of death. For a moment, he let his mind drift to a place that elevated death to a position far better than this camp of horrors. He snapped back to reality. Death was not an option. He would find Rahul. There would be payback for this deceit. What Rahul was selling to unknowing, but aggressive and driven young men was a complete fantasy of power and wealth. What he and others had unwittingly bought from this snake-oil selling charlatan was actually cruel slavery.

The long walk to the building at the end of the property was tough on Sanjay and the other handful of recruits that walked single file behind their handler, Arpit. The sand was already blisteringly hot and dug deep into the pads and heels of the recruit's feet. Sanjay felt far more like a prisoner than a recruit on this maddening morning trek. By the time they reached the small but sturdy looking building, Sanjay's feet were on fire, each step sending sharp daggers of intense pain from his toes to a part of the brain that simply wanted to give up, pass out or die. He had watched circus performers in Mumbai walk across red hot coals with no visible pain whatsoever. 'How could this be?' Sanjay thought to himself. His mind drifted to a memory of the third degree burn that he had inflicted on himself from sliding down a dry plastic waterslide when he was ten years old. The lifeguard had warned him that it was dangerous without the needed water. He remembered crying for hours. Today, there would be no crying, but the pain was far more intense.

Stepping onto the tile floor inside the building felt like Heaven to all that had made the molten sand walk with bare feet.

"Sit!" Arpit yelled at the six recruits as he pointed to a couple of ratty benches that sat against the wall to their left. Without argument, all six men quickly sat on the benches, happy to have their feet resting anywhere but on the sand.

Two men in surgical smocks and surgical masks entered the tiny waiting room through a door between the two benches. Their hands were held in the air, an undeniable indication of sterility, as if they had just scrubbed in for surgery and were simply waiting for a surgical suite to open.

Without a single word, they nodded in unison to Arpit, who grabbed the young man to Sanjay's left by the arm and wheeled him around towards the two men who, by Sanjay's assumption, must be doctors or nurses or other forms of medical professionals. He looked down at his hands which were trembling uncontrollably. Why were they here in this nondescript building that he and the other recruits referred to as 'The Office'? Were they here for vaccination, physical evaluation, organ harvesting, euthanasia?

A knock at the front door of the building got Arpit's attention. He almost sprinted to the door indicating that he knew the identity of the person that was knocking.

"Good morning, Arpit." Commander Sridhar Singha shook Arpit's hand vigorously. "How are our top recruits this fine day?" His sarcasm was obvious.

Sanjay recognized the necklace that the Commander was wearing. It was a shiny silver seashell necklace attached to a leather strap with a large reddish-brown chatoyant gemstone dangling from the middle, now adorning the chest of a monster instead of its rightful owner.

Sanjay had taken it from his sister's drawer the day after she had been brutally raped and killed by a group of thugs in a neighboring slum where she had been innocently playing Gilli

Danda, a crude form of Cricket, with friends from her school. On that day, before placing the necklace around his own neck, Sanjay sat on her portion of the bed which they shared, and wept for hours. Through the prism of his tears, he had imagined Mehlia sitting next to him before going out to play. With his eyes half closed, his mind drifted as he watched her take off the ornate necklace that had been given to her by their grandmother during a rare trip to the beaches just outside the city. She placed it gently on the bedside table so that she would not lose it or damage it while playing with her friends. She had looked lovingly at Sanjay and smiled. As soon as it had started, the vision of his sister faded into nothing as if the vision had been made of sand and carried off by the wind.

She had always referred to the necklace as her Tiger Eye and believed that this talisman not only acted as her protector but as a symbol of strength and beauty. For reasons unknown to Sanjay, she had chosen not to wear it on the day that she was killed. Mehlia was only fourteen years old and the overwhelming grief had consumed his family and surrounding community for months and continued to consume Sanjay to this very day.

Commander Singha was also wearing the recognizable pin-striped New York Yankees cap, a prized possession that Sanjay had been wearing confidently when he arrived at camp only a couple weeks ago. That confidence was now replaced entirely by fear and hate, fear of what might lie ahead and hate for his abhorrent captors and task masters.

"Sanjay, I want to again thank you for the hat. I guess I am a Yankees fan, now." Singha chuckled as he doffed the cap and then acted out the swinging of a baseball bat in a flaunting display of 'better not forget who the boss is, Sanjay!'

Anger swelled up in Sanjay, not because of the stupid baseball cap, but because of the loss of his sister's necklace to this disgusting pig. The necklace was the only physical reminder of his sister that Sanjay had kept, and he had worn it every day of his life until it was ripped from his neck on the day that he entered the camp.

Sanjay stayed silent, choosing not to respond to Commander Singha's bravado. Instead, he simply turned his eyes back to the floor and waited for his turn with the two orderlies, nurses, doctors, or whatever they were, to be escorted to the back room.

After two of the others had been ushered into the unknown behind the only interior door in the building, it was Sanjay's turn. Arpit grabbed him with unnecessary force and pushed him toward the backs of the men who were wasting no time as they reopened the door that led back to where they were obviously engaging in some type of medical procedure. Obvious smears of blood on the gloves and gown of the man in front almost caused Sanjay to faint in mid stride. What was happening? Why was there so much blood?

Without speaking, the taller man motioned for Sanjay to have a seat on the small gurney that was illuminated by a large surgical lamp. The gurney was covered in blue protective covering that had been rolled out of a large box that sat on a table at the foot of the gurney. The covering reminded Sanjay of the large box of aluminum foil that his mother kept under the sink, often used to cover food, but most importantly used as an alternative to curtains on the windows of the small urban dwelling that she shared with Sanjay and his sister.

Sanjay was shaking violently as he sat on the gurney. The two men straddled him on either side and moved him into a prone position before securing two large straps over his back and across his feet. One of the men moved a large cart to the end of the bed closest to Sanjay's head. After what seemed like an eternity to Sanjay, but that was likely only a few minutes, the other man wheeled a silver tray to the side of the bed. On top of the tray, Sanjay stared in horror at the two loaded syringes and what looked like an IV preparation kit.

The man next to the tray got to work immediately on Sanjay's wrist. In seconds, an IV was connected to Sanjay's arm and a bag of saline was hung on a large hook at the top of a crude pole that was attached to the gurney. After checking the flow of saline, the man introduced the syringe to the IV and plunged the unknown solution into Sanjay's veins. Sanjay could feel himself slipping out of consciousness as the cocktail started to do its work.

II

Sanjay woke up slightly dizzy and once again in a full sweat, the pleasant smell of lemon zest detergent from his new clothes just hours earlier, now replaced by the unmistakable stench of urine and heavy perspiration. His completely soaked pants stuck to his legs and thighs like wet toilet paper, indicating that he had lost control of his bladder while under anesthesia. The heat in his cell was unbearable, but what was most concerning was the pain he felt in his left ankle. Although still groggy and very nauseous, Sanjay summoned the strength to get to a sitting position on the dirt floor of the crude hut. He took a couple of deep breaths in a futile attempt to stop his head from swimming, before reclining against the coolness of the back wall.

He could see that his left ankle was completely bandaged, from the heel to the middle of his calf muscle. He felt along the gauze bandage, from top to bottom. Between his Achilles tendon and the pronounced bony prominence of his ankle, approximately three-and-a-half inches above the bottom of his foot, he pinpointed the area where the pain was most intense. He ran his fingers across the stitches that poked out of the crude, blood-soaked bandage. Just the slightest touch of these exposed wiry filaments sent shockwaves all the way up his leg. "What could they have possibly done to my ankle?" Sanjay was completely puzzled but was still in a state of semi-consciousness, wanting desperately to lay back down and rest rather than contemplate the possibilities.

The door to his crude domicile opened. Arpit, the always inappropriate watchman over the recruits, knelt next to the opening with a plate of food in one hand and a can of "Thumbs Up" soda in the other. "Finally awake, huh?"

Sanjay had a hard time focusing his eyes on Arpit. The intense sunlight made Arpit appear as a hulking silhouette, with no recognizable facial features. Arpit tended to be more aggressive and angrier than most of the guards, but Sanjay's curiosity overtook his fear. "What happened to me? Why? My ankle? What is wrong with my ankle? Hurts...so much pain... really sore..." The slurred words were almost unintelligible, a frustrated run-on series of questions and emotions, most likely a result of the residual effects of the anesthesia medications.

"Ha. You are like a dog in a kennel. You know people actually put microchips in their pets to be able to find them if they run away. You know that, right? Well...you are now Singha's little dog, except instead of a stupid microchip, you have your own GPS locator. Battery should last at least six months. Best if you don't mess with the stitches, would hate to see you get an infection." Arpit may have been rude, but he was obviously the most intelligent of all the other leaders in the camp. "Actually, mutt, this is a good omen for you. No one gets the GPS unless they are about to be deployed. If you prove yourself a worthy warrior, you might not need to get a replacement later. You are still on probation until Singha trusts you. I guess congratulations are in order. Now, eat up! Man, you stink of urine. You will need to shower soon with the others."

Arpit threw a large folder on the floor next to Sanjay's bare feet. "You need to read this. No. I take that back. Don't just read it, *memorize* it! You will need to sign it and give it back by tomorrow once you can recite it all by memory."

"What is it?" Sanjay croaked. "What am I signing?"

"The Liberation Resistance manifesto, you moron. I told you about it yesterday. It is our oath among brothers. Everyone must recite it out loud to Commander Singha before graduating. It also walks you through how you get paid. Read the part about bounties for certain key targets. Think about it. You could be rich someday, Sanjay. A little, worthless kid from the slums...now, with crazy, stupid money." Arpit laughed sardonically to himself. "The oath is pretty simple. Don't memorize it, you die. Don't sign it, you die. Sign it, memorize it, and don't follow it, you die. Pretty compelling choices, right?" Arpit spit chewing tobacco on the ground in front of Sanjay, splattering across the top of his bare feet. "Now, clean yourself up. You really do stink!"

Arpit slammed the crude door shut and fastened the lock that kept Sanjay a prisoner for now. Sanjay shifted his weight onto his hands and knees and crawled to the door. He peered through one of the slats and watched as Arpit walked past the bathing area towards the main building. Commander Singha walked from the building and met Arpit in the middle of the field that would be used for training the recruits later that day. They saluted each other and walked back to the building together.

Sanjay felt lightheaded, as if he were about to faint. He laid back down on his side and closed his eyes. His clothing was completely soaked through and clung to his body. His entire body ached. He desperately wanted to get some additional rest, but the damp heat made his head pound, a constant drumming that kept sleep just out of his grasp. He had no appetite at all. The food and drink would have to wait.

GOAN CURRY

There is no wisdom or understanding or counsel against the Lord. The horse is prepared for the day of battle, but deliverance is of the Lord.

- **PROVERBS 21: 30-31 (NEW KING JAMES VERSION)**

The God of my strength, in Him I will trust, my shield and the horn of my salvation, my stronghold and my refuge; my Savior, you save me from violence. I will call upon the Lord, who is worthy to be praised, so shall I be saved from my enemies.

- **2 SAMUEL 22: 3-4 (NEW KING JAMES VERSION)**

12

beth and Alisha followed Ganeeta into the fourth and final house on their house hunting tour for today. After arriving in Goa three days ago, they had seen a grand total of thirteen houses, four apartment homes, and several temporary housing options that were made available by local Christian churches.

"Mom, I really like this one." Alisha had stopped in the elevated foyer that looked directly into the extra-large kitchen area. She looked up at the skylight in the ceiling above that poured light into the large space. "This feels more like an American house and I like it."

"We haven't even seen the whole house, Ally. Patience, young lady," Beth smiled. Although more hesitant, she was thrilled that Alisha was finally positive about one of the showings.

Alisha bounded up the staircase in front of them, choosing not to engage in further conversation. She was already convinced that this was the one. All of the others had been either too small, too dingy, too dark, in a bad area, too far from civilization or just basically unlikeable.

Alisha yelled down from one of the rooms at the end of the upstairs hallway. "Mom. The bedrooms are huge and there are two bathrooms up here."

Ganeeta had already spread out the paperwork on the large granite island in the center of the kitchen when Alisha and Beth returned from the tour of the upstairs portion of the house. "Well, what do you think? Have we a possible winner?" Her soft voice, with a pronounced, yet very easy to understand Indian accent, was both calming and reassuring to Beth, who had become increasingly frustrated with the options from one stop to another over the last couple of days.

Alisha held Beth's hand tightly as an unspoken yet extremely clear message that this was indeed a "winner."

"Yes, Ganeeta. This is the one. Of course, we will need to get a better understanding of the area and I will need to chat with my husband." Beth took a seat on the bar stool next to Ganeeta and exhaled loudly in a reflexive show of relief.

"Dad will love it!" Ally exclaimed as she peered out the sliding doors that led out onto the large, covered patio. Beyond the deck, and through the heavy camouflage of tropical vegetation, Alisha could barely make out glimmers of light reflecting off the Arabian Sea that reached to the west from the town of Panjim.

She turned to look back at her mom, "I hope that Cade likes it, too." She bowed her head a bit revealing some residual sadness.

"We will bring him with on our next visit, honey. He will come around. Don't you worry. Just so glad that Trevor offered to let Cade stay with him for a couple of days while we narrowed our search for houses and for our trip to Mumbai. Right now, I have to think that video games with Trevor are a better option for him than house hunting or a trip to the slums." She winked at Alisha and turned her attention back to the paperwork that Ganeeta had presented.

13

With house hunting out of the way, the weekly trip to visit the slums of Mumbai seemed much less daunting to both Beth and Alisha. This would be their third trip of this nature and was quickly becoming one of Alisha's favorite parts of the week. It was a quick flight to Mumbai from Goa, and only a ten or fifteen minute taxi drive to where they typically met their host or hostess for the day.

The night before the trips, Dr. Nehru would provide them with their contact and a meeting place, usually a coffee shop or hotel lobby, where they could go over the plans for the day. Beth and Alisha always brought a box of bibles with them to give away to those that could read and showed interest along with boxes of American chocolate candies that always generated excitement from the kids that they encountered.

On this day, they were in a more remote area of old Mumbai that was a melting pot of many different religions. They would be meeting with Shilah Rokhi for the second time this month. Shilah was the lay leader of a small Christian church located just on the outskirts of their targeted, poverty stricken area of the city. The church had grown from only fifteen members to over four hundred members in just a matter of months. Shilah's charismatic approach to leadership and worship, and her unique ability to find amazing musical and teaching talent, led to a growth of the ministry that had spread like wildfire throughout the village.

When they had met Shilah for the first time three weeks back, they had been given a tour of the entire slum, the church building and the humanitarian center that served the church congregation and surrounding area.

Beth was excited to be able to provide money for rehabilitation of the church's run down and underfunded humanitarian center that helped to distribute water and food daily to the impoverished people in and around the slum neighborhood. The Global Calling international fund was able to provide over three thousand dollars for this initiative, an amount that would substantially impact the center from both an aesthetic and operational standpoint. Beth was super excited about the opportunity to present this during their trip.

"Shilah, before we discuss the plan for this morning, we wanted to provide you with this donation for your help center." Beth handed her an envelope full of rupees.

Tears welled up in Shilah's eyes as she quickly thumbed through the money. "There must be over one hundred and fifty thousand rupees here. We can't accept this."

"Yes, you can. And you will. This is the least of what we can do to help you and your community." Shilah's emotional response was infectious. Both Beth and Alisha now had tears streaming down their faces.

Shilah jumped out of her seat and hugged Beth and then Alisha. "You are truly sent by God. I don't know how I can thank you and your team."

"No thanks necessary, but you will have to excuse us. We need to get ready for the service." Beth was back to the business of the day. Wiping the last tear with the back of her hand, she motioned in the direction of the small church building where they would be hosting the short prayer service this morning.

As the three women made their way through this crowded section of the Dharavi slum, the pathway narrowed dramatically. They were abruptly forced to move to the far left side of the path when ten or twelve young boys and girls, each carrying what looked like large silver stackable plates in both hands and obviously in a hurry, entered the cramped space from the opposite direction.

"What are those? Smells delicious." Alisha watched as this peculiar group of kids sprinted towards the main thoroughfare that fronted Dharavi.

"Tiffins. You have never heard of a tiffin?" Shilah smiled.

"No, what are tiffins?" Alisha was more than curious.

"Those kids are called Dabbawallas." Shilah turned and looked back at Alisha, who was still watching the kids disappear into a large crowd. "Kind of like grub hub for many Indians, like personal caterers. Each silver tin is called a tiffin."

"What is in the tin?"

"Home cooked food is looked at as most hygienic here in India and is very highly valued," Shilah continued, "There are around five thousand Dabbawallas with over two hundred thousand customers. Each Dabbawalla can carry as many as forty tiffins at a time."

"Wow. That is really cool." Alisha turned back around, and they started to move further into the slum.

Shilah continued to teach Beth and Alisha about Dabbawallas as they walked the short distance to the small church building. "Most of the kids are illiterate. I think the average education is about seventh or eighth grade. They are grateful to have this important job in the community. It is a tradition that started in the 1890s."

"Where do they make the food? Who gets these jobs? Sounds like a lot to manage." Beth peppered Shilah with questions, showing a similar level of interest as her daughter.

"Great questions, you two. We will pass by the main cooking area on our way to the community center after the service. I will point it out when we get there. As for hiring, a Mukadam, kind of like a group leader, is responsible for hiring his own group of Dabbawallas. These are very sought after positions, so there is very little turnover."

"Very cool. What a great tradition!" Alisha was a sponge for learning about the traditions of India. The rest of the walk to the church was filled with interesting trivia and stories from Shilah about tiffins, Dabbawallas and the importance of this mid-day meal for so many in this country.

14

ndrew booted up his computer and went straight to his calendar to find the invite for the Global Calling Management Strategy Meeting that would start in five minutes. He clicked on the Microsoft Teams 'Join Meeting' link and his video jumped onto the screen.

"Good morning, Andrew," The warm and inviting voice of his friend Rajiv came through the laptop speaker.

"Good morning, Rajiv. Good morning, everyone."

The beeps from participants joining the call interrupted the greeting pleasantries. Their video boxes populated the laptop screen one by one until all seventeen attendees were dialed into the videoconference.

"Good morning, everyone." Rajiv repeated his welcome now that everyone was present. "Let us get started. First, let me say thank you for all of the efforts made by Andrew, Trevor, and Mr. Jaworski in getting all of the entertainment locked in for the event in Mumbai. The worship music is going to be truly amazing."

Muted clapping from many in the group interrupted Rajiv for a moment. "Before I continue with the logistics for the event, I have requested that Trevor give a brief update regarding the impacts of the Global Calling initiative in the U.S."

The group could hear the shuffling of papers as Trevor unmuted his line. "Thank you, Rajiv. I appreciate the opportunity to see all of your faces together here online, and I am glad to be able to report that truly amazing things are happening across a couple of large ponds, back in America."

Trevor cleared his throat before he continued, "As you know, Texas Governor, Barry Hatcher, a well-known and outspoken Independent candidate, will likely be running for election in 2024. His platform focuses on several controversial but important areas. His God-first political platform has gained overwhelming bipartisan support in the United States. This platform would allow God back in schools and would allow coaches and teachers to pray in both locker rooms and classrooms, and students would be allowed to recite the Pledge of Allegiance without unnecessary controversy. Over the last several years, the Global Calling Ministry has worked very closely with Governor Hatcher and he has expressed his commitment to helping us continue our important work in India and throughout the world. With him as President, there will be a healthy respect for all religions of the world, and within that context, there would no longer be limits placed on Christianity, but instead, the practices and promises of Christianity would be more widely accepted, if not encouraged."

Another round of applause lit up the speakers, this burst lasting much longer than the first. "The Unites States has also seen a lot of important and heated debate around scientific research and development. We are now seeing much more balanced ideas being generated around cloning, biopharmaceuticals, genetic engineering, and other critical and politically sensitive areas. Again, these controversial issues are specifically addressed in Governor Hatcher's platform."

Trevor's voice quickened in its cadence as he moved to the next point in his update. "The Call, the movement that started us on this amazing global journey, continues to gain momentum in America. Currently, we have over 3.2 million active members, approximately one percent of the entire U.S. population. Church membership has increased dramatically over the last two years and overall giving to churches and charitable organizations has almost doubled in the last twelve months."

Again, the sound of clapping took over, this time accompanied by shouts of adulation from many members of the team. "The young people in our country are creating a religious awakening that is amazing to behold. The zeal that they have for God and ministry is contagious and the long term effects on our country are certain to be well beyond our wildest expectations. As you all know, Satan's goal is to devour the influence of the people of God. This will not happen on our watch. We must continue to actively influence on God's behalf. We are in the midst of something that is truly God driven and God ordained. I can't emphasize how thrilled we are to see The Global Calling movement now taking this excitement and message of peace, love, hope and forgiveness to the rest of the world."

Seeing that Trevor had finished, and after the last of the clapping subsided, Rajiv unmuted his line and continued to brief the group on final preparations that needed to be made before the Mumbai rally.

"As you all know, India currently ranks as the tenth worst country in the world for Christian persecution." Rajiv cleared his throat and took a large sip of water, "Since 2016, incidents of persecution against Christians by both Hindu nationalists and other outside anti-Christian entities have increased dramatically with little or no consequences. In fact, there was a recent incident, in which radicals stuffed three Christians into jute bags and tried to throw them into a river. In a separate incident, a similar radical group tried to set two Christians on fire."

Rajiv closed his notebook and stared straight into his laptop camera. "The reason that I bring these to your attention is not to scare anyone, but to encourage all of us to be conscious of our surroundings at all times. Be careful and diligent in all that you do or say. These are dangerous and worrisome times, but we are to minister to the people of this country with confidence and not trepidation." He paused to allow this to sink in.

"This frightening and contagious crusade of religious intolerance has now reached unthinkable levels both nationally and internationally. The government here in India has been singled out by many countries and various Christian organizations to become more introspective regarding this situation. They have been asked to curb the recent antagonism towards religious minorities. Somehow, many world leaders have become accustomed to being ignored and side-lined because religious nationalism has been prioritized over the lives of people. A U.S. Commission on International Religious Freedom recently called on the U.S. State Department to label India as a "country of particular concern" for engaging in or tolerating systemic, egregious violations of religious freedom. My hope is that the Global Calling Movement can make a dramatic impact in this country, paving a way for more tolerance and a new benchmark for religious freedom in India. May God's will be done. I pray for his protection for all of those that have been chosen for this great mission."

Angels and Demons

Be merciful to me, O God, be merciful to me! For my soul trusts you; and in the shadow of Your wings I will make my refuge, until these calamities have passed by.

- Psalm 57:1 (New King James Version)

"Watch therefore, and pray always that you may be counted as worthy to escape all these things that will come to pass, and to stand before the Son of Man."

- Luke 21:36 (New King James Version)

Are they not all ministering spirits sent forth to minister for those who will inherit salvation?

- Hebrews 1:14 (New King James Version)

15

Mumbai, India
10:29 a.m.
May 2, 2022

the phone in Sanjay's pocket started to vibrate one minute before the anticipated time of the call from Arpit. Sanjay was annoyed that he was still in the facilities meeting that should have come to an end almost half an hour earlier. This was the third such meeting in the last four days in preparation for the upcoming event, and in Sanjay's mind, a complete waste of his time. He should have been on break fifteen minutes ago. The phone vibrated for the third time.

He had to create his own diversion.

Sanjay stood up abruptly holding his stomach. "Sorry boss, my stomach is not feeling well. I think I might blow chow, sir."

Hetal Patel stood up and vigorously pointed to the men's restroom just behind the group. "Go then! What are you waiting for? We don't want to be showered with your breakfast, Sanjay. Go now!"

Sanjay darted towards the open entrance to the men's restrooms. He quickly rounded the sinks and checked under the four stalls that housed a toilet. He entered the last stall, locked the door, pulled out his phone and took the call.

"What took you so long? Are you unable to follow instructions?"

"No, boss. Just a little problem with my micromanager. I took care of it." Sanjay crouched atop the toilet and spoke softly. "What are the orders?"

"It is a go. I assume your team is in order?"

"Yes sir, boss! I will be meeting with the team for final instructions in the morning." Sanjay was thrilled to have such an important role and was all too eager to provide details regarding his expertise and planning. "Hoss, we got it covered. They ain't gonna know what hit 'em." Sanjay slapped his knee with his free hand and smiled at his cowboy humor attempt.

"Alright, Sanjay. Giri and Singha are really high on you. You better not disappoint, if you know what is good for you." The phone went silent.

16

After the amazing worship experience in the heart of Dharavi, the walk back to our car would take approximately 30 minutes and would require all my skills in navigation and a keen memory of important landmarks to exit this complicated maze of buildings, shanties, store fronts, stray animals, discarded building materials, trash, and people. Manoj, who decided to remain with Dr. Nehru and his daughter because of the number of people that had stayed after the service for additional prayer time, had been our trusted guide as we made our trip into the heart of the slums. Forced to find our way back to the car without him, Alisha and I got turned around on several occasions. Dead end here. Wrong direction there. Repeatedly, we had to stop and carefully study the map given to us by Manoj. Unfortunately, Manoj's hand drawn cartographic representation of Dharavi usually demanded that we retrace our steps to get back on track. It was like trying to escape from a diabolical corn maze at one of the farms we would visit during the Fall as kids.

Alisha grabbed my hand as we continued toward the car. She pointed to a large poster that had been placed on the side of a small storefront. "Dad, check that one out!"

"Not too shabby. So many signs." I was amazed at how these placards were plastered all over Mumbai. Posters advertising the event were everywhere we looked. Around every corner. On the sides of buildings. On communal bulletin boards. Taped on restaurant windows. This particular banner that Alisha had pointed out was at least six feet tall and three feet wide, definitely the largest we had seen during our visit.

"Dad, listen. They are playing Christian music." Two teenage kids were sitting on either side of a large Bluetooth speaker that was on a ledge below one of the banners. Alisha waved and gave them a thumbs up. They both gave an exuberant thumbs up back to her as we continued walking.

"No kidding. Chris Tomlin, right?" I listened as the rhythmic thump and perfect harmony of All My Fountains echoed through the enclosed courtyard area that fronted one of the many small grocery stores. "I remember seeing him in concert a couple years back in Hershey, Pennsylvania. I think you were only seven or eight years old. You loved the 'sounds of the universe' presentation, by Louis Giglio."

"I remember, Dad. I was at least ten or eleven. Definitely one of my favorite concerts ever." She looked up at me and smiled.

As we maneuvered through the never ending twists and turns of Dharavi, seeing poster after poster, sign after sign and banner after banner, I found myself incredibly thankful that I was chosen to play a part in the spiritual awakening that was happening in both America and India. What was started as a youth ministry outreach organization in America, had turned into a global powerhouse of evangelism. The idea of 'The Call' that had sprouted in Trevor's kitchen just five years ago, now had close to three and a half million members in the U.S. and was still growing at over twenty percent each year. 'The Call' was making a remarkable impact in the lives of many young Americans. The overwhelming political division and intolerance that we had experienced as a country for the last several years was now being replaced with respectful dialogue, the tolerance of different opinions, a respect for others, a climate of inclusion and a love for God.

The spiritual revival in America had been a sight to behold for all of us in Church leadership. Instead of the continued erosion in Church membership and Christian affiliation, the exact opposite was now taking place. The Church was becoming a vibrant and integral part of life for many new and committed Christians.

Now, this same vision had made its way to India in the form of 'The Global Calling' Organization. In less than two years, under the inspired leadership of Rajiv Bansal, the organization had opened regional offices in thirty two cities across India. The response to the Christian message of peace, hope, and love had been remarkable. Lives were being changed on a daily basis and there was a palpable buzz of excitement across India. I could not imagine being more pumped for tomorrow's event.

17

Orion's powerful, billowy wings glowed brilliant white as he glided gently onto the perch where Maritius, Leshyra, Sariel, Zephia, Malachi, and Umbria had gathered only moments before. The seven angels looked down on the grand stadium that would be the setting for tomorrow's event from the top of the tallest building in India, the yet unfinished Palais Royal Tower, a structure that reached seventy five stories into the heavens above Mumbai.

For a somber moment, the majestic seven stared into the cavernous cricket stadium that would be the unfortunate backdrop for the carnage that would take place in less than twenty four hours. For Orion, the omniscience of God was amazing to behold. Heavenly Father already knew how every event would unfold, and the unfortunate pain and suffering that would result, but the responsibility of situational management was still a vital necessity. This assignment was no different. Their purpose was clear. They were responsible for their individual charges and would jealously protect the will of God for these

special people, but the overwhelming evil that so many innocent people would face tomorrow would be difficult to watch.

The angels watched as hundreds of people were already
milling about outside the stadium, many already forming
long lines in front of the ticket windows. Evidently, the public
had been alerted through the media that only four thousand
tickets were still available and could only be purchased on the
day of the event. They would camp out all night and through
the entire day tomorrow waiting for the green light from security to purchase their tickets. Armed guards were already stationed at every gate entrance, a gentle reminder that no one
would enter the stadium until approximately two hours before
the event was to begin.

Without speaking, all the angels gathered into a circle and
held hands. All were now in human form, as was customary
when meeting anywhere on Earth. Of course, the angelic form
was most convenient for travel between earthly and spiritual
realms, but once on Earth, Orion demanded that they utilize
only human form. This mandate served as a good reminder
to all the Heavenly Host gathered that spirit form, as inter-
preted by humans, could often lead to unnecessary confusion
between that which is good and that which is evil.

Although the guardian angels could communicate with their
charges in uniquely supernatural, and God ordained ways, creating what most humans counted as their own thoughts, feelings, or dreams, any direct and intentional contact could only
be delivered while they served in human form unless explicitly
approved by Orion, based on clear direction from God.

"Blessings to you all from our Father in Heaven." Orion
spoke in a heavenly tongue that was reserved for the heavenly

host. "Tomorrow, we will face an evil that is unimaginable. We pray for the restraint, wisdom, power, and protection that we will need to uphold the plan of our Heavenly Father. May God have mercy on the souls of all that gather here tomorrow and may he give protection to all of his people. For those that succumb to this evil, may He take them into his merciful and capable hands."

After a brief pause to allow everyone to pray their own individual prayers to God, Orion continued. "Tonight, we pray for the safety of all these important instruments of God's will on Earth, always keeping our eyes on those who would rise against them. God be with you all, and may God be with all of those that we have been sent to protect. Amen."

One by one, wings reappeared on the backs of the angels and brilliant streaks of light streamed through the sky as each angel soared to their prescribed station, based on the unspoken, yet fully understood orders given by Orion, so that they could protect their individual reports while standing against the evil spirits in this place. They would come together again as a group after tomorrow's event unfolded.

18

The back seat of the Audi A8 Long was almost as comfortable as my bed at home. I found the buttons on the door and reclined my seat to an almost fully flat position and stretched my legs across the extra-long back seat well and under the front passenger seat. My driver adjusted the rearview mirror and looked back at his now fully laid out passenger for the day.

"Are you comfortable, sir? Would you like cold water?" His smile suggested that he found humor in my childlike playing with the abilities that this car possessed.

"No, thank you. I just had dinner." Becoming aware of how silly I must look to the driver, I fumbled for the buttons again and inclined the seat to a relatively normal sitting position. "Sorry. Just checking out the car. Very nice."

"Yes sir. This is typically reserved for my normal passenger, Dr. Mangesh Dipali. He has instructed me to be your driver for the next two days. He is very pleased to be providing transportation for you, his good friend Rajiv and the rest of your team."

"Excellent. I feel like I may have won the car lottery for the next few days. The others might be a little jealous."

"Indeed. They will also be pleased with their mode of transportation. Dr. Mangesh was very particular in choosing the cars. He would like to know of your comfort." The driver readjusted the mirror back to the normal driving position.

"Please let him know that I am very comfortable." I smiled as I flashed the universal okay sign with my thumb and forefinger. "How long is the drive to the Paradox Hotel?"

"Approximately one hour in normal traffic. Might be a little shorter at this time of day." The driver turned left out of the hotel and merged with the mayhem that was created by pedestrians, mopeds, cars, trucks, and motorcycles heading towards the newer portion of the city where the meeting would be held.

This was the first time that I would be leaving Alisha alone at the hotel for an extended period of time. Although I was a bit hesitant, she had assured me that she would only leave the room for a quick workout and swim. She also promised that she was happy to order room service and would call me when they dropped off the tray so that I knew she was safely locked back in her room after the drop off.

I fumbled around in my pocket and fished out my phone. I scrolled down to Trevor's profile and placed a call. After only one ring, Trevor answered in his uniquely abrupt and consistently formal way. "Trevor speaking."

"Hey, bud. You on your way to the hotel?"

"Yeah. My driver, Omar, picked me up at the airport about half an hour back. How did the worship service go with Dr. Nehru and Dharvana?"

"Amazing. Absolutely amazing. God is moving in ways I have never seen. The impact is truly remarkable. We must have served lunch to over two hundred folks and many stayed after lunch to ask very probing questions and to pray with Dr. Nehru and his daughter. They were mesmerized by the message of love, healing, and compassion. The interpreter that Dr. Nehru picked out was amazing. It definitely made the preaching a pleasurable experience."

"That is fantastic, Andrew. I feel like everywhere we go and preach God's word the impact is powerful. The message of love and compassion has never been more important or desired."

"Definitely. People are hungry for a personal relationship with God. For many, this is the first time that they have ever received this type of message. The people are so kind, so caring, so devout in their own beliefs, but they lack that true connection to our creator. I couldn't be happier with what is happening throughout the country."

"Great stuff. Truly an amazing experience!" There was a short pause as we both reflected on our mission here.

Trevor broke the silence, "So, how close are you to the hotel?"

I covered the mouthpiece on my phone as I questioned the driver. Through my hand that blocked the speaker, I could still hear Trevor's muffled voice asking other questions. After a short back and forth with the driver, the scratchy sound of my hand moving off the microphone signaled I was back to our conversation. "According to my driver, we should be there in around thirty minutes."

"Perfect. I guess you didn't get my other questions?"

"No, sorry. What questions?"

"Never mind. Nothing that can't wait another thirty minutes."

"Alright. Any word from Hayward?" I couldn't help but be excited for a reunion with these two characters. We had been spread out over India for the past four weeks and this event provided a great excuse to get together for dinner to discuss the amazing things that were happening in this truly special place.

Trevor's voice became more animated as he poked fun at our mutual, high maintenance friend. "Yep. That chucklehead is on his way. He had his driver stop at the mall because he ran out of razors, diet soda and American snacks. You know how much he loves the Indian food after his chicken wing incident last month." We both laughed out loud.

"Alright, chief. I will see you soon. Looking forward to spending some time with you guys. I already grabbed some dinner, but if you beat Jaworski to the restaurant, make sure you convince the chef to prepare his typical lamb kabob order extra spicy, and when I say spicy, I mean the 'make the back of your head sweat' kind of spicy. It will be priceless." I sat back with a mischievous smile.

"You are evil, my friend, but I love it. Consider it done!"

19

etal Patel, the Executive Director of Facilities Management for the Kingsford Garden Stadium, had sent a text message early in the morning to all his direct reports, requiring their presence at a final preparedness meeting that would be held in floor seating section 101, immediately adjacent to the A gate concourse that led into the main concession area.

Each leader was asked by Hetal to provide a brief, only a couple of minutes at most, overview of their team's readiness for the monumental event that would take place in the stadium the next evening. Hetal was the prototypical micromanager. At only five foot, two inches tall, and barely weighing one hundred and twenty pounds, but with a desperate desire to be respected, if not feared, he tended to always wear his Napoleonic Complex tendencies on his sleeve.

As the last attendee took a seat in the third row, making the total count of twenty two invitees complete, Hetal stood proudly, steel faced and with immense focus, and addressed the small group. "Deepak, please begin with concession staffing and food storage." He sat down as abruptly as he had stood. He expected to waste no time.

More time means more preparation. More preparation means more money. And more money keeps the boss happy. Don't waste my time. This was the mantra that Hetal used over and over again with his team. Although always spoken in a jokingly playful cadence, he meant business and the team understood and respected this fact.

Deepak cleared his throat. He was not comfortable speaking in front of friends and colleagues. In an almost inaudible, high pitched creak of a voice, he gave his short report. "All is ready, Hetal bhai." His use of the word bhai when addressing his boss was an expression of honor and respect. Bhai literally means 'brother' in Hindi, and although sometimes used to describe a gangster in certain parts of India, this reference was purely respectful. "Yes, good sir. We have one hundred sixty eight people that will be manning the concession stands. One manager for each stall, and two to eight helpers, depending on the size of the stall.

Deepak continued, voice gaining confidence and becoming clearer, "Pleased to be letting you know that the Pepsi Company has provided all of the soft drinks, Hetal bhai, and have stocked each stall as requested. All profits made on the beverages will be donated to local Mumbai charities." His sun spotted face was covered with the smile of a proud grandfather as he delivered this message. This was unchartered territory for Hetal, who had worked in the industry for over thirty years but had never been witness to a company like Coca Cola or Pepsi providing soft drinks for such an immense crowd at no cost. Unbelievable!

"As for the food, we are fully stocked. We have been allotted one bag of masala peanuts for every ticket by Bikaji Foods...a total of eighty two thousand bags. This was again donated, Hetal bhai. We have also forty two thousand hot dogs, American style, with packets of ketchup and mustard at the ready along with popcorn, which will be popped only as necessary. As for Indian food, I do not have responsibility for them as they are not part of facilities management, but I am understanding that all of the twelve Indian food vendors in the stadium will have normal menu stocking, are following the same precautionary food-handling measures, and are fully prepared." Deepak sat down, fervently hoping that no additional questions would follow.

Hetal stood once again. "Sanjay, please inform on security staff." Mr. Patel spoke very matter-of-factly and then sat once again as Sanjay Swaminathan, newly appointed Head of Stadium Security stood up and flipped his long Bollywood inspired, John Abraham-styled black hair to the side. Sanjay wreaked of confidence and swagger, but always appeared to be more flippant and careless than Mr. Patel would have hoped for from a person in this type of position. Unfortunately, in Hetal Patel's view, Sanjay had been reflexively and prematurely hired by an outside agency after his predecessor, Pramod Sharma, was fired for running a privately managed, rent-a-guard security program using stadium employees as his side hustle security consultants. The business had become so lucrative that many of these cops on demand were leaving the relative comfort of stadium employment on a regular basis for the riskier, but much higher paying private security business being offered by Pramod.

Sanjay, a twenty nine year old product of one of the toughest areas of Mumbai, was an immature, fashion conscious prankster, known to everyone in the facilities maintenance group as S.S. He would consistently tell friends and family that his popularity and skills with the women had earned him the nickname 'Smooth Sanjay,' but all the managers gathered in the meeting today knew that S.S. really stood for 'Sissy Sanjay' in reference to his outlandish clothing choices and his abnormally high pitched, and often whiny voice.

Sanjay stood over six foot tall, which, in his mind, made him the veritable Gulliver among his group of tiny Lilliputian colleagues. His rigorous daily workout regimen, along with a steady diet of wheat germ and other GNC body mass miracle pills, gave him the stocky appearance of a rugby halfback or American football lineman. Although his dream for the past five years was to become ripped like his European futbol idol, David Beckham, the depressing prospect of a thirtieth birthday coming up in a matter of weeks had caused Sanjay to reevaluate his body goals. He was now comfortably resigned to simply being stronger and larger than most of his Indian counterparts. Getting ripped just simply took too much effort and demanded a far too limited diet. Extra pushups and crunches were fine, but avoiding Daal Makhani, Lamb Biryani, and Garlic Naan was simply not in the cards.

"Yeah. Yeah, Mr. P. We all good on the security front." His manner of speech was in many ways a bizarre and mostly poor mimicry of western gangster slang meets whimsical Walt Disney; a comedic mashup of Boyz in the Hood meets The Emperor's New Groove. Many of the younger, more unruly members of the security detail under Sanjay made regular attempts at imitating their boss, usually to the immense delight of anyone listening that had the unique, but typically annoying, pleasure of working with Sanjay.

"Thirty two security teams. All gates and exits will be manned. At all times, police presence will be outside the stadium and on stage. We got metal detectors stationed at all entrances and all bags will be hand checked." He paused, carefully eying his audience to make sure they were paying him the full and undivided attention that he required.

"And don't nobody forget...we got all the barricades up last week." He swayed back and forth in hip hop fashion. Sanjay's pomposity was on full display. "Ain't no one gots to worry 'bout nothin', Mr. P.! We all good." Smirks could be heard ripple through the small group. The collective 'what a moron' nervous laughter rattled on for a few more seconds before their boss slowly rose from his seat, his reddened face and visibly pounding temple vein indicating that he was obviously not impressed with Sanjay's lack of respect for his authority.

"Thank you, Sanjay." Hetal was more than happy to move to the next report.

One by one, the rest of the managers were called upon to provide an update on the readiness of their individual areas of responsibility. Will call staffing, janitorial services, seating ushers, stage crew, valet services, and bussing provisions all got their turn. The comprehensive reports on stadium readiness served to ease the mind of Hetal.

At the end of the hour long meeting, Hetal provided some final words of encouragement and instructed everyone to get home soon and get some rest. Tomorrow was to be a big day for Mother India. People from around the world would be tuning in to view what was being billed as the largest rally of its kind ever to be held in India, or the whole of Asia for that matter.

"We have a tremendous responsibility to our nation," Mr. Patel was beaming as he finished his pep talk with a flourish, his fist clenched tightly in the air. "Let us make India proud tomorrow."

20

The coffee was piping hot and surprisingly good at the Radisson Blu Hotel near the Mumbai International Airport. The bellman had brought up a full pot with my normal breakfast order of Masala Dosa, two eggs over easy, hash browns, and a side of bacon. I was now on my third cup of characteristically strong Indian coffee as I surveyed the culinary damage that I had just inflicted on the tray before me. The Dosa alone would have been more than sufficient, but when staying at a new hotel in India, I tended to always utilize the Yankee breakfast back up plan, just in case the Dosa was not to my liking. This morning, both the Indian and American offerings were equally delicious and were both completely, and certainly unnecessarily, devoured in their entirety. Although famished before the food had arrived, I was now uncomfortably full. I felt like a python that had just swallowed a Buick.

Alisha was still sound asleep in the adjoining room. It was certainly nice to have her with me for the last couple of days. As I watched her from the doorway, snoring lightly but soft enough to be more pleasant than annoying, my thoughts drifted back to my son, Cade, who had once again chosen to remain at home in Goa instead of joining us for the trip.

Since the string of murders and our family's kidnapping, Cade and Alisha had reacted in diametrically opposite ways. Cade had been a playful, fun-loving, easy-going, teenager before the unfortunate events that occurred only a couple years back. Alisha had been the shy, tentative girl that was always more comfortable playing alone with her new Barbie dolls and her Easy Bake Oven than having play dates with neighborhood friends.

Cade, Alisha, and Beth had been the unfortunate witnesses to the brutal murder of their friendly caretaker, Alfonso, who was responsible for guarding them in an abandoned bomb shelter near Chama, New Mexico that had been designated as an appropriate safe place for the family during the Christmas season in 2017, a terrifying period of time when leaders of 'The Call,' a powerful religious movement that started in the U.S., were being assassinated one after another. When targeted killing of the leaders of 'The Call' weren't getting the desired effect, my precious family was forced by gun point to climb into an unmarked van, where two less than gentle, wastes of humanity tied their wrists and ankles with uncomfortable zip ties and silenced all three with a heavy dose of duct tape. The tape fashioned gag was wrapped round and round their mouths so tightly that the tape dug into the skin around the nose, mouth, and ears, leaving scars that were still visible on Alisha's face to this day.

Cade had been so frightened by the two animals yelling unrecognizable instructions in what sounded like Russian that he soaked his jeans in his own urine, causing the back of the van to smell like one of those often misused stairwells that could be found in parking garages in many metropolitan cities. One of the men, the shorter fat one, kicked him squarely in the stomach after seeing and smelling the reaction to the abrupt abduction. Beth told me that she could see the tears of terror well up in Alisha's eyes as the driver gunned the engine, spinning the tires as they left the gravel parking area in front of what was intended to be the family's safety zone.

Immediately after these horrific events, Cade started to have regular anxiety attacks that would debilitate him for hours and sometimes days at a time. School, which had come easy for Cade until the time of the kidnapping, had lost its appeal and his grades had slipped dramatically. In the middle of the Spring semester of his Freshman year, after watching my son slide into a reclusive depression, we started to send Cade to a Christian counselor at Five Springs Community Church in Boerne, Texas, where I was the minister of music and church leadership for over three and a half years before accepting this new role in India.

This was an incredibly tough decision for me. For much of my adult life, until I met Beth of course, I viewed psychiatrists, psychologists, herbalists, and chiropractors in roughly the same light. Worthless as hen poop on a pump handle, as my late father would have said. Snake oil for the masses, basically. I often wondered, 'What is it about Americans?' The vast majority seem to be a malcontent group of misfits that incessantly search for the fountain of youth, the next great anti-depressant, or a miracle drug that lets us eat whatever our hearts desire without the annoying side effect of weight gain- that panacea for anything that might possibly be wrong with our bodies, minds, relationships, and overall wellbeing. Although I had witnessed firsthand the dramatic impact that Beth had on so many of her counseling patients, I still struggled with the residual, and very likely misplaced, negative associations. The decision to spend hard earned money for an outsider's opinion grated on my nerves for months, before I finally gave in to Beth's well intentioned desire to improve our son's mental health and stability.

The first few visits were tough for Cade. Unknowingly, my jokes about psychiatrists and chiropractors throughout his younger years had evidently helped to paint the same and completely unfair picture in my son's mind. He begrudgingly attended the sessions, but refused to discuss any of the conversations with his mother or with me, due to his obvious disdain for this required activity. But after about six to eight months, Cade would reveal to the family that, as usual, his mother had been right about the benefits of this kind of therapy. He felt much more at peace about the situation, was having fewer nightmares, and was now able to find forgiveness in his heart, a heart which for much of that year was virtually closed for anything in the forgiving business.

Living in Goa for the last several months had certainly continued to ease some of the anxiety for Cade, but he remained a bit reclusive, avoiding most social contact and preferring video games to any other options that might be available.

Fortunately, Trevor Haas, much more friend of the family than colleague, was also appointed by Global Calling leadership to join the team in Goa, and he had taken a personal interest in my son's wellbeing. Trevor and Cade had always enjoyed a close relationship. In fact, Cade referred to Trevor as Uncle T. Trevor's nickname for my son was Space Cadet, a nod to one of Cade's favorite video games that they played together when my son was a much younger, and perceptibly much happier kid.

I had watched, with more than a tinge of poor-dad jealousy on many occasions, Cade and Trevor spending hours playing Zelda or Super Mario Brothers, laughing, and conferring about castles, dungeons, secret passageways, tough puzzles and destroying various bosses.

One of Trevor's strengths was his ability to embrace the fun-loving, inquisitive child inside. He could speak teenager in a way that I had never quite mastered. He was up on the latest music, the latest social media trends, dressed far more fashionably than I would ever dare, and never came across as the creepy old guy in the group.

The first two months of our transition demanded that Trevor and I travel almost constantly throughout India to meet with the eight primary ministry teams scattered across the country, but for the last four months, Trevor had intentionally spent far more time with Cade, making a personal priority to eat lunch with him at least once a week and spending a couple hours on Saturday playing video games in our bonus room above the kitchen in our small, but comfortable Goa apartment. Although Trevor had not been blessed with children of his own, one would never know it based on his ability to connect with youth in the church, and in this case, most particularly, my son.

I could clearly see the positive effects of more time with Trevor, but a return to what I considered a normal Cade was slow going. Not particularly being blessed with the gift of patience, this slow yet steady process was difficult for me.

With only crumbs and plate smudges left as evidence of a huge breakfast, I placed the oversized, wooden, food service tray on the floor outside our room and I walked back to the desk next to the window. I opened my bible to where I had left off the day before, grabbed a pen and my journal and said a quick prayer before continuing to read in the book of Ephesians. Since the trauma that my family and I had experienced in Texas, New Mexico, and Colorado, I had come to find that this morning ritual was an absolute necessity for maintaining a proper state of mind, consistently providing me with the peace, strength, and conviction that I needed to be an effective leader in the Global Calling Organization.

Before digging into the Word of God, a subliminal voice reminded me that I had promised Beth a phone call as soon as we woke up in the morning. Since the kidnapping, Beth was not only a huge support to me and the kids, but she had also become far more invested personally in the Global Calling movement. On one of our weekly date nights in Boerne, about six weeks before we were set to head to the subcontinent of India, she set down her glass of wine, looked me straight in the eye and said, "Honey, I want to be a part of this movement. God has protected us, and I feel that he is calling me to become an active participant instead of just a supportive companion. What do you think?"

I remember sitting for a couple of seconds in silence, initial feelings of excitement, pride, curiosity, and concern flowing through my mind as I let this question percolate before giving an answer. My wife of sixteen years was as serious as I had ever seen her. She meant business!

Beth had never been a shrinking violet. In fact, she was quite the opposite. She had been a leader in everything she had ever done. She was captain of her Volleyball team in high school. She was a Texas All-State French Horn player. She had graduated Magna Cum Laude from Baylor with a degree in Psychology and had worked for five years in private practice as a Christian Psychologist, until she made the decision to step away after our second child was born.

"Andrew," she continued before I could provide an answer. "I know that the original plan was for me to go back into private practice, but I am not sure that private practice is where I am being led. You know what I mean?" A gentle but nervous smile came across her beautiful face, highlighted just perfectly by the glow of the two candles that sat in the middle of our white tablecloth covered table. Hers was a face that could always ease my fears...a face that I could always count on to provide comfort or redirection when needed. It was also a face that could jerk me back in line whenever I needed it, which tended to be more often than not. She could be tough as nails when needed, yet soft as a trusted wool blanket when the situation demanded otherwise.

"I have been thinking about going back to work a lot lately. The kids are older. The nest is going to be without baby birds sooner than we can imagine. I feel that I can use my talents as a professional therapist to help both those that are leading the ministry as well as for others outside the ministry that we think could benefit from this type of therapy. Not that there would be a need for payment, a salary...you know...maybe later if it becomes a more time consuming and necessary service...I could simply do this for the benefit of the Organization. They take care of us just fine where money and living arrangements are concerned. Why not give back a bit?"

I smiled and winked at Beth. "I don't think I tell you enough how spoiled I am to have you as my wife. I love the idea. I think you would be a remarkable addition."

"What do you think Trevor will say?" She asked with a tinge of nervousness.

"I don't really know, but I think that we should talk with him tomorrow. I truly think he will be all over it."

Fast forward to this morning, with me now sitting in a hotel in Mumbai and Beth probably already counseling someone in her new office in Goa, I was excited to talk to her about the day ahead. It was 8:45AM and I hoped to catch her before her first appointment of the day.

I reached across the desk and grabbed my iPhone, pulling up Beth's profile and pressing the FaceTime button. The screen stuttered for a moment but then came to life with Beth framed by the credenza that stood behind her desk in the office, "Good morning, honey." As usual, she looked amazing. I was a complete mess, still in an undershirt and pajama pants. Seeing her reminded me that I hadn't even brushed my hair yet today. Maybe FaceTime was a mistake. Sometimes a conversation without the accompanying video is more appropriate.

I laughed at the thought of what I must look like to her. "What is so funny, Andrew?" She asked as my laugh must have seemed to come from nowhere.

"Nothing, I just looked at my picture that is being seen on your end. What a disaster. Still a little early this morning."

She smiled and continued. "I have seen worse." She gave out a warm chuckle. "How is Alisha doing on your road trip?"

"Great. She is still asleep, but I think that she is excited about tonight, especially about the concert."

"What time are you guys leaving for the stadium?" She moved in closer to the camera on her laptop.

"Not sure, yet. Probably after I work out and we have lunch." The question reminded me that I needed to send a text to the team regarding our meeting time this afternoon.

"How are the counseling sessions going?" For the last month, Beth had launched a management training program that required the twelve regional leaders of the Global Calling movement based in India to undergo weekly counseling sessions. The two primary goals of this program were to provide them with an outlet to discuss any issues or concerns that they were dealing with in their individual ministry areas and to provide them with additional training on discipleship and leadership within the organization and among the people that they were ministering to across India.

"They have been amazing. It is hard to express how overwhelming the response has been from all the participants. It has been particularly encouraging to see the transformation of mindsets regarding women in leadership. This has been a country dominated by men for centuries. To a large extent, women are still viewed as inferior. I have enjoyed challenging some of these long held beliefs with both the men and women of the group."

I was so incredibly proud of what Beth had been able to do in such a short time. Her main role was centered around psychological issues that faced many of the senior leaders as they often faced significant legal, religious, and cultural challenges. Her efforts had helped many of the members of the Global Calling management team better understand how to communicate with one another and how to handle the overwhelming stress associated with taking a Christian message into areas that were not always welcoming.

Beth continued, "So many great questions and concerns have been brought up in the individual settings. I have taken copious notes and can't wait to share some of my ideas. You really have an amazing group of Christian leaders here in India, honey. Lives are being changed every day and I am simply happy to provide a kind ear, and occasional helpful advice, for some of these people that have never been especially good at expressing their emotions."

"Give me a couple of the ideas," I said with a burst of curiosity.

"Not now, honey. Once you get back. It will take some time." She was always the calmer voice of the two of us. Today was no different. "You have a very important day in front of you, Andrew. Focus on that today and we will have plenty to discuss when you get back home. This I *can* tell you. Words simply cannot express how thrilled I am to be working with this amazing ministry, doing something that really makes a difference in the Kingdom. So incredibly humbled and thankful."

"Great to hear, Beth. I am so happy for you. You sound great." I leaned back in the office chair and sighed, "Everyone seems to really appreciate the service that you are providing. Can't tell you how many calls I have gotten from the team about how much they love working with you. Keep up the good work. Sounds like really cool things are happening."

After another few minutes of trivial conversation about the hotel and what we had for breakfast, we said our goodbyes and I promised to give her a call immediately following the big event tonight.

I placed the wireless phone back in its cradle on the desk and opened my bible, where I had secured a bookmark the night before, to Acts, Chapter 13 and started reading aloud to myself once I made it to verse 47, "For so the Lord has commanded us: I have set you to be a light to the Gentiles, that you should be for salvation to the ends of the earth. Now when the Gentiles heard this, they were glad, and glorified the word of the Lord. And as many as had been appointed to eternal life believed. And the word of the Lord was being spread throughout all the region. But the Jews stirred up the devout and prominent women, and the chief men of the city, raised up persecution against Paul and Barnabas, and expelled them from their region. But they shook off the dust from their feet against them, and came to Iconium. And the disciples were filled with joy, and with the Holy Spirit."

I stood up and walked over to the window that looked out over the crowded streets of Mumbai, a special place that still felt much like the 'ends of the earth' to me and started to pray. As I was finishing my morning prayers, a ritual that always gave me a special feeling of peace and contentment before starting the day, I heard the bedroom door creak open. I closed the Bible that laid in front of me on the small hotel desk, opened my eyes and turned around in my chair.

"Good morning, Daddy," Alisha rubbed her eyes with her fist and then stretched both arms towards the ceiling, "What's for breakfast?"

"Good morning, little one." I was truly glad that she had chosen to join me for this trip. "Yogurt parfait with fresh fruit, as requested. I think that there is some coffee left as well."

"Yuck!" She said as she rolled her eyes. "You know I hate coffee, Dad. Can we call down for some orange juice or milk?"

"Sure, honey. Give room service a call. Shouldn't be too long to get it to the room."

Alisha, still in her pajamas, laid down on the small couch and closed her eyes, signaling that she wasn't fully awake yet and really not in the mood for a normal conversation. Not taking the bait, I continued our morning chat. "So, I thought we would finish up breakfast, go grab a quick workout, and then head over to meet the team at the stadium."

"Wow, a workout? Really? Mom would be shocked." My daughter gave a half smile, half smirk as she poked fun at me. She was right. Beth would be shocked, but very pleased. Being on the road with plenty of tasty Indian food at my disposal had put some extra weight on my already stocky frame and my much fitter, goes-to-the-gym-every-single-day wife had been gently...well, maybe a little more than gently, reminding me that I need to get back into a normal workout routine for the last several weeks.

"No better time than the present, young lady. Not gonna hurt either one of us."

"Okay, dad. Give me an hour to wake up and I will go with you." Her words tailed off in lukewarm protest, but I knew that she would be more committed after some orange juice and the yogurt parfait.

I walked over to the couch, kissed my precious daughter on the forehead, and headed back to the bedroom to put on my workout clothes.

21

As I started my five minute cool down that followed a brutal forty minute climb on the Radisson's early 2000s vintage elliptical machine, Trevor's picture appeared on my iPhone which was sitting in its stand above the machine's digital workout monitor. I slowed down my pace, took a couple of deep breaths, and hit the green button to accept the FaceTime call.

"What's up, buddy?" Trevor was staring at me in all my sweaty and out of breath glory. "Seriously? Better take it easy. Looks like you might be closing in on a heart attack."

"Funny, Trev. Just finishing up." I gulped in another breath, "Yep, not in my top form right now, but who could pass up the opportunity to work out in this amazing training facility where ancient workout equipment evidently goes to die?" We both gave out a short chuckle. Trevor and I had stayed in this Radisson Blu hotel on a couple of trips to Mumbai, so the joke wasn't lost on my friend.

"You ready for tonight? I can't believe that the event is completely sold out, Andrew. Completely sold out! That is almost one hundred thousand people for those keeping score at home." A giant thumbs up came into full view on my screen. "I just arrived at the hotel. What time do you think we need to be at the stadium, and did you call for car service? Oh, and what are you planning to wear to the event?"

Trevor, always the detail guy, waited for my answer. When I stepped off the machine and grabbed my towel without giving an answer, he continued. "You haven't checked in with Rajiv, have you? Hmmm..."

"Yeah. I know. I will call him as soon as I get a shower. I would guess we should get there around four o'clock. I think that will give us plenty of time to get situated."

Having spent five years under Trevor's hands-on style of pastoral leadership at the Rittenhouse Square Methodist Church in Philadelphia, I was not a bit surprised to field these questions. Trevor was a lot of things; focused, trustworthy, truthful, hard-working, faithful, diligent, honest, but always, at least in my experience, detail focused.

Our already close friendship, that had initially blossomed during my time as the Director for Music and Youth Ministries at Trevor's church, had grown even stronger after our family moved to Boerne, Texas. Fortunately, our work together continued as leadership partners in The Call ministry, which had exploded across the United States in the last few years and had now grown into the renamed Global Calling Ministry, a powerful movement that led both of us to India and was now making its mark on the entire world.

"By the way, did I mention that I have been seeing someone online?" Trevor's abrupt segue caught me flat footed.

"Come again? You are what? I thought you were completely against online dating sites?" I grabbed the phone out of its cradle and looked directly at my friend who was now smiling like the cat that swallowed a canary.

"I know. I know." He shook his head. "Kind of kept this one under the radar. It has been over fifteen years since cancer took my Christine. It just seemed like the right time. Sorry to keep it from you guys, but I didn't want to jump the gun."

"Dude. Seriously. That is, uh...great...I mean *fantastic* news." I was completely shocked by this unexpected news. "Man, oh man. How long? When did this start?" I was giddy with excitement for my friend. In my opinion, interest in finding a new relationship was way overdue. If anyone deserved to find love again, it was Trevor.

"You know, when we were in Colorado together, and when we found your family, and I saw the love and connection that was missing in my life, I started to ask myself if I was just scared or selfish?"

"So, how long have you been seeing each other?" It was my turn to be Mr. Detail.

"Long story, short. I didn't really get out of the blocks for over a year and a half. When you are out of the game that long, your dating confidence, as one might say, is a little lukewarm. I finally pulled the trigger in the daunting world of social media dating late last year."

"Over six months? You kept this a secret for over six months?" I was smiling but still annoyed, even though that feeling might be out of line. "You know, if I were with you, I would punch you squarely in the shoulder."

"I know. The old punch-buggy special." Trevor referred to a favorite road trip game from our childhood where you punched your opponent in the shoulder and yelled 'punch buggy,' whenever you saw an old style Volkswagen Beatle.

"Congratulations, my friend. Beth is going to be ecstatic."

"Thanks, bud."

"What's her name?"

"Lisa. You are going to love her. She lives in Colorado Springs. Doesn't really have a strong desire to move to India at this time but the relationship is definitely moving in the right direction. Who knows, maybe I can convince her to come visit for a couple of weeks after the weather gets a little bit less hot and humid."

"That would be amazing, Trevor. I can't wait to meet her. You definitely need to convince her to make a trip to India."

"Patience, grasshopper. All will be revealed in due time. Huuaaaa." He gave his best sensei pose.

I laughed. "Yeah. Yeah. I got ya." I threw the used towel in the wicker hamper before exiting the workout museum. "Let's plan to leave at three thirty. Will check in with Rajiv, and if he thinks that we need to leave earlier, I will give you a quick call."

"Sounds good. See you in a bit."

22

anjay Swaminathan, known only as 'Swami' to those that had been handpicked for today's mission, addressed the group of ten men who had arrived on time at the proposed meeting venue, a tiny and long abandoned newspaper vending stall on the back side of a two acre park that had most recently become overgrown, due to neglect by city officials. The park now served mainly as a resting place for several homeless families and a playground for stray dogs, feral pigs and emaciated cows that would come and go as they pleased. The many presents left by both animals and humans in the way of defecation and urination had given the once beautiful plot of land an almost unbearable stench whenever the monsoon was not in full effect. The ten by fifteen foot structure where they would be meeting had seen better days. Only one third of the roof remained, but the walls were somehow still intact and stable. Trees had grown around the building over the last several years, creating a camouflaged tree-fort of sorts out of the once bustling convenience store.

Sanjay had found the abandoned and well-disguised building on one of his walks through the park, a short cut that he had found to cut a few minutes out of his pedestrian commute between his workplace and his mother's small abode that he shared with her. The walls were completely stable and were impenetrable, due to simple construction using cement blocks. Seeing that the building was otherwise forgotten about by the city and those that semi-inhabited the park, Sanjay purchased four sheets of three quarter inch plywood and enough sheet metal to cover the two large openings where magazines were once distributed along with sodas, candies, and other various sundry items. It was perfect. No one would even notice, much less care about half-baked renovations to a camouflaged and rundown building on this desolate, forgotten waste of public land.

There was one door on the side of the building that seemed to be very sturdy, but that hung on only one hinge when Sanjay had stumbled onto it. After installing three much more sturdy hinges to the door frame and incorporating two deadbolt locks, no one would be able to pry their way into his convenient make-shift storage unit. Sanjay had spent the last thirty days stocking the small shack with everything needed for the upcoming event. By the time of the meeting, there was very little room left in the space for anything more to be stored. Sanjay had carefully cleared out a four or five square foot area just inside the door where he could sit in a steel grey folding chair that had been swiped from a gazebo a few blocks away. The small space was perfect for the time consuming searches on his laptop to find the required ammunitions and materials.

It had become his office, his headquarters of sorts. Sanjay was proud of his renovated, personal shanty.

The event would take place in less than ten hours. Sanjay was giddy with excitement but nervous and fidgety. He had been chosen by Commander Singha. What an honor! He would make sure that this assignment would go off without a hitch.

One by one, those chosen by Swami to carry out tonight's mission started to congregate just outside the small building. Sidhar, Ravi, Ahul, Anil, Samir, and Tarik were trading stories of their recent training that had obviously been specifically designed for this important mission. They recounted lesser recruits that had been broken to the point of tears, some even dismissed from the program, never to be heard from again by family or friends. What had happened to them? This was the question being discussed when Sanjay walked out of the building to address the group. With great bravado, Ravi exclaimed, "They are dead, of course. What do you think happened, you morons? They were weak! They failed the test and must be disposed of properly. Otherwise, we risk everything. We can only carry out Singha's will if the brotherhood is not compromised."

Ravi was very bright and obviously very well spoken. Sanjay counted him as his top lieutenant. But today, he needed to bring Ravi back into alignment with the task at hand.

"Ravi, enough of your yapping," Sanjay spoke very calmly but with powerful effect. "This is not the time for such thoughts. Pleased to be asking you to maintain your cool and focus on the day in front of us. Those who are not with us are dead to us already."

"Yes, Swami." Ravi bowed his head slightly as a show of respect. He hated when Sanjay clipped his wings in front of the group but was not about to dare lose his place as the second in command for this high profile mission.

"I just...I mean...I was just saying..." Ravi's voice trailed off, indicating to everyone, most importantly to Sanjay, that the message was understood.

Sanjay abruptly cut him off, "I need two of you to help me bring the provisions out of the shed." Sanjay motioned to one of the stronger recruits, Anil, "You, you. Come with me."

Anil and Tarik followed Sanjay to the side of the building. Sanjay stepped inside and came back out with a large box. He handed it to Anil. It had the name Samir scribbled on the top in black ink. "Give this to Samir, the kid in the yellow shirt." He pointed to Samir once the box was in Anil's hands. Sanjay had made sure that the recruits didn't know one another. Sanjay was convinced that familiarity breeds risk as well as contempt. This anonymity was important for the mission, as he couldn't afford any last minute reservations to spread like the flu inside the group.

Anil walked to where Samir was standing and set the box down at his feet. Sanjay sidestepped Anil and reached down to open the top of the box. "Samir, you have one nylon vest that is lined with two sticks of C-4 plastique. The trigger is already set and is activated by your cell phone. I will text you the number this afternoon. Also, I have provided you with a 9MM handgun with two magazines that hold 25 rounds each. Your vest has two internal pockets for the magazines, and you will need to carry the gun in your back holster, which is also in the box. You will receive instructions regarding the entry gate where Bhargav will allow you to gain entry. This will also be texted to you once he is assigned to one of the ticketing gates."

Sanjay reentered his shed, and after a couple of minutes, he exited with a dark green canvas-backed wheelchair in front of him. He had installed a crude ramp from the door of the building down to the ground, allowing him to navigate the nine inch drop from inside to outside with relative ease. Once Sanjay reached the hard packed dirt, he wheeled the chair directly in front of Sidhar.

Sidhar eyed the wheelchair with palpable apprehension. "Why do I need a wheelchair, Swami?"

The question stood unanswered for several tense seconds. Sanjay eyed his recruit, searching for any sign that there might be a lack of necessary commitment. Feeling that this was indeed a natural question, Sanjay answered his question, "Trust is required. We have spent countless hours in preparation for this event. We have put together a plan that will work. The chair is an important part of that plan. I am not asking you to commit suicide in the chair. You will simply be responsible for the appropriate positioning of the chair to create as much carnage as possible." For an uncomfortable number of seconds, Sanjay maintained his deadly serious stare, as he waited for the right answer.

"I understand." Although less than exuberant, Sidhar was back on board with his role in the plan.

"There are two pockets under the seat that hold two large bricks of C4 explosive and both pockets are packed full of nails, glass, and pellets that will explode into the crowd. Most of this shrapnel should be lethal up to fifty to one hundred feet from the epicenter of the explosion. This might be the most important part of the entire operation. You will receive a text immediately before the event, which will provide clear directions as to where the chair must be positioned for ultimate effect. Are you clear?"

"Very clear, sir." Sidhar reached out and touched the firm seat of the wheelchair. With his forefinger, he traced the vague outline of both bricks of C4 plastique that would act as his uncomfortable seat for a couple of hours.

Sanjay retraced his steps back to his storage facility and quickly reappeared carrying what looked like a musical instrument case. "Ahul, it is my understanding that you were taught how to fire a bazooka. Is this correct?"

"Yessir, Swami. Uhhh...I mean, yes sir." He quickly corrected his initial, far too familiar response.

"This baritone saxophone case has been altered specifically to house a folded M9 Bazooka." Sanjay set the case in front of Ahul, turned the key that was already inserted in the oversized Master Lock that was obviously not part of the original case, and opened the case fully, exposing the ominous military grade weapon.

"How in the world do you expect me to get this past security?" The size of the case deserved this type of concern.

"You speak the best English of all of us, Ahul. For this reason, you will be acting as one of the members of the band that will be playing at the event. Tarik will be accompanying you as one of the vocalists. We will be providing you both with credible U.S. passports and you will arrive four hours before the event starts. You will check in with a woman named Sharya at the will call ticket window. She will allow you both entry through the VIP gate next to the will call booth. She will escort you to a small janitorial closet that is not currently used in the facility. You will be able to lock it once inside. The closet is located in a lower level corridor and is adjacent to the south stage entrance. The concert stage has been set up in a way that only utilizes the north stage entrance, so there should not be any interference. I doubt that anyone will be in this part of the stadium when you need to be in place."

"Wow. That is one amazing piece of machinery." The sun poked out of the clouds for a moment and the M9 came to life, the bright reflection causing Ahul to squint as he continued to examine his new wielder of death to those that deserved it.

"Tarik, Ahul will brief you on the loading of the bazooka. It is very important that you run through test firings in the closet. There should be plenty of room." Sanjay pulled a small .38 caliber pistol out of his waistband and handed it to Tarik. "This will be used if there is anyone that keeps you and Ahul from gaining an appropriate firing position in the tunnel. Understand?"

Both Tarik and Ahul answered in unison. "Yes, sir."

"As you can see, there is also a 9MM handgun in the large pocket of the case with one fully loaded magazine. "Like I just told Tarik, this will only be necessary if you find that people are blocking your position at the south stage opening where you will kneel in firing position. Your target will be the posts that hold up the right hand portion of the stage. Once they are destroyed, the entire stage should collapse to the turf twenty feet below. Timing and any changes to the primary target will be provided via text while you are in the closet."

"Can I touch it?" Ahul was reaching for one of the large, silver tipped mortars that were secured by large Velcro strips on either side of the main housing.

"No. Do not touch until you reach the closet. These are not toys." Sanjay turned and headed back to his office of horrors.

"Anil, come with me." Anil followed in lock step with Sanjay until they were inside the building.

Sanjay handed Anil an assault rifle that he had just retrieved from a large cardboard box. Anil instantly recognized it as the Omni Hybrid Maxx P3 AR-15 semi-automatic rifle with a 60+1 magazine. Sanjay reached back into the box and retrieved two additional full magazines and handed them to Anil as well.

Sanjay retrieved a similar rifle for himself and placed it on the small tray table behind Anil. He reached back into the box and pulled out two pieces of clothing that looked like hunting vests, each having a number of Velcro strips that hung unsecured down the back of the vest.

Without speaking, Sanjay lifted his rifle and placed the vest face down on the table. He carefully laid the AR-15 into place and secured the gun in three places. The most complex strap had a thick piece of Velcro that wrapped around the stock and a secondary strap off the main strap that curved around the bottom of the stock to keep the gun from sliding down the back of the vest. The top strap nearest the neckline secured the sixteen inch barrel, while the middle bifurcated strap, circled the main handle and wrapped around the trigger housing. Sanjay checked the security of the Velcro around the weapon and then pulled the vest over his t-shirt to model for Anil how the gun would be holstered for entry into the stadium.

Anil followed the same steps, and once both were wearing the required clothing, Sanjay reached into a smaller box to his left and handed two fully loaded magazines to Anil. "Place these in the side pockets on the front of the vests. Once we start shooting, we will only have a couple of minutes before they find our positions. I will give you further instructions before we head over."

"Yes, sir!" Anil was ecstatic that he had been chosen to accompany the boss.

After removing the vests, they both exited the building and Sanjay motioned all the recruits to move closer to his position near the building.

"Comrades, we will not allow this threat to take over India. We are called to take action today. This is not just about religion. This is about the Indian way of life. All that we hold dear about Mother India. We must control this outright lying and deceit from the West. You have all lived in poverty for your entire lives. You have tasted the bitter life of the unspoken world that we know as the slums of Mumbai. These people say that they are here to help the poor of India. They say that they are here to spread love and kindness. Do not believe these lies. They are immoral infidels. They have turned their backs to Allah. They are here to pilfer India. They have hoodwinked the people and they have pulled the wool over the eyes of India's government. They seek to take all that India has to offer the world for their own benefit. They prefer to own us as slaves to their greed and imperialism. They seek to rule our country and the world. We must take this seriously. We are the *only* hope for Mother India."

Sanjay reached into the left rear pocket of his jeans and pulled out envelopes for each recruit gathered in the circle with him. "These are your instructions for this evening. You will find a map of the stadium with your entry point circled in red ink. You will also see the name of the person that you will seek out to let you gain entrance. You must be adamant that someone find this person, or you will jeopardize the entire mission. Only these people can get you through security without further scrutiny. Further instructions will come via text throughout the day. Do I make myself clear?"

No answer.

"Do I make myself clear?" Sanjay screamed his repetition of the question, spittle flying from his lips into the faces of those gathered.

Every one of them answered loudly and in unison. "Yes, sir."

23

The line from every ticket gate that led into the stadium wrapped through a maze of red, velvet ropes that stretched some two or three hundred feet from the actual entrance to the streets that surrounded the venue. On all sides, the streets that abutted the stadium had been barricaded early in the morning by law enforcement and had now become an outdoor waiting room for people trying to gain access to the entry queue for the event.

The energy was electric. Crowds were singing hymns and shouting hallelujahs and small groups were singing contemporary Christian chart toppers at the top of their lungs in both Hindi and English. Many in the crowd had been standing in the hot sun for hours, their energy waning until just this moment. The indication that the gates would open quickly circulated through the masses reenergizing the mob of anxious ticket holders.

After receiving the official green light to open the gates at exactly six thirty, Hetal Patel sent a text to all the gate supervisors. Red lights above each metal detector were illuminated, indicating that they were now ready for use. A mighty roar rose from the crowd as the ticket checkers removed the barricades that were the last obstacle between their place in line, where most had been standing for hours on end, and their comfortable assigned seat in the stadium.

A steady stream of excited ticket holders quickly flooded all concourses. Within a matter of minutes, there were long lines at every concession stand and concert t-shirt vendor kiosk as excited fans from all walks of Indian life grabbed plenty of food and souvenirs before heading to their seats where they would settle in for the next few hours.

Sanjay, after receiving the text from his boss, sent his own green light text to his chosen team of mercenaries, all of them now making their way to their assigned positions in the stadium as per the plan. The message was clear and concise:

SWAMI: GO TIME... EXACTLY 7:14PM

Sanjay tucked his cell phone in his front pocket and worked his way upstream through the entering masses, until he was safely outside the stadium. As much as he craved attention from Commander Singha and Giri, his stomach was in knots, knowing that so many innocent Indians would die at his hands this night. He could feel the stock of the AR-15 digging into his lower back. He turned back and scanned the large crowd, realizing that he did not have the stomach for killing innocent people. How would anyone know if he left the stadium before the carnage began? His pace quickened as he headed in the direction of his parked car. He was unable to stop the unexpected tears that now clouded his eyes. What had he just done? The increasingly intense pain in his gut caused him to double over just as he reached the driver side door. He dropped to his knees and breathed deeply as he looked back over his shoulder towards the arena.

Unseen by all humans in attendance, a swarm of hundreds of angels floated majestically above the stadium as the first explosion rocked the foundations of the building. With anger and frustration in their heavenly eyes, they watched as the unspeakable carnage began. They would protect all that they could amidst this wave of irrational evil. They could see many bands of demons in the stadium below, swirling like angry hawks in search of prey. Their inability to look in the direction of the Angels indicated the vast limitations of their loudly professed, yet feigned power.

"His will be done! On this Earth and today in India!" Triskal raised his shining sword high into the air as he yelled his exhortation to the Heavenly Host.

One by one, angels knifed through the air into the chaotic stadium, ready for the battle against evil.

The Aftermath

No temptation has overtaken you except such as is common to man; but God is faithful, who will not allow you to be tempted beyond what you are able, but with the temptation will also make the way of escape, that you may be able to bear it.

— 1 Corinthians 11:13 (New King James Version)

"Whether or not you believe in God, you must believe this: when we as a species abandon our trust in a power greater than us, we abandon our sense of accountability. Faiths... all faiths... are admonitions that there is something we cannot understand, something to which we are accountable. With faith we are accountable to each other, to ourselves, and to a higher truth. Religion is flawed, but only because man is flawed. The church consists of a brotherhood of imperfect, simple souls wanting only to be a voice of compassion in a world spinning out of control."

— Dan Brown, Angels & Demons

24

MUMBAI, INDIA
9:00 P.M.
JUNE 3, 2022

Orion and Maritius glided onto the only part of the main stage that was still standing. They stood for minutes looking over the brutality that had just been handed out by the evil one. Demonic spirits continued to shoot back and forth across the stadium, stopping on occasion near the bodies of those that littered the stands and the turf, as if they were hunters on safari surveying their human prizes. Orion and Maritius could hear the hissing cackles of pride and mockery when some of these spirits were close enough to their position on stage.

"My brother," Orion addressed Maritius as his eyes scanned the destruction that was all around them, "Why must these tragedies take place in order to fulfill our Father's plan for this world?" His question was rhetorical but clearly indicated the sharp pain that he felt at this moment.

"His will is greater than even our understanding, Orion. May God welcome these chosen few, those that have given their lives on this fateful day, into His kingdom forever." They both bowed their heads in reverence to their God.

Leshyra, one of Harut's minions, saw the two angels standing on the stage and flew directly towards Orion, abruptly stopping and hovering only inches from his face. Orion didn't flinch, knowing that this imp had no power when it came to the Heavenly Host. Leshyra's nostrils flared with glowing red capillaries and his yellowish eyes squinted into the Dark blue eyes of his nemesis. "What ya think about this, you apologists for weak humans?" He spit through his perfectly white teeth as he mocked the Angels. "What is wrong? Are you so very sad?"

"Some of the lost may not always be able to pick the evil spirits out of a crowd, Leshyra." Orion took a commanding step forward pushing the demons to the edge of the stage. "Some may not realize when you poison their minds with your evil, but be assured that the Heavenly Host will always be there to protect and preserve those who are called by His name. We will continue to work for the glory of God so that the lost will be found." Orion raised his left hand to Heaven and closed his eyes only for a millisecond.

Without warning, and with one wave of his mighty arm, Orion flung Leshyra into the Mezzanine section of the stadium. He tumbled clumsily into the last row of seats and bounced off the top wall before flopping down in the aisle directly beside the exit ramp that led to the concession area. The other demons in the stadium laughed hysterically, chiding their partner for his stupidity in fraternizing with the angels. Leshyra, having been reminded that his power would always be far inferior to that of the angels, brushed himself off and angrily darted out of the stadium to avoid further embarrassment.

Orion looked at Maritius who was now simply gazing heavenward as he watched Leshyra leave this world with his wings figuratively clipped.

Maritius turned his eyes back to Orion and motioned towards the back of the stadium complex, "Let's go! We have seen quite enough evil for today." His brilliant white wings unfurled with a snap before leading the way for he and Orion to pass over the remarkable damage that had been done by these godless humans at the behest of the demons that still littered the arena.

25

ergeant Neeraj Valsangikar approached the makeshift podium that had been set up in the Leela Hotel lobby located approximately two miles from where the arena massacre had taken place. A press conference had been scheduled only an hour before to formerly address the media and the residents of Mumbai. The news reporting thus far had been all over the map, some blaming terrorists, others claiming it was a random act of violence, others claiming that it was being overblown and was simply a minor incident. The death toll reporting was also questionable. The many Hindi, English, Punjabi, Marathi, or Gujarati news channels that broadcasted news across India had all raced to get the latest information to the Indian public, many times without adequate confirmation or vetting of the minute by minute information being received from their correspondents at ground zero. Estimates from tens to hundreds to thousands killed were frustrating and confusing at best.

Sergeant Valsangikar tapped the microphone before he began to speak. "Good evening," he paused with obvious emotion trapping the words in his mouth. "This is a very sad day for Mumbai." He paused again and cleared his throat, "It is a sad day for India and a sad day for the world."

Flashbulbs lit up the small lobby of the Leela as reporters moved their microphones and iPhones up and down and side to side to try to get the best audio or video position among the crowded pack of rabid news gatherers. Every reporter was in it for themselves with an almost unnatural focus on the task at hand, each with a self-centered view of their value as a reporter. The art of decorum and respect had long since left these ranks, just like it had throughout the rest of the world. They were there to get the story at whatever cost, and they needed to do it better than anyone else in the room.

"Thus far, we must report approximately three hundred and twenty two deaths at the hands of these animals and over one thousand wounded. Unfortunately, these numbers will continue to rise as we get updated reports." Sergeant Valsangikar bowed his head as he continued to read from his handwritten notes. "We have far more questions than answers at this time but will continue to update you on the situation as we receive more information. We ask that you maintain calm and stay patient as we attempt to manage this disaster."

"It has been confirmed that this attack was at the hands of IBAWIF, the Islamic Brotherhood Against Western Infidel Factions. This particular attack was carried out by one of their smaller, regional factions, the Indian Liberation Resistance Organization, a militant group that has continued to target Christians, Jews and even Hindus here in this country for years.

This is their most brazen show of indiscretion and a continued attempt to terrorize our country."

Neeraj cleared his throat before he continued, "We will not stand idly by as this cancer continues to seek the destruction of that which is good and right in India. The people that were targeted and killed tonight, although many are not Indian by birth, they are part of the diverse and rich fabric of India. They were here for the benefit of the people of this country. They came with a message of peace and love. Unfortunately, our world is filled with evil and hate that we can't even begin to fathom."

Neeraj paused just long enough for the cacophony of shouted questions to start again from the ranks of the rabid media mob. A young woman in the front row respectfully raised her hand. Sergeant Valsangikar had a reputation for only answering questions from those in the media that were respectful during a press conference.

"Quiet, please!" The Sergeant's face swelled with the redness of anger as he shouted over the almost deafening shouts coming at him from almost every direction. He looked down from his podium and pointed to the reporter still raising her hand. "We only have time for one question. You. Light blue shirt in the front row."

"Yes, sir. Thank you, Sergeant. It was reported that the stage was almost completely destroyed during the attack. Were any of the leaders or musicians that were on stage killed or injured?" She lowered her hand as she finished.

Valsangikar looked down at the scribbled notes on the podium. "At this point, we know that at least two security guards were killed and two of the band members were injured and taken to a local hospital. Not sure about the severity of their injuries. Reports are coming in every few minutes."

The reporter raised her hand but did not wait to be called on before asking a follow up question. "What about Rajeev Bansal or the gentleman from America that were the keynote speakers?"

"No, ma'am. I am sorry, but we don't have any word yet on either Rajeev or Andrew Morrison, the gentleman from the United States." The gaggle of anxious reporters started to yell over each other again trying to gain the Sergeant's attention.

"Enough. Enough. Quiet, please!" The crowd noise continued to boil out of control. "No more questions!" Sergeant Valsangikar stepped back away from the podium until the noise died down. He stepped back to the microphone and continued, "I will not be answering any more of your questions at this time. We have much to do and this is clearly not the time."

The frenzied circus of media personnel cowered back into their seats and the furious shouting turned to muted whispers between one another as they fought for space in the crowded lobby.

Neeraj bowed his head again as he looked back at his notes. "We will find the people behind these unjust and cowardly attacks on innocent people. The ignorance and hatred will not be tolerated. We will schedule another press briefing for tomorrow night at the same time. Thank you."

The Visitation

"You can take the Indian out of the family, but you cannot take the family out of India.
— **Amit Kalantri**

"Make yourself familiar with the angels and behold them frequently in spirit; for without being seen, they are present with you."
— **St. Francis de Sales**

"May your neighbors respect you, trouble neglect you, the angels protect you, and Heaven accept you."
— **Irish Saying**

26

Sanjay woke with a start. The tiny back room of his mother's home that had once been his sister's room was awash with light. The fierce intensity of the light caused him to blink and close his eyes. He threw back his sheets and backed up against the wall that acted as his headboard directly behind the twin sized mattress that had served as his bed for the last five nights.

Slowly, his eyes became more accustomed to the light and he was able to squint towards the light source. To his amazement, two glowing figures, dressed in flowing white robes, stood at the end of his bed. Their hair was dazzling white, possibly even brighter white than the garments that they were wearing. Their eyes were a breathtaking blue, with a focused intensity that he had never experienced.

Without saying a word, the two figures floated effortlessly to each side of Sanjay's small bed. Orion reached out his right hand and placed it on the top of Sanjay's head.

Sanjay closed his eyes as a feeling of remorse and sadness washed over him. In his mind, the evil that took place in the stadium a week back flicked through his mind frame by frame, as if he were watching a highlight reel on a news channel. Each image jolted Sanjay with its realism and sheer horror. The explosions that maimed and killed women, children, entire families. The visions of snipers shooting innocent victims one by one as they looked for escape. The collapse of the stage that only seconds before acted as the platform for what Sanjay remembered to be beautiful music. What had he done? For what purpose? How could he have orchestrated these horrific acts of pure evil?

As Sanjay opened his eyes, tears flowed down his cheeks. Both angels were now floating in the corner of the room, still glowing so brightly that Sanjay could barely keep his eyes on them. Their outstretched wings spanned at least twelve feet and beat slowly against the warm air that filled his room. Their magnificent beauty was overwhelming. Sanjay could feel the breeze from the wings briefly intensify as the two bowed their heads, turned, and abruptly shot through the wall behind them.

The room was dark once again, his visitors nowhere to be found. The wall was still fully intact. He sat on the bed for several long minutes before dropping to the side of the bed on his knees. "God, who are you? I do not know you. I am scared, God. Why were they here? Did you send them?" Sanjay paused, hoping for an audible answer to his questions. "I am so sorry for my actions. Please forgive us. Please forgive me." Sanjay continued to pray for hours. For the first time in his life, he felt the presence of God. For the first time in a week, he felt like he could breathe again. Triskal and Maritius hovered momentarily above Sanjay's tiny bedroom. They watched as he knelt in prayerful consideration of their visit. With their brilliant wings now beating in perfect unison, they soared back into the dark night of Mumbai.

'Who were these mysterious visitors? They had to be angels.' Sanjay was now wide awake. He sat in his bed until almost noon and wrestled with these thoughts. 'Ghosts aren't real. Could it be just a dream?' He knew in his heart that this was not the case.

The visitors had not spoken a word, but the message that they were able to convey by laying hands on Sanjay's head was overwhelming. He was given a mission, an opportunity to right the wrong that he had helped to create. There was no question in Sanjay's mind that they had been sent from above. They had kindness and love in those piercing blue eyes, but their message was serious and undeniable. Sanjay grabbed a pen and started to write down the angel's unspoken instructions on the back of a used envelope. He would be faithful to their command.

27

ROORKEE, INDIA
8:47 A.M.
JUNE 16, 2022

Sleep had once again been difficult for Sanjay. He had not been to work in almost two weeks. Was Hetal looking for him or did they just think he was afraid to come back to the stadium? Did they have any idea that he might be tied to the vicious group responsible for the Mumbai massacre? His mind twirled endlessly in pursuit of a reasonable plan to reach out to the leaders of the group that had put on the show at the stadium. But how could he schedule a meeting with these powerful people that he had never met before? He could not remember any of the American's names or if any of them lived or worked in Mumbai. He had spoken briefly with one gentleman named Rajiv, who seemed to be one of the main speakers at the event. Rajiv had been extremely polite and seemed to be a very capable and trustworthy individual. This was the person that Sanjay needed to contact.

During his restless night of intermittent dreams that usually featured his recent angelic visitors, his convincingly alive sister prodding him to turn himself in, the horrible sights associated with last week's attack, or the recurring hunt for Commander Singha at the training compound, Sanjay had come up with a plan to make contact and confess to the appropriate authorities what he had done.

He would make an unscheduled visit to the office of his former boss at Kingsford Garden Stadium. Hetal Patel knew everyone in management at the stadium and had been in close contact with the group that hosted the event. He would know exactly who to talk to about this situation. The burning question in Sanjay's mind still lingered. How could he trust Mr. Patel not to immediately turn him over to the authorities? Sanjay wanted to speak with the leaders of the group first, before turning himself in to the Indian police. He desperately needed to apologize in person. If already in jail, an apology might not come across as genuine. The other, likely unconscious driver of Sanjay's strategy was the fact that growing up in the slums of Mumbai had not necessarily instilled a great deal of confidence in Indian law enforcement.

As Sanjay walked the twenty or so blocks to the stadium, he practiced the speech that he planned to give to Mr. Patel, "Sir, I am in desperate need of a favor. I know of very important facts related to the recent attacks here at the stadium." He paused and restarted, speaking out loud to himself, "Mr. Patel, good morning. I am needing you to provide me the name of the leader of the group that was putting on the show last week when the bombing and killings happened."

The words just never seemed to come out right. His message needed to be perfect so that he would not cause unwanted concern that might lead to Mr. Patel prematurely contacting law enforcement, thereby keeping him from achieving his goal of speaking with those in charge of the rally first.

Sanjay arrived at the stadium only two minutes before nine o'clock in the morning, his normally expected start time. The security was much tighter at the stadium. As he approached the employee entrance next to Gate B, he noticed two heavily armed guards sitting in folding chairs on either side of the double doors.

"Can we help you, young man?" The officer held up the palm of his hand in the traditional stop position.

"Uh, yes, officer." Sanjay pulled out his wallet and fumbled for his security clearance card, "Sanjay Swaminathan, sir. I work in security for Mr. Patel." His heart raced as the other officer scanned a clipboard.

"Alright. Head of stadium security, are you? Seems like you have been a no show since the event."

"Uh, yeah. The event really scared me and my family. Took some time off to gather myself. I am here to tender my official resignation to Hetal bhai." Sanjay's confidence started to fade a bit.

"We understand. You can go up," The officer with the clipboard opened the door for Sanjay.

Out of habit, he went straight to his timecard slot located on the wall outside of the facilities administration office. Not surprisingly, his timecard was no longer in the slot and his printed name plate had been removed. The well-used, and certainly older than Sanjay, time clock machine maintained its second by second clicking cadence as Sanjay stood pondering how he would start the conversation with Mr. Patel.

Instead of walking down the main concourse to his tiny security office on the east end of the stadium, he took the stairs on his left that led up to Hetal Patel's facility management suite located on the west side of the main entrance.

Sanjay knocked twice on Mr. Patel's door before turning the knob and letting himself in. "Good morning, boss. Do you have a couple of minutes?" His voice cracked due to his intense nervousness.

"Sanjay. Where have you been? With some of the bodies still not identified, we thought you might have been one of the victims of the attack?" His eyes squinted just a bit as Sanjay took the seat in front of his desk. Hetal sat back in his black leather office chair and clasped his hands behind his head. He studied his head of security carefully, "I am curious. What brings you back here today after being missing in action for two weeks?"

"Uh. Yes. Yes sir," Sanjay stammered a bit as he launched into his prepared speech, "Um, yeah. I am needing of a favor, boss. A huge favor."

"O.K., Sanjay. I am listening."

"Please, first...." Sanjay's words trailed off. He hesitated a couple of seconds and then continued, "I have to apologize for my unforgivable actions. I have very important information regarding the attack last week that I must provide to Rajiv, the man I met at the stadium before the event started. Is he one of the leaders or something like that?"

"What do you mean by important information?" Mr. Patel was now laser focused on his employee, "You had something to do with this?" His face swelled red with anger.

"Wait, boss. I am not able to discuss the details, until I meet with Mr. Rajiv. You have to understand that if I am not able to convey the message to him, I will not be providing any additional information." Sanjay sat back in the chair with his arms crossed waiting for the reaction.

"What details, Sanjay?" Hetal sat straight up in his chair and placed both hands firmly on the desk in front of him. "Why would you need to talk with only Rajiv? I don't understand." He pushed himself into a standing position, "You better hope that you have not brought shame to me or to this team." He picked up his cell phone that had been resting on the desk in front of him and started dialing.

"Who are you calling? Hetal bhai, please! I need to speak with Rajiv!"

"Yes, good morning. Agent Pai please."

Sanjay jumped up and slammed his hand down on the button with the red LED light that indicated the line being used for the call. "I told you, Hetal. I will only talk with Rajiv. You have my phone number. Tell him, and only him, to call me." Sanjay yanked the cord out of the back of the phone and ran out of the office. He couldn't chance exiting through the employee entrance because of the guards, so he ran towards the emergency stairs near Gate C. He crashed through the exit door after descending four flights of stairs. Although loud alarms rang throughout the stadium, Sanjay was across the street in a matter of seconds and lost in a sea of people waiting at one of the city's busiest bus stops.

At the back of the crowd, he casually removed the easily recognizable red sweater that he was wearing over a white undershirt and tucked it into his pants. He gazed back in the direction of the stadium, and with no perceivable threat of being spotted, he continued his retreat from the stadium for several blocks until he reached another bus stop where a Mumbai City Transit bus was in the process of boarding. He jumped on at the last minute, looking over his shoulder to make sure he had not been followed. The bus destination didn't really matter to Sanjay. He would get off at the first stop and walk back home.

28

As promised by Rajiv the morning after the unscheduled meeting in Hetal Patel's office, Rajiv's customary driver pulled up to the Gate J entrance at a quarter until seven in the morning. The driver got out of the Mahindra Scorpio SUV and offered a hand to pick up Sanjay's one piece of luggage. "Good morning, sir. I am Manish and I will be pleased to drive you to Pune today. Please allow me stow your luggage."

"Thank you," Sanjay had never traveled to Pune but remembered his grandmother telling him stories of the remarkable beauty of the drive between Bombay and Pune. "How long is the drive, Manish?"

"Approximately three and one half hours, only. We will go straight away to the JW Marriott in Pune. I have been told that you should check in to the hotel, freshen up a bit and we will head to the Oxford Golf Club to meet the group for lunch."

"That is fine. Thank you." Sanjay's heart rate quickened as he thought of the impending meeting and the information that he would be forced to deliver.

Sanjay was stunned at the grandeur of the mountains and pristine countryside between Mumbai and Pune. His grandmother was absolutely correct. The area around Lonavala was gorgeous. The rain this morning caused waterfalls to gush over cliffs, often dissecting the brilliant green forested hillsides with many of the streams in the valleys running much higher than was typical during this early part of the monsoon season. Sanjay was mesmerized by the dense mist that seemed to dance around the peaks of the mountains and dip into the deep valleys of this resort area. This was a playground for the rich, not for a poor slum dweller like him. His mind drifted into a dream state where he fantasized of owning one of the mansions on a hill overlooking this beautiful land.

The loud honking of the Tata truck behind them snapped him back into reality. "How much longer until we get to Pune, Manish? Could really use a restroom."

"Not to worry, sir. We will stop at the roadside station in only a few minutes. I could use the break myself."

The line of cars waiting to be cleared for entry to the drop off area for the JW Marriott hotel in Pune was at least ten cars deep. Sanjay watched as each car was carefully surveilled by armed guards before getting the green light to proceed through the gates. A large flat mirror was rolled under each car to check for explosives and all of the doors were opened to check the luggage situation. He watched as the new hotel guests exited their vehicles and proceeded through the metal detectors before heading into the lobby. His mind danced with thoughts of what these obviously important people must do for a living. Were they famous? Where did they all travel from to get to Pune? Why were they here? His curiosity ran wild.

Manish stopped the car directly in front of the main entrance, exited the vehicle, and pulled Sanjay's bag out of the back of the truck. He gave the bag to the bellman to run it through the metal detector. "Pleased to be picking you up again in only one hour, sir." Manish put his hands together and bowed in a traditional Namaste manner. "You will be meeting Rajiv bhai for lunch at the Oxford Club at half past noon."

"Sounds good. Thank you." Sanjay meekly walked towards the door but was quickly redirected to take out everything in his pockets and asked to step through the metal detector before entering the lobby.

Manish pulled back into the loading zone precisely at noon and motioned for Sanjay to hop into the back seat of the car. Thirty minutes later, the limo assigned to him for the day crested the hill above the Oxford Golf Club. Sanjay could see all eighteen holes laid out across the valley. The view was breathtaking. He had no idea that India contained such beauty.

Manish dropped off Sanjay near the entrance to the golf shop where a sharply dressed white man was waiting on a bench next to the bag drop area. Sanjay bowed his head in shame, as Andrew stood up and started walking in his direction.

"Good afternoon, Sanjay," Andrew reached out his hand.

Sanjay's hand was visibly shaking as he shook the stranger's hand. "Don't be frightened, Sanjay. You are safe here. Mr. Bansal, Mr. Haas, and Mr. Jaworski are waiting inside."

"Thank you, sir. Thank you." Sanjay followed Andrew through the pro shop and into a small courtyard next to the Greenside Grill restaurant.

As they approached the table where Trevor, Rajiv, and Harold were sitting, Sanjay noticed that Rajiv had a full cast on his leg and two crutches propped against the wall behind him.

"Please know that I am so sorry, sir. I know that you all must be hating me so much. I can see it in your faces," Sanjay stammered as he continued, "Uh, uh, I don't know how to say... I am so very disappointed in my actions."

"Sit, please," Rajiv, stone faced, motioned towards the seat next to him, "Please, have a seat. We don't hate you. While we still struggle with our anger, we appreciate that you are here today."

Rajiv waved to one of the servers standing in the doorway that led to the kitchen. He hurried over to the table, "Yes, sir. What can I get you?"

"Would you be so kind as to bring another glass of water for our guest?" Rajiv adjusted his chair, so that he was now directly facing Sanjay. He placed his right hand gingerly on Sanjay's forearm, "We are not here to judge anyone today, but we would like to know what information that you might have concerning the events that took place in Mumbai."

For over an hour, Sanjay recounted all the events that led up to the attack. From his recruitment by Rahul to the misery of the training camp under Commander Singha to his role in the Mumbai cricket stadium massacre. The story flowed out of Sanjay, interrupted only by the occasional outburst of emotional tears for what he and this terrorist group of murderers had done to these innocent people.

As Sanjay described the visit by the angels, everyone at the table was mesmerized by the vivid details presented by the young man in front of them. These men of God had never had such a visit in their own lives, and each felt a tinge of jealousy that Sanjay had been witness to such an event.

Once the story was fully told, Rajiv placed his hand on the slumped shoulders of the still sobbing Sanjay. "Thank you, Sanjay. Thank you for your honesty and bravery to come visit us today." Sanjay looked up into the eyes of this remarkably kind Indian gentleman.

"As you know, we have to place this in the hands of the Central Bureau of Investigation and the police here in India. You will need to give them your statement as well."

"Yes sir. I know, sir. I am ready."

"Of course, we are all very angry and feel a great pain of loss, but we forgive you, my son. God can also forgive you. After what you told us yesterday, we have prayed about this situation very fervently and have worked with law enforcement here in India to come up with a possible plan."

Sanjay sat up abruptly and looked feverishly around the room. He had not contemplated the possibility that law enforcement would be involved this quickly. Rajiv tightened his grip on Sanjay's shoulder ever so slightly, "Don't be afraid. Our proposed plan involves you only if you are a willing participant. Are you willing to hear us out, my friend?"

Sanjay nodded sheepishly and looked down at the floor. "Yes, sir. I owe you at least that, sir."

Rajiv reached into the leather satchel at his side and retrieved a manila folder that he placed in front of Sanjay. "Based on what you had told Hetal regarding your involvement in the Indian Liberation Resistance Organization, and what you have now confirmed today, we have outlined a preliminary plan that both the Central Intelligence Bureau, India's internal intelligence agency and the FBI from America believe will help us infiltrate this group and bring them to justice."

Rajiv waved to another table at the opposite side of the restaurant where two Indian gentlemen in dark blue suits were eating lunch. Both stood up, pushed their chairs back under the table and joined Rajiv, Sanjay, and the rest of the group. Trevor and Andrew gave up their seats directly across from Sanjay and Rajiv to the newcomers.

"Let me introduce Agents Pai and Bandela. They will be walking you through the plan that we have put together," Rajiv adjusted his casted right leg, sat back in his chair, and exhaled loudly.

"Good afternoon, Sanjay. I am Agent Bandela, and I will be the lead in this investigation." The confidence in Agent Bandela's booming voice was palpable, "For us to successfully stop future attacks of this nature, we will need your full cooperation and a large measure of bravery and fearlessness."

Sanjay squirmed slightly in his now very uncomfortable chair. Agent Bandela continued to lay out the plan, utilizing the documents that he had now taken out of the folder and laid in front of his prospective under cover recruit. "First, I must ask what orders have you been given by the IRLO? What does the organization expect from you? Do they have any immediate attacks planned? Are you back in Mumbai for good or do you expect to rejoin the group in Roorkee at some point?"

Sanjay cleared his throat, "Yes, sir. I have received a text from Commander Singha this morning itself requiring me to be back in Roorkee next week for further training and instructions. Not much information was given, as usual. All planning and assignments are given only in person. I am worried that they have used the GPS tracking device in my ankle to determine that I am now in Pune. This might have caused them to request for my return." Sanjay carefully assessed Agent Bandela's reaction. He was impressed by the way Agent Bandela carried himself. If he were to agree to this mission, he would have to decide if this man of justice and honor could adequately protect him.

"A GPS device, is it?" Bandela stroked his manicured goatee as he pondered this. "Excuse us, Sanjay, I need to have a private word with Agent Pai.

"Yes, sir," Sanjay watched as the two law enforcement professionals stepped outside the restaurant. After a quick conversation, Agent Pai took out his cell phone and placed a call. After what seemed like an eternity to Sanjay, the two agents rejoined the others at the table.

"Sorry for the interruption, gentlemen. The GPS device mentioned by Sanjay might be an unexpected gift. We have added an element to the plan that we think might be very helpful." Agent Bandela's piercing stare sent a message that what he would be saying next was non-negotiable.

"Agent Pai just made an appointment with Dr. Mandahar Singh at a surgery center in Pune for later this afternoon. Dr. Singh will be inserting our own GPS device into your ankle utilizing the same incision that was made when the first GPS unit was surgically inserted. The other device will remain intact. He will go through the same scar and will close the wound internally so that it will be very difficult to notice."

Agent Bandela paused to let this sink in. "This will allow us to know exactly where you are at all times, and if things become dangerous, we will be able to extract you when and if necessary. This is more for your protection than anything. Are you willing to proceed, Sanjay?"

"Yes, sir."

Agent Pai placed a new phone on the table in front of Sanjay, "We are providing you with this untraceable mobile phone for use only to call the number that is already programmed." Agent Pai's voice was a bit raspy due to many years of smoking, but his level of confidence rivaled that of Agent Bandela, "It is not to be used for any other calls. Do we have an understanding?"

"Yes sir, Agent Pai," Sanjay nodded his head in agreement.

Agent Pai continued, "You will need to find an appropriate place to keep the phone. You should not have it with you while you are on the Roorkee site. You will use the phone to give us all details related to all future plans of the organization. We will give you instructions based on these details."

For the next fifteen minutes, both agents went through the entire plan with Sanjay and once Sanjay had agreed to the mission, they had him sign the appropriate documents that made the partnership official. "After the minor surgical procedure, we will have Manish drive you back to Mumbai tonight. There will be no need to stay tonight in Pune as this might put you in jeopardy. We will be communicating all of this to the FBI from the United States as well. You will be well protected. We appreciate your cooperation and although we can make no promises regarding how you will be treated in the court system for your participation in the Mumbai event, we can assure you that your cooperation will be looked at favorably by the judge."

After the agents had finished the briefing, Trevor stood up and shook both of their hands. "Gentlemen, thank you. Please know that we are at your disposal. Anything that you need from us, please don't hesitate to ask."

"Thank you, Trevor." Agent Bandela said as he waved goodbye to the rest of the group.

"Sanjay, I will ask Manish to take you to the hospital immediately. We have to get back to our meetings here at the resort, but from all of us, thank you for coming forward and for your willingness to help us stomp out the evil in our midst. You are being used by God in a mighty way to protect the country of India and the rest of the world. Thank you."

The rest of the group stood and made their way to where Sanjay was seated. They all put their hands on the shoulders of the young man and silently prayed for his protection before they made their way back to the conference center area. Rajiv asked Andrew to hand him his crutches. Once they were stabilized under his armpits, he reached out his hand to Sanjay, "God be with you, my friend. Until we meet again."

Sanjay followed the group out of the pro shop and watched them walk through the parking lot towards the cluster of buildings where their meetings were likely being held that afternoon. In only a couple of minutes, Manish would pull the Scorpio around to his position next to the first tee box and chauffer him to his surgical appointment.

29

ajiv, Harold, Trevor, and Andrew took their assigned seats around the conference table. Sixteen senior leaders of the Global Calling Organization were already in their seats, most of them engaged in casual conversations with other members of the team, an opportunistic way to both fill the time while the senior most leaders were still in the meeting with Sanjay, and to catch up with some of their close friends and colleagues around the table.

Rajiv picked up his pen and clinked his water glass to reconvene the meeting. "Sorry for the delay, everyone. We had a very productive meeting with Sanjay and are anxious to fill you all in on the plans that have been made surrounding his involvement in stopping this violent group of criminals that he was unfortunately associated with over the last several months."

"Trevor, would you please go over the minutes from our last conference call regarding the World Leadership Summit to be held in Goa?" Rajiv pushed the conference phone speaker to

Trevor so that the six other members that were on via phone could hear Trevor more clearly.

"My pleasure, Rajiv," Trevor rolled his leather backed conference table chair to a position directly in front of the speaker, "Thank you. As agreed in our last meeting, we will not be cancelling or postponing the upcoming leadership summit in Goa. It will be held during the third week of September, as originally planned. Our faith dictates that we continue this global mission with the confidence and expectation that God's plan supersedes any fear or trepidation that we might have because of the events that took place in Mumbai." Trevor looked around the room and was greeted by many confident nods from a number of those around the table. "Of course, we will be taking some very serious steps that we believe are necessary to increase the level of protection for our leaders and the conference attendees, and we will be providing an outline of these new security initiatives within the next several days. Most importantly, we will not allow this kind of violence and fear mongering to derail this very important movement in our world. We have spoken to leaders across India and, in all cases, faith trumps fear. Everyone to a person has been fully supportive of our desire to continue to move forward with the Goa summit."

Orion and Triskal floated above the meeting, each having the unique otherworldly ability to see through physical structures, almost like a supernatural sonar. They felt an overwhelming calm and great pride, due to the measure of faith and devotion being exhibited by these devout leaders that had been called by God to do His great work in the world. They continued to watch as Trevor outlined the plans for the World

Leadership Summit and then heard Rajiv carefully describe how Sanjay would be used to thwart any future terror threats that they might encounter.

A Mission from God

Let no one deceive you by any means; for that Day will not come unless the falling away comes first, and the man of sin is revealed, the son of perdition.

- 2 Thessalonians 2:3 (New King James Version)

Where lambs have nibbled, silent moves the feet of angels bright; unseen they pour blessing, and joy without ceasing, on each bud and blossom, and each sleeping bosom.

- WILLIAM BLAKE, *Night*

30

MUMBAI, INDIA
10:50 P.M.
JUNE 18, 2022

anjay was seated on one of the concrete benches outside of the stadium just beyond where yellow crime tape and oversized orange cones sealed off one of the main gates when his mobile phone began to vibrate in the oversized front pocket of his camouflage cargo shorts.

He retrieved the phone and stared for a long moment at the name that was flashing on the screen. Aakesh Sharma. Aakesh had been promoted to Lieutenant by Commander Singha and was typically used to give Singha's orders or clean up messy situations. Sanjay pressed the green button, "Lieutenant Sharma. Sanjay speaking." He could feel his pulse quicken as he waited for the response.

"Good evening, Sanjay. We will be expecting you to return to camp tomorrow. We fully expect you to have the capability to find your way to the train station in the morning. Am I correct?"

"Yes, sir. I will be on the first train in the morning. May I ask how long I will be in Roorkee this time?"

"You are not to ask questions!" Aakesh was suddenly yelling through the phone. "When Commander Singha gives an order, it is not to be questioned. You will stay as long as is required."

Sanjay pulled the phone a few inches away from his ear to lower the volume of Aakesh's angry outburst, "I understand, sir. I will arrive by late afternoon."

"Excellent," His tone was now much more subdued, "You have done well, and Commander Singha has bigger plans in store for you. You have shown yourself to be a dependable force against these infidels. You shall be rewarded upon your return."

"Thank you, Lieutenant." Sanjay couldn't help but feel mixed emotions. He had never received a compliment from any of the leaders of this cruel and inhumane group and was curious about what type of reward might be in store for him. Although intrigued and even a bit excited upon hearing this news from one of the people he feared most in this world, his mind quickly circled back to the reality of his recent visit by the angels, the commitment that had been made to Rajiv and the IB of India and the overwhelming fact that God had different plans in store for him.

"We will see you tomorrow. No delays," Sanjay's home screen popped back up on his phone. In typical Aakesh form, there was no 'goodbye' to indicate the end of the conversation.

31

As Sanjay disembarked from the train, he noticed a large sign with his name written in red letters being held by a well-dressed, taller gentleman in a white turban that was at the front of the large crowd that typically awaited those passengers arriving on the train. Somewhat confused, he walked towards the man. As he approached, the man took Sanjay's suitcase and motioned towards the parking area at the south side of the train station.

Sanjay followed the man as he quickly made his way to the parking lot. "Good afternoon, Sanjay. How was the trip?" His command of the English language was pure perfection.

"Who are you, sir?" The size and demeanor of this imposing individual had sent a very clear message to Sanjay that he should be respected.

"My name is not important. All you need to know is that I work for Singha. He has requested that I transport you personally to the camp. He is waiting for you."

Sanjay listened carefully, trying to read whether this was a good or bad thing to be told that Singha would be waiting for him. With no clear indication and without another word to his new driver, he climbed into the back seat of the Suzuki Maruti and settled into the cloth, rear passenger-side seat feeling a bit uneasy about what might be in store for him. Did Singha know of his meeting with Rajiv in Pune? Had they been tracking his every move with GPS? Why did he agree to come back to Roorkee when he had so much hatred and distrust for these people?

When they arrived at the gate to the compound, two heavily armed guards immediately unchained the large metal gate and swung it to the inside, away from the vehicle. The two sentries saluted the driver without saying a word and they continued the short drive to the main building.

Commander Singha was sitting on large stump outside of the building as the car pulled up. He stood up as Sanjay got out of the car and said, "Welcome back, my friend." The welcome seemed genuine and far more pleasant than expected by Sanjay.

"Good afternoon, Commander." The driver placed his only piece of luggage on the ground next to Sanjay. Without saying a word to Singha, he got back into the Maruti and quickly drove away.

Through the front door of the main building, three others joined Singha. Lieutenant Giri, Lieutenant Arpit, and one gentleman that was unfamiliar to Sanjay joined Commander Singha on the gravel driveway.

"We want to thank you for your service, Mr. Swaminathan." The unknown man reached out his hand, "Corporal Mohammed Masad, sir. Very glad to meet you."

"Uh, yes. Good to meet you as well." Sanjay could not kick the nervousness that he felt. The reception seemed very calm, a massive departure from the treatment he had come to expect at the compound, "Where shall I place my bag, Corporal, sir?"

Singha jumped in before Masad could answer, "You will be staying in the main barracks with the other officers, Captain Swaminathan. You have been promoted." Sanjay couldn't help but smile as a huge wave of relief overtook him.

"You have performed admirably, my friend. The stadium plans, your recruitment efforts, the tactical planning, your execution of the plan. You exceeded my expectations, and we have much larger plans in store for you."

Sanjay took all of this in as he wrestled with his allegiances. This level of safety and security was very enticing, not to mention the possibility of real wealth that might be a part of the package. He shook off the curiosity and focused on maintaining his composure. He was here for God's purposes, now. Nothing else mattered. The Angels had been clear. He had been forgiven and would be protected. 'Focus, Sanjay! Focus!' he thought to himself.

His room back at the compound was nothing special, but it had a relatively large bunk bed that could sleep two people, clean sheets and pillows, a small wooden desk, and a wall-mounted sink. It was a far cry from the six by three foot dirt-floored hut that had been his disgusting home during the training program that almost broke him.

Commander Singha followed Sanjay into his new room, "What do you think, Swaminathan? Definitely an upgrade, correct?"

"Yes, sir. Thank you, sir." Sanjay looked back at Commander Singha and found his eyes drawn to the necklace that he was wearing, "I see that you still have my Tiger Eye necklace."

"Ah, yes. So, you like Tigers, my friend. I have something quite amazing to show you. Put your bag on the bed and come with me," Sanjay did as he was instructed.

Sanjay followed Singha across the central courtyard, passing by the bathing area and thatch roof huts that obviously now had new inhabitant trainees. They walked the length of two football fields, until they reached what looked like massive, make-shift zoo cages.

"Like you, Sanjay, I also have a passion for tigers." As they approached the cages, three large Bengal tigers stood on their hind legs and let out a spine tingling roar that stopped Sanjay in his tracks. The two smaller animals had the traditional Bengal coloring of light brownish orange with black stripes. The largest of the big cats was bright white but with the same black stripes. The dark blue eyes of the white tiger almost glowed against the snow white fur on its angular, albino face.

"That one is special," Singha pointed the electric wand towards his prized white tiger, "A very rare find. Only one in every ten thousand tigers."

"He is much bigger than the others," Sanjay remained a few feet behind Commander Singha.

"Indeed. White tigers tend to grow faster and heavier than the plain orange ones."

"How much do they weigh?" Sanjay feigned interest in Singha's pets.

"The big one is over two hundred kilograms. Maybe two-twenty."

The ominous, but gorgeous beasts darted back and forth, ramming the back wall of the heavily reinforced steel cage hoping with all their power and might to break through the sturdy enclosure, hoping to escape from their hated captor.

Commander Singha continued towards the main entrance to the cage. "Good girls!" Singha grabbed a large rod like staff that was hanging from a pole that extended from the top of the cage. He pushed a button on the handle and an arc of electricity crackled at the end between the two electrodes. The cats immediately reeled around towards Singha and backed up against the far side of the cage when they heard the sound made by this tool of submission. "I find this stun gun to be very effective, my friend. Works for bad tigers, as well as bad recruits." Singha smiled with a devilish grin as he waved the wand in the direction of the now terrified animals.

Singha opened the six foot wide and eight foot tall cage door and brazenly walked towards the large cats, all three now lying next to each other with their heads cocked back in fear. Singha stopped just short of the largest of the three, almost close enough to pet her, before zapping the air immediately above the tiger's head. Singha turned back towards Sanjay and motioned to him with his left hand, "Come on inside, boy. They won't bite unless I let them."

One of the wild animals let out a cautious roar while Singha's eyes were turned away. The Commander snapped back his head and jabbed the cat with the prod, sending

950,000 volts of electricity into the shoulder of the now cowering tiger. The stunned cat let out a loud whimper, as it gingerly got back on its feet and slid away towards the other side of the cage.

Singha cackled in sheer delight, "You want another, kitty cat?" His power and control over these large animals fed perfectly into his narcissistic and sociopathic tendencies. The other large cats slowly moved towards their recently shocked cell mate, their eyes never leaving Singha.

"Lucky day for you, Captain Swaminathan. It is feeding time at the Singha Zoo." Behind a small shed that was attached to the cages, Sanjay saw Lieutenant Giri walking in their direction, dragging a large grey Igloo cooler behind him. Giri stopped next to a long ladder that led to a platform that was at least twelve foot above the floor of the cages. He grabbed two large quarters of what appeared to be the remains of a lamb or small deer and started up the ladder. After three trips up and down the ladder with the carcasses of at least two dismembered animals, he removed a piece of plywood that covered a small opening in the steel cage that had been carefully cut out of the top of the cage, obviously designed to be used as a feeding chute.

Commander Singha backed his way towards the cage entrance. Sanjay didn't need to be asked to leave the cage. After they were both safely outside, Singha closed and secured the cage by sliding two heavy duty steel bolts into place at the top and bottom of the steel door. "Don't worry, young Captain, these bolts were specially made with these beasts in mind. They can't be broken or bent by the tigers."

Although Sanjay was not fully convinced about the safety provided by the bolts, he could feel the frantic rapidity of his heart beats returning to normal. At least they were no longer in the cage. Although Sanjay and his sister adored the beauty of these animals and spent hours talking about going to see them at the Mumbai Zoo, until today, he had no idea how large these cats were in real life or the fear that a cat's roar could instill when only a few feet away from the animal. His glorification and adoration had now turned quickly to awe and respect.

Singha and Sanjay stepped back to get a better vantage point for the feeding. One by one, Giri dropped a quarter of an animal and before the meat hit the ground, one of the hungry tigers would rip it out of the air with its' huge claws before taking it to his or her designated feeding area inside the cage. In a matter of minutes, all the meat had been consumed, only a few large bones were left as evidence that mealtime had been observed.

Giri climbed back down the ladder, pulled the Igloo back behind the shed, rinsed it out quickly and came around to where Singha and Sanjay were watching the tigers lick their large paws after the meal, "Come with me, Sanjay. Now that you are an officer," his sentence was briefly interrupted by his muttering "Mmhmm" under his breath. "We have some business to take care of with a couple of recruits. I think you may know one of the worthless little weasels."

32

After the short walk back from the tiger cages to where field training was taking place, Sanjay noticed four of the recruits, all of them completely covered in dirt and sweat from head to foot, wearing only what looked like a homemade diaper that was tied around the waist on both sides of each young man. Giri was now brandishing the electric prod that had been used minutes earlier by Singha to frighten and terrify the tigers.

"One of you pigs stole extra bread last night during bath time, when the guards were not watching carefully enough." Like an angry drill sergeant, Giri moved down the lineup one by one, tapping the stick on the hard packed dirt in front of each recruit. "I will give you one chance to step out of the line and admit the betrayal of your oath and the stealing from your brothers."

None of the recruits moved, but the second from the left was shaking violently. Giri slowly circled back to this terrified youth's position in line and abruptly jerked his head around until he was eye to eye with him, only a couple of inches separating the two. He whispered something that only the recruit could hear.

Sanjay noticed a puddle of urine pooling around the feet of this terrified recruit. He looked very familiar to Sanjay. Was this Kirit from his old neighborhood? Sanjay studied him more carefully. He was much skinnier than Sanjay had remembered. His ribcage was fully visible, appearing more skeleton than human.

Without turning, Giri asked. "Recognize this thief, Captain Swaminathan?"

"Yes, sir. I believe so, sir." Sanjay was now sure that this was Kirit. Although Kirit was at least three years younger than Sanjay, he had always been one of the better cricketers in the neighborhood and seemed to always be getting in some form of trouble. Sanjay never had a problem with him and remembered him to have a keen sense of humor. Today, as he shook in abject fear of Commander Giri, that sense of humor would not be on display.

Giri stepped back away from Kirit, and without warning, stabbed the electrodes into the stomach of the now whimpering recruit. The crackle of the electrodes sent Kirit sprawling onto his back and into a convulsion fit. "Get up, pig!" Giri stood over the quaking body with the wand of terror hovering just above Kirit's face.

Sanjay's stomach was in knots.

"This is the second offense," Giri said with nonchalance, "Immediately after our successful mission in Mumbai, as we were planning to celebrate the victory with everyone here, this imbecile had the audacity to question Singha regarding why we would kill innocent people of India. When Singha explained that these people were the rich and powerful of the West and only here to rape and pillage all that is India, he informed Singha that Christians were not all evil. Today, because of his disloyalty, he has cemented his fate."

From the corner of his eye, Sanjay could see Commander Singha sitting on a crude bench in front of the cages with his legs crossed, watching the situation unfold at the hands of his trusted protégé, Giri.

Lieutenant Giridhar placed the tip of the rod on Kirit's neck. "Any more words of wisdom for us this fine day, you thieving little piglet?" Giri pulled the trigger, sending a continuous stream of electricity into Kirit for over thirty seconds. Kirit's body jerked into a reflexive prone position until Giri let go of the trigger.

Giri backed away and surveyed the damage that he had inflicted. He walked back around the remaining three recruits and turned to face them. "Let this be a lesson today! Without loyalty and respect, your life is worthless here. Do you understand me?"

The three meekly spoke in unison the response as they had been commanded to provide when questioned by an officer. "Yes, sir. Giri, sir."

Sanjay felt week in the knees as he looked over at the motionless body of a kid from his neighborhood. He lifted up a silent and quick prayer, "God, please be merciful to Kirit. Please forgive him."

"Sanjay, have these recruits take the body out past the tiger cages. There is a cooler behind the shed. Put the body in with the rest of the meat. We will cut it up later once he is frozen. Hope them hungry cats develop a taste for humans."

Giri bellowed out a visceral laugh that made Sanjay cringe, "And after you put Kirit in the freezer, pleased to have you freshen up for dinner. We will be taking dinner at the home of Commander Singha at nine o'clock this evening. I will drive you. Will pick you up at quarter 'till nine."

Triskal and Maritius watched in horror as Sanjay was forced to supervise the two raggedly dressed recruits as they dragged Kirit's lifeless body toward the oversized freezer behind the shed. The angels could see tears welling up in Sanjay's eyes and immediately Triskal flew directly behind him and placed a hand on his shoulder, providing Sanjay with a renewed sense of calm.

Two demons suddenly flanked the recruits that were carrying out the body concealment mission. They both stared into the piercing bright blue eyes of Triskal. Triskal never broke his gaze into the deeply set, blood shot eyes of these evil minions of Satan.

Verum and Leshyra were perplexed as to why they were unable to affect Sanjay. As they reached out to touch him with their ornate swords, trying to perpetuate evil thoughts and seeking to push Sanjay towards cruel treatment of the recruits, the swords were deflected as if a force field protected one that had once been firmly under their control.

Triskal brandished his holy weapon, "You have lost this battle. You no longer have dominion over Sanjay. He is now one of the chosen. Depart this place." With both of his mighty arms, Triskal swung his glowing silver sword, creating an overwhelming arc of fire and wind that blew both demons through the veiled entrance to Earth and back into the dark abyss from whence they had come.

33

ommander Singha's home was surrounded by a twelve foot tall rock wall, creating more of a fortress feeling rather than a family dwelling. Just outside of the gates, piles of dirt and discarded bricks littered the walkway between the wall and the street. Two armed guards with machine guns approached the vehicle and performed the required automobile checks before allowing entry. Once the attendant sitting inside the small guardhouse had recorded the license plate number and name of the driver, he waved for the armed guards to open the oversized, and obviously very heavy, wrought iron gate.

Once inside the gates, the grounds were immaculate. Sanjay looked across the perfectly manicured green grass that spread out to either side with large marble fountains at the center of the side yards. The cobblestone driveway weaved through several well-kept gardens, until it reached the circular driveway at the back of the property.

Giri stopped the car directly in front of the steps that led up to the front entrance of what Sanjay thought looked like the palace of a king or queen. A man dressed in black with white gloves bowed in front of Giri as he accepted the keys to the car. Without saying a word, he drove the car back in the direction of the main gate.

Sanjay mused to himself, 'Valet service at Singha's home? How did he have such wealth? Wasn't valet service reserved for parliament or hotels?'

Sanjay followed Giri up the steps and through the open front doors that led into a large living area complete with vaulted ceilings, a large fireplace, and opulent pieces of framed art on the walls. Commander Singha was sitting alone in a high backed lounge chair directly in front of the fireplace, a cup of coffee or tea sitting on a saucer in front of him on the marble coffee table.

"Good evening, Singha bhai." Giri said in a voice that was more fearful than respectful.

"Welcome, Sanjay." His entire dismissal of Giri was obvious and uncomfortable. It was obvious that this meeting was primarily called for a discussion with Sanjay. Evidently, with the success of the Mumbai massacre, Sanjay had become Singha's new 'golden boy.'

"My friend, please," Singha waved his left hand towards the oversized couch next to his chair. Without a formal invitation, Giri remained standing at attention next to the fireplace.

Sanjay could feel his mouth becoming dry, as if he had swallowed a bag of cotton balls. Why had he been summoned to the Singha palace? Would he be asked to orchestrate another bloodbath?

"You have proved yourself to be a most valuable asset, Sanjay." Singha took a sip of tea and motioned to the Chaiwallah who was standing in the foyer. In a very terse voice, he commanded the young man, "What are you waiting for. Are you lazy or incompetent? Am I to drink my tea alone?"

Singha turned back to his honored guest. "We have come to know that our enemies are planning a meeting in Goa. It seems that this Global Calling Organization did not receive the message that you have helped us clearly deliver in Mumbai. We must crush these arrogant and greedy infidels that intend to take what is rightfully ours here in India. They are like roaches among us. We must destroy them all, at whatever the cost. When we create fear and division in the hearts of many, control will be ours. India will be ours. Do you understand?"

"Yes, sir, Commander Singha," Sanjay squirmed just slightly, causing the leather of the couch to give a quiet squeak.

"Wouldn't you prefer to live like this rather than where you and your family are forced to live today?" Singha raised his hands and eyebrows in an obvious gesture that indicated he was talking about his opulent estate.

Receiving no comment from Sanjay, the Commander continued, "We have people on the inside, much like you prior to the Mumbai mission. They have confirmed the time and location of the meeting. You have been chosen, along with ten of our finest soldiers, to carry out a very important part of our plan to eradicate these foolish Americans and Indian sheep that follow them blindly."

Singha took another sip of his tea as Sanjay's tea was placed in front of him by the dutiful, yet diminutive Chaiwallah. After placing the cup of tea on the saucer, the young man bowed quickly and retreated back to the kitchen.

Commander Singha turned his gaze towards Giri. "Where is it, Giri? Did you forget?"

"No, sir. I have it here with me," Giri unclipped the back holster from his belt and handed it to Singha.

The holster held a Sig Sauer .45 caliber pistol. Singha slid the weapon out of the holster and placed it in front of Sanjay. "A gift for you, Captain."

Sanjay picked up the pistol and checked to see if it was loaded. He was careful to show that he had taken his training seriously. The magazine was fully loaded, and one round was already in the chamber. He engaged the safety and placed it back on the table in front of him.

"This will be your tool to wipe away those that do not belong in India. Giri will outfit you with additional ammunition and he will be leading the team in Goa. Failure is not an option for this assignment. Further instructions will be given in the next few days." Commander Singha stood up and crossed his arms, indicating to both Giri and Sanjay that the business portion of the meeting was over.

Sanjay fumbled for the gun as he stood facing Singha, "Yes, sir. Thank you, sir."

Singha started to walk in the direction of the dining room. Sanjay sidestepped Singha's chair and followed him with Giri closely behind.

The Abduction

"Now when these things begin to happen, look up and lift up your heads, because your redemption draws near."

- Luke 21:28 (New King James Version)

The eternal God is your refuge, and underneath are the everlasting arms; He will thrust out the enemy from before you, and will say 'Destroy!'

- Deuteronomy 33:27

34

As Rajiv was finishing his initial briefing, he surveyed the room. Around the large horseshoe of long tables that faced the podium, these amazing men and women of God, who each felt an individual calling to bring the message of Christ to the world, stared back at him with wide-eyed and careful attention to every word. Their commitment to ministry was both encouraging and exhilarating for Rajiv. After the long weeks that followed the tragedy in Mumbai, spending time with these fellow warriors of God was exactly what the doctor ordered.

After a deep and thankful breath, Rajiv continued, "Brothers and sisters, we are faced today with insidious evil in India that we could never have imagined. We face a radicalized militia here in this country that not only hates America, but hates the West, all Christians, and frankly, any formal religion for that matter. They refer to themselves as liberators, but in truth they are demented terrorists bent on destroying any person or group that they feel might pose a risk to their grandiose plans of greed and control. They trade in terror and feel that power for them can only be gained when fear overpowers the people of this great country, giving this evil group the opportunity to continue their corruption and extortion throughout India."

"The Bible is clear. Christ Jesus has taught us that love is the most important fruit of the spirit, and out of love and obedience to our Father, we are providing a message of hope, security and the promise of eternal life to many that have never heard such an important message."

Rajiv took the glass of water from the shelf inside the podium and took a sip before continuing, "While we were never promised that a missionary life would be easy, I believe that we all share the same commitment and determination to continue our work here in India." Everyone at the table voiced their agreement with vigorous applause.

With a thunderous boom that rang the eardrums of everyone in the conference room, an explosion blasted open the locked double doors that acted as the only entrance to Panjim Room 1A. Rajiv watched as a smoke bomb was tossed through the doors into the middle of the room and all the participants jumped out of their chairs and dropped to their knees, many crawling under the tables for protection.

In seconds, the room was filled with men dressed in camo fatigues with ski masks covering their faces, all carrying assault style weapons. Gunshots rang out from the back of the room. One of Rajiv's closest friends and Sr. Vice President of the Global Calling Institute, Srini Rhokar, ran towards one of the shooters but she was cut down by a barrage of bullets from two of the intruders. Two of the bullets intended for Srini cut through the flimsy tabletop in front of Andrew, one piercing his chest just below the shoulder and the other hitting him just below the knee, shattering his shin bone. Andrew cried out in sheer agony.

Two of the other leaders stood up and charged towards the assailants, only to be mowed down as well by additional gunfire. One of the terrorists climbed onto the nearest table at the back of the room using a chair as a step stool. "Do not move. If you move, you die. We are here for Andrew, Srini, Trevor, and Rajiv." He looked down at the body of Srini with two exit wounds through her head and chest. "Looks like Srini may no longer be on the list," he laughed under his breath at his inappropriate attempt at humor as he waved his AK-47 assault rifle around the room looking for his other named targets. Everyone else in the room remained still.

Orion floated invisibly through the smoky, people filled room, until he was immediately next to a suffering Andrew. With a touch of his angelic fingertip to Andrew's forehead, Andrew drifted into unconsciousness, his heartbeat now virtually untraceable by the traditional pressure on the carotid artery in the neck.

One of the terrorists closest to Andrew's position swung his rifle around his back on its strap while he reached down to check his pulse. "Looks like this one is off the list as well, boss. Looks like Andrew."

"Forget him, then. Maybe today's lesson will be a little more powerful." The obvious leader of the group dismounted the table and walked to where Andrew's body was lying in a pool of his own blood. He spit angrily on the body and yelled at the top of his lungs. "Your family is next, arrogant Christian infidel! This is not finished." He walked back to join the others, "Grab

Trevor and Rajiv. They are all we need. The rest of them don't matter. If they know what is best for their families, they will give their resignation today."

Sanjay was inadvertently knocked out by the initial blast as one of the doors blew back and caught him directly under the chin. Now awake again, his eyes were filled with tears that he would later blame on a concussion and the thick smoke. He felt nauseous and wanted desperately to throw up. What he and the rest of the gang of kidnappers and killers could not comprehend was that Triskal had actually guided the door perfectly as to render Sanjay unconscious, while not causing any serious physical harm. Maintaining Sanjay's anonymity and alleviating any need for Sanjay to inflict additional harm on other humans were integral parts of the overall plan.

"You two. Grab the Indian traitor." The leader, Giri, waived two of the men in the direction of Rajiv who was still on the small stage that held the podium.

One of the men kicked Rajiv squarely in the stomach causing Rajiv to gasp for breath as he curled into a fetal position. The other joined in, both kicking Rajiv in the back, side and stomach until Rajiv started to spit up blood. "Enough! Enough! Just get him to the truck!" The leader instructed his team in no uncertain terms.

Cries and whimpers could be heard around the room as the gravity of the situation started to set in with the Global Calling team members that had survived the attack.

"Stand up, Trevor." The leader was now standing behind Trevor Haas, who was still semi shielded under one of the tables. Trevor slid out from under the table and stood with hands raised. He looked over at the motionless body of his best friend and hung his head in sheer disbelief.

One of the men grabbed Trevor's arm and yanked him towards the opening where the doors had earlier been attached to the wall. Outside of the Taj Fort Aguada Hotel, which was promised to be a safe location to hold the World Leadership Summit Planning Meeting, three other men with machine guns held all the employees at bay while the abducted leaders were roughly ushered into the waiting Range Rover SUV. As the car exited through the main gate, Trevor noticed the bodies of two men lying next to the guard house, one still holding the mirror that was typically used to inspect the underside of each arriving automobile. It was painfully obvious how the terrorists had gained entry.

Without warning, the same ski masks that had been used to disguise the captors while at the hotel were turned backwards and put on the heads of Trevor and Rajiv to avoid any possibility that the two abductees could determine the location of what would be their new place of residence for the foreseeable future.

Angels in our Midst

How wonderful it must be to speak the language of the angels, with no words for hate and a million words for love!

EILEEN ELIAS FREEMAN, *THE ANGELS' LITTLE INSTRUCTION BOOK: LEARNING FROM GOD'S HEAVENLY MESSENGERS*

Lord, give Thine angels every day / Command to guard us on our way / And bid them every evening keep / Their watch around us while we sleep / So shall no wicked thing draw near / To do us harm or cause us fear / And we shall dwell, when life is past / With angels round Thy throne at last.

JOHN M. NEALE, *HYMNS FOR CHILDREN*

35

ROORKEE, INDIA
6:22 A.M.
JULY 4, 2022

On the wall, just below the level of the steel cot bed frame and obscured by the remarkably uncomfortable single mattress that he had slept on for the last seven days, Trevor scratched another mark on the wall as a way to keep track of the number of days he had been held captive. After replacing his one pillow, he placed the small rock that he used as a writing implement back inside the small tear in the dilapidated mattress.

Trevor sat at the edge of the bed and remembered that today was the fourth of July. That usually meant hot dogs and hamburgers with friends in Rittenhouse Square, followed by a dazzling firework show directly over boathouse row in Philly. He desperately wished that this might become his own Independence Day.

Like clockwork, there was a knock on the door indicating that breakfast had arrived. A small window at the bottom of the door, just wide enough for a tray of food and tall enough for a small carton of milk, slid open so that the usual portion of eggs, toast and yogurt could be pushed along the floor into the dimly lit room. The minimal, but much appreciated light was provided by a tiny window in the back corner of the room that served as the only measure of day and night for Trevor.

"Good morning, Trevor." The calming voice from beyond the door of his cell was welcomed each morning by Trevor. The greeting this morning, as was the case on every morning, always came just after he had finished his breakfast. "How was your rest?"

"As good as could be expected, I guess." Trevor rubbed his sleep filled eyes with the knuckles on the back of his hands as he walked towards his breakfast. For the last five days, the only conversation had been with this kind stranger, after breakfast and dinner meals were served, the only two meals provided each day. The majority of the day was instead filled with cruel expletives and ridiculous orders being yelled out by the inhumane guards, as Trevor was put through the same grueling and demoralizing beat-down process that the recruits were forced to endure.

Trevor assumed that his kind visitor must also live in the building that was now his prison. Every evening, after midnight, Trevor would hear a chair slide across the tile floor until it rested just outside of his locked door. Although Trevor was exhausted beyond what he believed possible, due to the brutality and cruelty that was inflicted daily by Commander Singha and his vicious minions, he craved this personal interaction, and their conversations would often flow deep into the early morning hours.

Trevor had learned from his new friend on the other side of his door that Andrew had survived the attack and that this unknown kind purveyor of food was appalled by the kidnapping and unfortunate executions. He promised that he would do anything he could do to help keep Trevor safe from harm during his stay. Trevor had also learned that his name was Maritius. No last name was given, but this did not seem that important. Showing a keen sense of humor, Maritius told Trevor that his friends usually referred to him as Mari, "Pronounced Mawree, not Mary, just so we are clear." As a new friend, Trevor was encouraged to use the shorter version as well.

Trevor found the stranger to be remarkably intelligent and very thoughtful in his conversation. He would take his time before speaking and would carefully choose each and every word. He never raised his voice and everything he said seemed to be kind and gentle, completely out of line with the group of people that raided the Global Calling meeting before killing many of his friends and ultimately kidnapping he and Rajiv.

Trevor placed the breakfast tray on the end of his bed. For all of the conversations with Maritius, Trevor would sit on the stainless steel toilet that was attached to the wall in the front corner of the room, allowing him to have an almost whispered conversation through the few inches of wall that separated the two.

"How is Rajiv doing, Mari?" This was always the first question that came to Trevor's mind each morning.

"He is well," Mari always sounded upbeat, "Like you, he is not always thrilled with the cuisine, but we had a very nice chat last night regarding his guiding faith and the Global Calling Institute."

Trevor paused to reflect on this, "Really. Great. Um…. Yes…. The institute." He paused another moment before he asked the next question. It dribbled out more meekly than expected, "Are you a man of faith, Mari?" Although hopeful, he could feel a tinge of nervousness as he waited for the answer.

"Yes, Trevor. Faith and obedience are my guiding lights," Maritius smiled a wry smile as he gave his answer. The angel's guidelines were clear. This must be what it felt like to be a secret service agent, making sure that you build a strong relationship, while trying not to blow your cover.

Maritius continued, "Thomas Aquinas may have said it the best. To one who has faith, no explanation is necessary. To one without faith, no explanation is possible."

Although Trevor did not completely understand this answer, he chose not to continue down this potentially conversation ending path, "Why do you work for these people? You seem so compassionate and sympathetic."

This time, the pause was on Mari's end, "Trevor, there are many times in our life where we are given direction that we are compelled to follow because it supports a far greater calling than we are able to fathom. I am my Father's son, and by His perfect will, I must be here at this time."

Trevor often found himself intrigued by the way that Mari seemed to answer his deepest questions with what seemed like exotic riddles. Although his instincts told him to dig deeper, something more subtle in his heart pushed him to leave it alone.

"You have been sent here for a reason, Trevor. Run the race that has been set before you. I am here to support you as you continue to train for this race."

Trevor's mind was swimming in questions. 'What did Maritius mean by this? Why was he so supportive and encouraging? Was he putting himself at risk? Why was his English so perfect? Where did he come from?'

Before he could ask another question, he could hear his friend's footsteps heading back down the hall. Trevor walked back to his cot, opened the carton of milk, and started to eat his now lukewarm breakfast. He quickly inhaled the meal, placed the tray next to the food slot, and laid his head on the lumpy pillow. He closed his eyes and dreamt of fireworks, parades, and American freedom.

36

The screech of chair legs on the tile woke Trevor with a start. "Trevor, are you awake?" Maritius patiently waited, as Trevor put on his shirt and shuffled through the dark towards his required toilet seat perch. The last thing he wanted was to put Mari in an awkward position with these morally corrupt animals.

"Tough day, Mari. I must have drifted to sleep," Trevor yawned and stretched his arms up high against the wall.

"My heart aches for you, my son," Trevor lamented, the sympathy in his voice almost overwhelming to Trevor, "I was witness to the horrors that have been placed upon you on this day. I watched as they whipped you and Rajiv, wanting desperately to intervene. Watching Rajiv fall unconscious due to the pain was almost impossible to bear. I am so sorry, Trevor, that I was unable to stop them."

"What could you have done, Mari? They are monsters and you are just one man?"

"When the time is right, this evil will be vanquished. You have my word." His words were forceful and resolute. This was the first time that Trevor sensed anger from this typically calm and collected harbinger of peace.

Trevor redirected the conversation, "Mari, there has been something I wanted to ask you, but I wasn't sure if it was appropriate."

"Please Trevor. Please. Do not be afraid to ask me anything. My purposes here are not like the others. You are safe while I am near."

Trevor took a deep breath, as he contemplated his safety with or without Mari being present, "Are you familiar with a young man named Sanjay?"

"Why, yes. Of course. In this place full of evil, he is known as Captain Sanjay Swaminathan, but I do not believe that he fits the mold of the others."

"Do you know where he is right now?" Trevor worried that the question might be slightly over the line.

"Yes, he just returned yesterday from Delhi. I believe that he was making preparations for a meeting there under orders from Commander Singha and Lieutenant Giri. After he was promoted to Captain, he was given sleeping quarters in the officer's building."

"Is there any chance you could let him know that we are here?" Trevor bowed his head with a simple prayer that the answer would be yes.

"Consider it done, Trevor. He will know as soon as I leave your presence." The confident message took Trevor by surprise.

"Really? Are you sure that I am not putting you in harm's way? That is the last thing that I would want, Mari." Trevor pulled himself to a more upright position as he listened intently.

"It will be done. Fear not, my friend." The squeak of the chair and scratching sound of the shuffling feet moving back down the hall indicated that the conversation had ended.

37

ROORKEE, INDIA
2:17 A.M.
JULY 5, 2022

two large raps on the door jolted Trevor out of a deep sleep once again. A muffled whisper penetrated the darkness, "Trevor? Trevor? Wake up! It is your humble servant, Sanjay."

Trevor almost jumped out of the cot as he bolted to the door. "Sanjay, I am so relieved to hear your voice. You are risking your life to come here tonight. I didn't mean for Mari to ask you to come visit me."

"Ask who? Mari? I don't believe that I know a Mari, Trevor."

Trevor was confused by Sanjay's response. Was it just a weird coincidence that Sanjay would come just hours after he had asked Mari to alert him of his presence? "Okay…. Um…. Never mind, my friend. How did you know where they were keeping me?"

"Are you kidding, Trevor? You and Rajiv are more famous here than any cricketer in India. All that they talk about is how they will use you to crush those that they call the 'anti-India, religious infidels.' They plan to make you an example to the world. They want to strike mortal fear into those that are not welcome here in India. I am fearful for your lives, Trevor. You are in grave danger." Sanjay whimpered like a scared young boy as he finished giving his assessment of the situation. "It is all over the news. No one knows where to find you. They fear that you are already dead."

"Fear not, Sanjay," Trevor immediately recognized the irony that the same words had just been provided to him by Mari only hours earlier, "We are part of God's master plan. He will guide us and protect us, even when we don't fully understand his ways."

Sanjay stammered, "Yes, yes, yes. I am aware of this, but it does not make it any easier. I am surrounded by blood-thirsty, vicious dogs that seek only to kill and destroy. I am frightened, Trevor. I am truly terrified. But tonight, tonight was different. I was awakened by a bright light that shone down through the window in my room. Maybe a shooting star or something, I don't know. But whatever it was, something told me that it would be safe to come visit you right now. I can't explain it."

"No need to explain, San..."

Sanjay cut Trevor off in mid-sentence, "So, I opened my door and no one was awake, even the guard at the front door was nowhere to be seen. I ran through the darkness to get to your building, which we call 'the hospital,' because this is where they perform the surgery."

"What surgery are you talking about?" Trevor was curious but, again, somewhat confused. Surgery in the middle of nowhere? Where were the surgeons? Who were the patients?

"When they implant the GPS device in your ankle. All new recruits that pass the test have a chip placed in their ankle for tracking purposes."

"Oh, yes. I remember the federal agents mentioning that. That is horrible." Trevor sat on the toilet with his ear pressed against the wall so that he could hear Sanjay more clearly, "It did, however, provide us with a covert way to implant a second device, through that same scar."

Sanjay continued, speaking as quickly as his tongue would allow. "So, I get to the building where I expected to see the normal night watchman, but again, no one was in sight. I figured that I would have to speak to you through the window from outside of your room, but I was able to just walk by the empty guard desk and straight back to your door. I don't know how long I will have until I need to get back."

"Don't worry, Sanjay. God has obviously cleared this path for you, and He will continue to protect you. If for some reason, someone questions you during your return, simply tell them that you couldn't sleep and wanted to check to see that the new prisoners were adequately detained."

"Yes sir, Mr. Trevor. That is a very good story. Give me a second. I will be right back."

Trevor could hear Sanjay's footsteps as he walked down the hall. In a matter of seconds, Sanjay was back at the door, "Coast is clear, Trevor. I wanted to give you the latest information."

"Yes, please. Go ahead," Trevor stood again and placed his ear against the door.

"I have been in Delhi for the last several days setting up a planning meeting for Commander Singha. All of the sick and ruthless leaders here in Roorkee are meeting with other despicable monsters from around the world to plan another massive attack. They are filled with hate and jealousy. This is evil that you cannot describe. The meeting is only three days from now."

Sanjay paused for a moment, "Trevor, are you still there?"

"Yes, go ahead. What are they planning, Sanjay?" Trevor could not disguise his curiosity or his fear of another possible attack.

The pace of his speaking quickened dramatically, as Sanjay nervously continued. "Delhi was chosen to host one of the largest global information technology conferences of the year at a giant conference center just outside of Gurgaon. There will be over fifty thousand attendees each day, and the meeting will be held in seven large conference center buildings for three days in late August. Their goal is to kill or injure at least ten percent of those that attend. This has become much bigger than just religious persecution where they started. Their goal is complete anarchy and creating insurmountable fear, so that they can continue to take advantage of an opportunistically corrupt marketplace."

"Will you be attending this meeting?" Trevor's voice quivered a bit, "If they find out…"

"I know, Trevor. I know. I am scared, but yes, I must be attending. If I choose not to go, they will kill me. I have come to ask you to pray for me. Pray for the police. They provided me with a phone when I left Mumbai and I was instructed to call them if I came across any information that might help them locate those that were responsible for the death and destruction at the Cricket Stadium. And like you said, they placed a second GPS tracking device in my ankle, so that they always know my location. The agents told me that they will do everything in their power to keep me safe when they raid the place."

"I can assure you that I will be praying for you, my brave young friend. Please know that you were carefully chosen by God to serve a mighty role. I hope that you can understand how important this is for the safety of your friends, your family, Christians, your fellow Indians, all of God's children, the entire world."

"Yes, sir, Mr. Travis, sir. I am honored to be one of the chosen. Please. I just ask you to pray."

Before Trevor could respond, he could hear the rapid pitter patter of bare feet on the tile as Sanjay ran back towards the front entrance of the building. Trevor collapsed in a heap with his back against the door and started to pray.

38

The entire camp had become a mud pit due to the powerful rains during the night. Over three inches of rain had been dumped on the compound in less than five hours. Giri banged the bottom of a large steel pot with a soup spoon next to the head of Trevor, a brutal, but effective alarm clock. "Get up, you lazy mutt!" Giri yelled down at a shocked Trevor. The neurons in Trevor's brain were still working out the unexpected wake up call.

Trevor could see Rajiv leaning on crutches in the hall just outside of Trevor's room. After quickly getting dressed, Trevor followed Giri and Rajiv as they exited the building. The two prisoners marched barefoot through the muddy clay behind Giri, an evil task master with waterproof boots, past the tiger cages, across the field operations training field, and into a small, wooded area at the back of the property. Rajiv's left leg was throbbing in his now waterlogged cast.

"What happened to your leg, Rajiv?" Trevor spoke quietly without turning to look back at his friend. He kept his eyes trained on Giri, who was now over thirty yards ahead of his slower moving captives. "One of Giri's men kicked me in the knee during field exercises yesterday. I think I may have some torn ligaments."

"We will make it through this, my friend. Our prayers will be answered," Trevor glanced back at Rajiv and gave him a quick thumbs up.

Moving through the thick mud with the use of crutches proved terribly frustrating for Rajiv. Giri was getting more and more flustered with the pace and circled back behind Rajiv, the obvious cause of delay. Each time Rajiv slipped or slowed down, Giri would step forward and yell a litany of expletives, as he whipped him across the back with a thick leather belt.

After walking a quarter of a mile into the woods, the cover of the trees ended, and the path took them into a large treeless area that had what appeared to be a large fire pit at its center with two wooden guillotines on either side. Next to each guillotine, a half dozen large plastic bottles sat on the ground in the mud. As they made their way towards the instrument of death on the left, and at Giri's whistled command, two of Giri's men appeared out of nowhere and pushed Trevor and Sanjay to their knees in the gummy mud that surrounded the pit.

Giri turned and kicked Rajiv squarely in the stomach. He screamed in an almost frantic rage, "Imbecile. You have betrayed your own country. You have turned your back on India. Where is your God today, you idiot? Today is your day of reckoning, my friend!"

One of the men moved in behind Trevor and cracked him over the skull with the butt end of his rifle. Trevor could feel the warmth of blood as it trickled around his ear and down his cheek. Rain drops pelted his face as he lay on his back looking up at his aggressor. "You have something to say, pig? Look at the poor piggy in the mud. Awwww, poor little piggy, poor little piggy."

Giri firmly addressed the armed guard that was still standing over Trevor with his gun raised, as if he were going to give the prisoner another whack over the head for good measure. "Shut up and put the gun down, Harik. Do you think this is a game?"

"No sir, Lieutenant Giri. No sir." He stepped back a couple of paces as he cowered back into place.

Giri returned his attention to Rajiv. "You know what that is, right?" He pointed to the fire pit. Without waiting for an answer, he continued. "That is our special barbeque pit, specifically made for worthless traitors like you that fall for religious lies and the promises of those who would take what is ours while trying to spread lies."

Rajiv could barely see over the rocks that made up the perimeter of the pit. The middle of the pit was made up of waterlogged pieces of wood on top of grey ashes that were now completely soaked by the rain. He could see hundreds of bone fragments and a number of charred skulls strewn around the outer edges of the pit, protected from where the fire would be intense enough to completely incinerate any human tissue, soft or bony.

"The tigers think it tastes like chicken," The three captors roared with laughter at what was obviously a joke told on all similar trips to this location. The fear in the eyes of the two captives spoke to the fact that this joke was completely lost on Trevor and Rajiv, as it was for all of those that had come before them.

"First, we must teach them about the power of water." Again, laughter erupted from the two armed men that served as Giri's captive and appreciative audience. "Put them on the tables and tie them down."

Trevor was first. The two guards grabbed him under the armpit and dragged him through the mud to the guillotine on the left. They fastened his hands and feet to the legs of the table using zip ties. On his back, with his arms pulled uncomfortably behind and below his body, Trevor watched as one of the guards slid his forefinger along the blade in an obvious gesture to check the sharpness of the heavy machete like blade that was perched two feet above where Trevor's neck was now positioned. The sharp stainless steel head removal implement was held at bay by only a small safety clip that could easily be released by the prescribed executioner.

The men performed the same positioning ritual on Rajiv, before returning to Trevor's table. Giri stood above Trevor and covered his entire face with a wet, white bath towel. He grabbed a role of duct tape and secured the towel by taping completely around Trevor's head at both the forehead and the chin. The tape was fastened so tightly that Trevor could feel every pulse of his heartbeat from his neck to the top of his head.

Without warning, the two men started the 'power of water' ritual. One of the guards grabbed Trevor by the chin and forcibly opened his mouth, as the other man started to pour water into Trevor's mouth from a large two gallon jug. The glug, glug,

glug of the bottle being emptied was only interrupted by the choking and gasping coming from Trevor's throat.

Rajiv craned his neck in order to see the water boarding exercise from across the pit of death, his eyes filling up with tears of both immense sadness for his friend and uncontrollable fear of what would surely be his fate as well.

The two men shouted obscenities at the top of their lungs as they continued their torture of Trevor. This was not an attempt to gain information, as was the typical aim with waterboarding, but was simply a show of power, an unmistakable act of pure evil. Giri smugly grinned as he sat on one of the larger rocks that outlined the fire pit. He pulled a Camel light cigarette out of his jacket pocket and took slow drags of the cigarette, as he watched Trevor suffer at the hands of his eager comrades.

Orion and Triskal had seen enough. They could sense the life being drained from Trevor. With a swoosh of their wings, they soared into the black clouds that had gathered above the horrible acts which were on display on the ground below. With mighty swords drawn, the two angels directed two massive bolts of lightning in the direction of the scene that was unfolding, one bolt hitting the largest tree at the south side of the open field and one bolt hitting the ground directly behind the guillotine where Rajiv had been secured.

The first bolt of lightning exploded the tree trunk, splitting the large Sheesham tree from top to bottom and sending a small fireball into the air like a mini atom bomb. The guard that was engaged in the near drowning of Trevor jumped back in fear and flung his almost empty bottle of water into the fire pit and started running for the camp. The other guard glanced back at a sprawled out Giri, who had fallen backward into the pit due to the blast, before quickly running to join his fellow scared-out-of-his-mind colleague in a sprint to the safety of the camp.

The blast of the second bolt splintered the table that held Rajiv, flipping him into the air back towards the fire pit. He landed face first in the mud, briefly stunning him. With ringing in his ears, but with no additional injuries, Rajiv stood and hobbled to the table where Trevor was still gasping for air. Rajiv untied his friend and helped him into a sitting position, as his breathing became more regular.

Giri had his gun drawn as he stepped back over the stone ledge towards his two prisoners. "Don't move! I said don't move!"

Rajiv froze with his back to Giri. He slowly raised his empty hands into the air in a show of submission. Orion and Triskal streaked down from the clouds in a blaze of light, until they were face to face with the one last demon that held control over Giri. The other demons had departed with the two frightened guards. "Azazel, your teaching of the evil arts is not wanted or appreciated here," Triskal stood over a foot taller than this diminutive, yet menacing, pot stirrer.

Azazel hissed back at Triskal, spitting venom as he spoke. "Leave us, you weak and worthless birds of the air. We will not be stopped. We own these souls."

Orion grabbed Azazel by the nape of his neck with one hand and his leather belt with the other and flung him into the trees. Azazel pinballed his way through the trees, until he slid to a stop next to an old stump. Knowing that a battle with these two mighty angels was a losing proposition, he drew his sword and opened a tear in the earth, creating an escape for himself back to the place of evil below the earth.

The arrogance and confidence had drained out of Giri. Rajiv and Trevor now faced a young man that was more of a scared, confused, and worried young plebe than a Lieutenant, his gun now shaking in his hand as he gave his orders, "You. Both of you. Today is obviously your lucky day. We will deal with the both of you later. Trevor, grab the crippled traitor's crutches and help him get back to camp."

Trevor and Rajiv stood and watched as Giri stomped his way through the thick mud, until he disappeared into the tree lined path that led back to the large courtyard between the tiger cages and the main building.

39

The parking lot at Seven Hills Health City was jampacked this evening. This was not a huge surprise to Beth, since visiting hours started promptly at six o'clock and only lasted for an hour and a half. The line of cars waiting to drop off visitors extended almost a quarter of a mile back onto Marol Maroshi Road, the main thoroughfare that fronts the sprawling seventeen acres that provide a scenic backdrop for the Seven Hills health care complex.

"Shuti, do you think that we are safe to walk from here?" Beth tapped her driver on the shoulder from the back seat of the Maruti.

Shuti removed the air bud from his left ear and looked back at Beth, "Excuse me. So sorry. Were you asking a question?"

"Yes. Is it safe for us to walk from here?"

"Come on, mom! The hospital is right up there." From the third row, Cade inserted himself into the conversation, clearly communicating his frustration from being forced to sit in the hot car for over twenty minutes. "If we stay in this line, we

245

might not make it to the front door before visiting hours are closed. Let's just walk."

"Yes, ma'am. I am thinking that it should be safe." The driver bobbed his head in a motion indicating that he felt there would be little danger associated with the short walk to the hospital. "I can see the front doors from here and will keep my eye on you."

"Perfect!" Cade was already climbing through the center of the second row captain's chairs where his mom and sister were sitting, "Let's go Lisha, I am really tired of sweating in this back seat."

"Calm down, mister McSnippety," Beth said, trying to diffuse the situation before it started, "Give us a second. A little patience, son?"

"Sorry, mom. Just want to see dad."

"I understand. Me too," Beth handed the driver a tip of five hundred rupees and a card with her phone number on it, "Just in case you don't see us after our visit."

"No worries, ma'am. I will find you. Please just walk out of the front doors and I will drive around to collect you." The driver placed the card and the tip in the center console for safe keeping.

Beth, Alisha, and Cade piled out of the car and walked with a quick pace towards the large main building at Seven Hills. After waiting in another line at reception for almost half an hour, they were finally given the necessary passes to head up to the fifth floor where Andrew was still recovering.

As they approached room 577, they almost collided with Agent Bandela, who was backing out of Andrew's room, still maintaining a conversation with Agent Pai who was seated in a winged back chair under the wall mounted television set.

The three new visitors stopped in the hallway just long enough for Agent Bandela to turn in their direction. Startled by the unexpected visit, he jumped back a half step. "Whew. Seems like I almost ran over you guys. Sorry 'bout that."

"Our fault, Agent Bandela. We should have let out a quick warning when we saw you coming." Beth ushered the kids toward Andrew's room.

"Didn't know you guys were coming today. I thought you were headed back to Goa for a few days."

"Late change of plans. After finding out that Andrew might be released as early as tomorrow, we thought we would stick around and take him home with us. Hopefully, that is not an inconvenience."

"Not at all. In fact, I think it is a fabulous idea. I know he will appreciate the family escort." The agent's kindness was, again, on full display. Beth felt overwhelmingly fortunate that Pai and Bandela had been assigned to the case.

Agent Bandela motioned towards the hospital room door, "I think someone might like to see you."

"Thank you. Thank you for everything." Beth gave Agent Bandela a quick hug before joining Cade and Alisha at the side of the bed.

40

Beth walked around to the right side of my bed and stood next to Alisha. I let go of my daughter's hand and took Beth's. "I thought you guys were heading back this afternoon?"

"I know, honey. We talked to Dr. Shetty this morning, and she indicated that you could be released as early as tomorrow morning. We thought you might enjoy some company on the trip home."

"Would love that. I guess the patient is always the last to hear the news of an impending release from hospital prison, right? Don't think for one minute that I am not thrilled to get the news from you guys." He looked up at Cade and gave him a wink.

"Dad, you have only been in here for a week or so. With what happened to your leg, I would count yourself pretty lucky." Cade reached down and traced his own signature with his forefinger. He had been the first to sign his dad's full leg cast on the day after the assault, choosing the most open area he could find between the ominously large pins that were attached to a cylindrical cage-like framework, constantly suspended like a cruel and evil swing from an anchor on the top of the bed frame.

"Yep, sport. Ten days, actually, but who is counting," I smiled and shifted my weight from my left to right side. The one thing about this injury was that it never allowed more than an hour or so of comfort before I felt the need to shift to a different position.

"How do you go to the bathroom with this thing still attached?" Cade thumped the metal cage for effect.

"Let's not go there for now, son. There are ladies present." They all laughed together for the first time in a week and a half.

"Did Agent Pai or Bandela know anything about Rajiv and Trevor?" Beth turned the focus of the visit back to more serious business.

"Uh. Well, yes and no, I guess." I had to clear my throat, as I thought about the update received only minutes earlier. With a lot of Vicodin still on board, I sometimes found that the recollection of even a recent conversation was typically more foggy than crystal clear. "They said that they had some good leads from a new informant named Sanjay. They are evidently in regular contact with him and they hope to locate Rajiv and Trevor soon."

I looked directly into Beth's eyes. "Wait until you hear the entire story of the young man that I told you about. Sanjay Swaminathan. It will give you goosebumps. First of all, Angels of God appeared to him in a vision, encouraging him to come forward to help. And from what Agent Pai just told me, I think that they may have visited him again."

Beth placed both hands over her gaping mouth, "Seriously? Angels?"

"I know. I know. Amazing stuff, right? He is acting as kind of a double agent and has agreed to go back to the camp where he was trained in order to find out additional information, hopefully including where they are holding our friends."

"Wow, honey. Sounds pretty scary." Beth grabbed my hand again with both of hers. "Do they think that they are still alive?" Her eyes started to well up with tears.

"Faith, Beth. Faith. We have to believe that God has them in His capable hands. The agents seemed to be optimistic. We simply need to pray as hard as ever for their safe return." My rear end was starting to fall asleep again, so I shimmied back and forth until the tingles started to subside. "Evidently, a meeting is scheduled somewhere in Delhi where they think they might find some of the leaders of the terror organization. They said that they should know more in the next several days. In the meantime, why don't you guys pack up my stuff over on the counter and let's get ready to roll out of here in the morning?"

New Delhi, India

He who dwells in the secret place of the Most High shall abide under the shadow of the Almighty. I will say of the Lord, "He is my refuge and my fortress; my God, in Him I will trust."
- **Psalm 91:1-2 (New King James Version)**

The angels are so enamored of the language that is spoken in Heaven, that they will not distort their lips with the hissing and unmusical dialects of men, but speak their own, whether there be any who understand it or not.

Ralph Waldo Emerson,
"Intellect", *Essays*

41

DELHI, INDIA
11:18 A.M.
JULY 8, 2022

When the Indian Railways train #452 from Roorkee finally came to a complete stop at the New Delhi Railway Station, Sanjay stepped off the packed economy train car into the massive crowd that was waiting for trains to arrive from both directions.

Even though he had been told by Commander Singha that he was now a trusted associate and no longer had the need to be tracked using the GPS device in his ankle (of course, this was likely more a function of limited battery life rather than a matter of trust), Sanjay scanned the crowd for anyone that looked even remotely suspicious. He could not help but feel that he was still under surveillance.

Sanjay swam through the sea of people in a slumped position to avoid being picked out of the crowd if he was being followed. After ascending the two flights of stairs from track level to ticketing, he exited through the main turnstiles into the massive lobby where the train schedules and track assignments were displayed on a large jumbotron screen hanging from the ceiling.

With residual anxiety about a possible tail, he jogged to the escalator that led to street level and bounded up the moving staircase three steps at a time. Once outside, he continued to jog down Hamilton Road for a quarter of a mile until he reached a packed bus stop that would provide good cover for a quick call to Agent Kumar of the Intelligence Bureau.

Sanjay had been given strict instructions for providing information to the Bureau. It would be given in coded form in order to protect against any possibility that someone had gained access to the phone at any time without Sanjay's knowledge and to protect against any ability to intercept the call from a sophisticated device while the phone was being used by Sanjay.

"Good day. Please, go ahead." No "hello." No name provided. The person on the receiving end of the call was very matter of fact. "Go ahead, please."

"Ummm…. yes…. yes…. good morning, sir." Sanjay's head was on a swivel as he surveyed the crowd around him. Nothing out of order. "Gobi Manchurian. 13324 Lodhi Road. Today evening. Eight thirty is fine. Approximately twelve orders."

"Your order is complete. Thank you." The line went dead. Password, location, timing, and number of targets, in exactly that order. All information had been transmitted as required.

He had been instructed by the agents during the meeting in Pune that he was to act as if everything was normal when in the company of the terrorists. He was cleared to attend all meetings and was instructed to intentionally misfire his weapon if he was required to engage a target with deadly force. The most important instruction was given at the end of the Pune meeting. When Sanjay was able to provide a meeting location, number of attendees, and a time that a raid should be executed, and if the response received when the call is place indicated that law enforcement officers planned to engage the enemy, Sanjay was to leave the location an hour earlier than the specified time using an appropriate and believable excuse. If he was unable to leave for any reason, Sanjay was further instructed to feign illness exactly five minutes prior to the suggested time of the raid and was to lock himself inside a bathroom in the building, using a bathtub or shower for cover, until the raid had been completed and he was given the safe sign by the officers on site.

As a DTC city bus pulled into the loading zone in front of the stop, two ladies stood up from the covered bench where they had been waiting, leaving an open seat for Sanjay. He sat down, slid the phone back into his pocket and placed his head in his hands. He dreaded what this day, and more likely what this evening might hold for him. He whispered a short prayer for protection under his breath, stood up and stretched his arms towards the overcast sky, and then started to make his way towards the rickshaw queue that was only a couple hundred steps from the bus stop. He was expected to arrive for the meeting in less than an hour.

42

One by one, the angels soared in from all directions, until they were all hovering in a perfect circle above the residential location given by the Heavenly Father. The same mighty seven that had protected Rajiv, Andrew, and countless others at the Cricket stadium the month before had been asked again to protect the officers and agents engaged in tonight's important next step in God's master plan. They joined hands and closed their eyes in prayer as they floated high above the Earth.

As it had always been since the angels had been created, those that were assigned to tasks associated with protecting God's children would gather to pray for protection, wisdom, and heavenly power prior to any interaction with their human reports. Sariel, the mightiest in stature of the seven angels, with wings sparkling as if covered completely with diamonds, led the prayer using the language reserved for the heavenly host. This spiritual telepathic style of communication required no physical speaking as would be expected in human definitional terms but could be clearly heard and understood by all of those gathered together in the sky tonight.

"Our father in Heaven, how mighty is your name. May your perfect will be done on Earth tonight. May you grant us with wisdom that can only be derived from you and heavenly power against the darkness, against the evil spirits that will war against us and against the wickedness that plagues humanity in so many forms. May we defeat the enemy and may evil have no dominion over those that know and love you. For your glory and yours alone, Father God."

Each angel provided their own portion of the collaborative prayer. Once they had finished, Sariel provided final instruction to each angel regarding their assigned positions and responsibilities.

With the briefing complete, and a final squeeze of holy hands in the circle, the mighty clap from the unison unfurling of wings created a violent whoosh of air that catapulted each angel outward from the circle into their own individual arc of flight towards their required positions.

43

Delhi, India
8:27 p.m.
July 8, 2022

Agents Mosur, Singh, Jain, Pai and Mandan peered through the fourth floor window of an abandoned office structure at the two story bungalow across the bustling traffic of Palam Marg, a stretch of the Outer Ring Road of New Delhi, which serves primarily as an access point to some of the most affluent neighborhoods of Vasant.

Agent Jain picked up the walkie talkie on the table in front of the window and depressed the talk button. "We have positive confirmation of two key targets. Operation Lightning Bolt is a go. I repeat. Operation is a go. Three minutes and counting. Three minutes and counting." In less than sixty seconds, an oversized black Mercedes transportation van made a right turn into a relatively obscured driveway just over a quarter mile down from the meeting residence that had been provided by Sanjay. The large double doors on the opposite side from the target building opened and twelve COBRA team officers (the COmmando Battalion for Resolute Actions), clad in full body armor and brandishing assault weapons, sprinted in single file to positions behind the building where the van had parked.

One by one, each officer was dispatched to locations closer to the target building by the team leader on the ground. The four agents that were watching from the windows across the street watched the COBRA officers carefully maneuver into position. All the officers were dressed in dark blue camou-flage fatigues, making them virtually invisible at times as they moved through the trees and bushes at the back of the four properties that separated them from the building of interest. The ominous dark clouds and the rapid onset of dusk added another measure of additional coverage as they took their assigned starting position.

Agent Mandan turned his attention back to the targets of the raid and trained his binoculars on 13324 Lodhi Road. "Current ground zero situation. Three possible shooters." He relayed the message to Agent Jain in a quiet and measured staccato. "Target one, left front corner rooftop with large cal-iber rifle. Target two. Front entry gate, side arm, no rifle in plain sight. Target three. Front courtyard area. Machine gun strapped on his back. Unable to make out caliber of weapon. Side arm in holster on right side of belt."

Agent Jain relayed the identically worded message to the Operation team leader using the walkie talkie.

"Ten four. Will engage." The line clicked back to static as the team leader switched to a different channel to communicate to those engaged in the raid on the ground.

Two of the twelve moved toward a side window of the house immediately next to 13324. They could see an older man sitting in a recliner in front of the television only a few feet from the window. The officer tapped lightly on the glass, holding his badge up to the window for the man to see.

The man inclined his chair to the normal sitting position, stood up, and walked slowly to the window. He had his hands in the air as if he were under arrest. In Hindi, the officer gave clear instructions, "Open the window. You are not in any trouble." The officer loudly whispered near the glass making sure that his voice did not carry far enough to alert the armed men next door. "Do not be afraid. We are here to protect you and your family."

The man did as he was told. He unlatched the lock at the top of the window and slid the pane up some six inches, until he could hear the officers more clearly.

"Sorry to startle you. I am Officer Venkat Patel. How many people are in the house?" The officer spoke softly but with purpose.

"There are six of us. My wife, my wife's parents, and our two children. May I ask why you are here?" The man was calm and did not seem frightened.

"Do you have a car?"

"Yes, we have a car, sir," the man was a bit perplexed.

"I need you to have everyone in the house get dressed and you need to leave the residence at once. Other officers will give you directions when they stop you at the end of the road. We have official business next door, and we are concerned for everyone's safety. Do you understand?

"Yes sir. We will leave immediately." The man started to walk towards the staircase.

"Sir. Excuse me. We will also be needing the use of your rooftop. Would you allow the two of us to use the roof as a lookout? No one else will enter your home."

The man stood still in the dim light of the hallway as he pondered the question. "Yes, I believe that I do not have a choice. Am I right? You may use the house."

"Thank you. We will be entering through the window. Please act in a normal manner as you leave the house." The man turned and headed up the staircase. The two officers pushed the window to its maximum height and lumbered clumsily into the living room.

By the time that they made it to the roof, they could hear the car's ignition, a sign that this compliant Indian family had dutifully followed their orders and would be safe from harm.

Both agents set up their sharp shooting positions behind what appeared to be a three foot tall and ten inch thick adobe brick style wall that had been erected on the rooftop patio as a safety barrier that would be tall enough to keep kids or careless adults from potentially falling off the roof.

The wall would be perfect for the officer's purposes. At floor level, spaced out every three to four feet, a twelve inch by nine inch opening in the otherwise solid concrete wall had been designed for drainage purposes so that the roof would not retain water. These openings at the bottom of the wall were just tall enough so that the two agents could set up their rifles on three inch mounted tripods while lying flat on their stomach in prone position. The wall offered the necessary cover while allowing sufficient field of vision for identifying their targets in the adjacent building using high powered infrared scopes.

After radioing their readiness, they focused in on the three confirmed armed targets that had been identified as immediate threats and patiently waited for the next command from the team leader below.

Sanjay nervously watched for any movement from the Arora Super Shopee convenience store on the opposite side of Lodhi Road from where the raid was likely imminent. He took a sip of his Thumbs Up cola beverage as he sat on the concrete bench outside of the small store, a perfect location to watch the raid unfold.

"Come on! No action yet?" He whispered the question to himself as he searched for any agents that might be lurking around the buildings.

As the darkness swallowed the targeted meeting place for the Indian Liberation Resistance, he could barely make out a silhouette of the guard at the front gate but could clearly identify the orange burn of a cigarette each time that this unknowing sentry would take a drag.

Through the binoculars, Agent Mandan watched as an incendiary device lit up the inside of the right side of the house like a mini explosion. Smoke billowed out of the front and side doors. From across the street, the unmistakable sound of gunshots rang through the night, sounding more like a pack of black cat firecrackers than large caliber weapons. The shots were obviously muffled by both the building itself and the cacophony of beeping horns from the heavy vehicle traffic between their vantage point and where the raid was now taking place.

Officer Kolunkar, the COBRA marksman on the left side of the next door neighbor's roof watched as one of the armed guards on top of the target building ran to the roof's edge above where the smoke bomb had just been deployed. The guard propped his rifle on the wrought iron railing that circled the rooftop in an attempt to unleash his weapon on as many officers on the ground as possible. Without warning, the railing seemed to buckle under the weight of the rifle, causing the shooter to fall to the floor. He removed the oversized magazine and replaced it a couple of times. The gun seemed to be jammed. He stood and angrily shook the weapon as he attempted to adjust the slide.

Before the active shooter was able to adequately resolve the issue with his firearm, Officer Kolunkar took out the threat with one fatal shot to the head. At less than fifty yards, hitting the target within a few centimeters of where he had trained the crosshairs was virtually guaranteed.

Agent Mandan continued to watch the building, moving from window to window. The gunfire had stopped completely. As if it had come out of nowhere, a bright yellow Suzuki Jimny, the Japanese equivalent to the Jeep Wrangler, jumped out of the darkness from behind the building, spewing small pebbles and a trail of dust, as it bounded over the dirt courtyard. It carved a huge swath through the carefully manicured gardens that lined the front of the house before bouncing back onto the cobblestones of the main driveway heading towards the main gate. Gunfire erupted once again, this time much louder as the shots were being fired at the Suzuki from both the front porch and from behind the building. Agents were on their knees at their assigned spots on the property, trying desperately to stop or slow the escaping vehicle.

"Where did that come from?" Agent Mandan screamed in surprised anger.

"Follow me. We have to follow that vehicle." Agent Mosur was already halfway out the door as he gave the instruction.

"You go. Hurry. The police are already staked out on both sides of Lodhi. They will engage the vehicle." Agent Mandan continued to follow the Jimny with the binoculars as it crashed through the main gate, sending pieces of steel and wood flying into the street. The Jeep knock off skidded across the pavement, precariously teetering on only two wheels, as it bounced into the traffic. The Jimny regained its balance and continued West on Lodhi, weaving in and out of the heavy traffic until it was finally out of sight.

To his left, in the building adjacent to the mini mart, Sanjay noticed Agent Mosur running at full speed across the courtyard towards a car parked only forty feet from where he sat. Sanjay dropped his soda and ran in the agent's direction, circling around the brick wall that separated the apartment building from the convenience store. He was completely out of breath when he made it to the car. Agent Mosur had already fired up the ignition in the agency issued vehicle, a nondescript brown Tata Altroz which he had parked in the underground garage. "Sir, sir," Sanjay stammered and fought for air as he pounded on the hood of the car. "That was Singha. He escaped. Giri is with him. I could see them when they drove past me. I must go with you. God is counting on me to help you find them."

"Alright. God, is it? Yeah, whatever you say. Jump in. We have no time." Mosur shook his head and tapped his fingers on the steering wheel as he watched a desperate but committed

Sanjay head for the passenger door. Mosur hit the gas before Sanjay was able to shut the door completely. The sharp turn out of the garage flung the door wide open, almost sending Sanjay onto the pavement as the obviously impatient agent made the jerky turn into the street. Sanjay yanked the door shut and frantically fastened his safety belt.

The raid had been fully executed with only three fatalities, all in the ranks of the radical terrorist camp. With a great deal of coordination and unseen help by a large host of angels, no officers were killed or wounded. Seven in the house were arrested, two of them with serious injuries. One of the four captured during the operation was a primary target and on the most-wanted list in India for multiple crimes against humanity. His recent involvement and planning of the Mumbai attack had elevated the urgency of this particular mission. Lieutenant Rami Shirkan, a radical extremist from Yemen was confirmed as second in command to Commander Sridhar Singha in the Indian Liberation Resistance Organization. Unfortunately, the two main targets had escaped from an unknown underground garage, likely one of the main reasons that this house had been chosen as a meeting place.

44

anjay was beginning to feel carsick. The game of chicken that Agent Mosur had played for over thirty five minutes through the erratic and highly unpredictable traffic had turned his stomach sour, his recently eaten chicken tikka pizza, from the Arora Super, felt like it might soon become an unwanted projectile inside Agent Mosur's impeccably clean service vehicle.

With only minutes or maybe seconds to spare before the food eruption, Agent Mosur slammed on the brakes of the small Tata, barely avoiding a collision with the large food truck in front of them and skidding to a stop between the truck and a large concrete divider that separated the major thoroughfare from the dirt sidewalk that fronted the entry to one of the largest slums in the city.

Just three car lengths in front of them, awash in the headlights of the many cars now stopped in the road, Sanjay and Agent Mosur could see the unmistakable yellow Jimny, which had been T-boned from the right side by a BMW that likely had the right of way based on the way that the driver was screaming in the direction of the Jimny driver.

Agent Mosur jumped out of the car just in time to see Commander Singha pull a handgun from his waistband. He trained the barrel on the driver of the BMW who was no longer yelling profanity, but instead opting to fall silent and raise his hands in the air, as if under arrest.

Agent Mosur, gun drawn as well, screamed at the fugitive over the dozens of cars that were now stalled behind the accident. "Put the gun down, Singha. We have you surrounded." This, of course, was not an accurate statement, as there were no other officers in the immediate area. During the course of the chase, Mosur had carefully coordinated three police road-blocks using his car's old school CB radio, but unfortunately, the accident happened a full half mile from where the nearest blockade was in place.

Singha jerked his head in Mosur's direction when he heard the command. He wheeled around and drew aim, firing three shots at the agent who was fortunate to find sufficient cover behind the open door of the truck in front of them.

"Get down! Get down! Get back in your cars!" Agent Mosur yelled, as he waved his arms frantically in a downward motion that clearly indicated to the curious rubberneckers that they needed to hit the ground immediately.

The car ride, compounded by the sheer intensity of the situation, caused Sanjay to throw up his entire dinner behind a barricade of mopeds that were also stymied by the crash.

With no more shots being fired, Mosur peered around the side of the door that he was using for cover and could see that Singha and his passenger were running directly towards one of the alleyways that led into the heart of the Munirka slum area. Without hesitation, Agent Mosur sprinted after them. Feeling much better after launching his dinner into the street, Sanjay jumped to his feet and quickly caught up to the older and less nimble agent.

Because of his experience growing up in a slum area, Sanjay was much more adept at navigating the dark labyrinth that made up this vast overpopulated area in the heart of Delhi than Agent Mosur and soon took the lead in pursuit of Singha and Giri. The small alleys and tiny streets were littered with trash, discarded tires, large concrete blocks that had fallen from the walls of decaying buildings, and filled from side to side with people, cows, chickens, and dogs, a dangerous collection of obstacles that made following anyone almost impossible.

After only a couple of minutes, Sanjay turned back to look for Agent Mosur, but he was nowhere to be found. He would have to track down Singha alone. Nothing was going to stop him. He remembered the words of the angels. God had big plans for Sanjay.

A gunshot split the night air and a piece of plaster on one of the buildings shattered only inches from where Sanjay had stopped to catch his breath. The crowd of people in the immediate area flung themselves against the walls and into open windows when they heard the shot ring out. Sanjay ducked into a small doorway and reached behind his back, retrieving the 45mm handgun that had been given to him by the same man that was now trying to kill him.

Just as Sanjay peeked around the small wall that separated him from the shooter, another bullet shattered one of the clay pots that was sitting on the open windowsill just behind his position. Sanjay needed to find a more secure position. Lacking the courage to take another look around the concrete wall, Sanjay chose to simply shoot his 45 directly into the large pile of dirt and trash against the building in front of him, hoping to send a message to those that were now hunting him that he was armed as well. How could they know it was the young Captain Sanjay? They might erroneously believe it was the agent, a much more formidable opponent.

His plan seemed to work. He heard the sound of trash cans clanking on the ground and the shrill cries of older ladies in Hindi chastising the men for their actions. Sanjay had always found it fascinating and amusing that those fortunate enough to grow very old in the slums would refuse to cower in fear when threatened by bullies or thieves but would instead opt for giving these thugs a piece of their mind. Sanjay, on the other hand, was still shaking violently as he left the safety of the door frame and resumed the chase.

Sanjay could make out the shadows of two men jumping back and forth, avoiding people and objects that littered their narrow path. In just a matter of seconds, they had created the distance of half a football pitch between where they were and his position. Both of the men stopped and looked back down the alley.

A bright spotlight from one of the shanty dwellings reflected off the necklace that one of the men was wearing. It was his sister's necklace, the Tiger Eye. A wave of anger and resolve swept over Sanjay. The hair on the back of his neck bristled with electricity. He was livid.

A rubber ball bounced next to Sanjay's left leg, causing him to almost jump out of his skin. He looked up and noticed several young children looking down from the roof in front of him, obviously searching for their lost ball. Sanjay noticed that the roofs on that side of the alley seemed to be at uniform height, stretching out far beyond where his two former leaders were now standing and the ladder that was obviously used by the kids was leaning on the front of the building.

He ascended the ladder two rungs at a time, until he was standing on the roof top with the kids. Sanjay gave the "shhh" sign with his pointer finger over his lips and then pointed to where they would find the lost ball. Standing atop the run down ruins of the thousands of dilapidated shacks that melded together haphazardly to form the Munirka slum, Sanjay could see the reflection of poorly hung streetlights dancing over the tops the corrugated sheets of scrap metal that served as roofing material.

Sanjay started to run across the uneven tin roof tops, some more sturdy and steady than others. As he approached the end of the roofline, he was more careful to keep his footsteps as silent as possible. Twelve feet below his position and in the very back of a dead end alley, he could see Singha and Giri, guns drawn, walking quickly towards two men that were sitting on idling motorcycles.

One of the men dismounted his cycle, placed his helmet on the seat and walked slowly away with hands held above his head in a show of surrender. The other maintained his position on the bike in obvious defiance, yelling obscenities at the two potential hijackers. Giri fired two shots at the ground in front of the bike. The driver flipped his right leg over the top of the bike and slid off the seat onto his knees, his hands now in the air as well. Giri moved to the side where the now compliant driver was kneeling and kicked him squarely in the chest, then another swift kick to the side of the head that knocked him onto his side. Giri ripped the helmet off his head and spit in the wheezing young man's face.

Singha was already on his bike and revved the motor twice, a gloating gesture for sure, as well as a warning to the two rightful owners that their bikes were now in other hands.

Sanjay watched as Singha put the motorcycle in gear and started down the narrow alley in his direction. Sanjay closed his eyes and whispered out loud, "God, please be with me."

As Singha slowly drove under the roof's overhang where Sanjay was perched in a crouched position, Sanjay jumped off the roof into the dimly lit alleyway, catching Singha under the chin strap of his helmet, sending Singha's body headlong into a large iron gate that acted as a front door into one of the makeshift homes in the slum. Sanjay rolled a couple of times on the hard dirt, until he was back on his feet with his weapon drawn. He looked over at Singha, who was completely unconscious, due to the vicious collision of his head against the unforgiving iron.

Sanjay turned his attention back in Giri's direction.

"Well, looky here! I tell you...our little Captain is a spy and is obviously ready to die. Isn't this a surprise? If I were you, sport, I would put the gun down!" Giri spoke calmly but sternly, as he sat on his recently acquired Suzuki Gixxer 250.

Giri's hands were on the handlebars indicating to Sanjay that he must have holstered his gun before mounting the bike. Giri was at least twenty-five yards away from where Sanjay was standing. Sanjay trained his gun on the chest of Giri, feeling less than confident in shooting from this distance. He shouted angrily at his prior boss down the moonlit sliver of walkway that separated the two men, "Get off the bike, Giri! I mean it! I am not afraid of you."

Without warning, Giri gunned the engine and shot forward, lurching the bike into a wheelie, with only the back wheel touching the ground for a couple of seconds before both tires found footing and accelerated directly towards Sanjay.

Sanjay stood his ground, and with only seconds to act and nowhere to take cover in the tiny alley, he fired two shots into the chest of Giri, flipping him backwards off the bike. Sanjay, with eyes completely shut and violently shaking out of intense fear, was completely unaware of the presence of a calm and determined Triskal standing next to him, his angelic hand gently guiding the barrel of the pistol to ensure that the required target was hit. The driverless motorcycle wobbled clumsily for another few yards, as it quickly approached Sanjay, bounced off a short stone wall on the left side of the alley and took Sanjay's legs out from under him as the collision flipped his body sideways. The force of the impact slammed Sanjay into a stack of wooden crates that made up the outer wall of one of the shanty dwellings. The wooden crates exploded into splinters, helping to cushion what might have otherwise been a fatal collision if Sanjay would have been propelled into a less forgiving surface such as stone or metal.

45

When Sanjay regained consciousness, he was laying on a small hammock surrounded by two older Indian women, both taking turns patting his temples with cold wash cloths. They were dressed in colorful Saris, familiar garments that sparked childhood memories of his grandmother and great aunt back in Mumbai, "Owwww…. Where am I? What happened to my leg?" Sanjay whimpered, due to the intense pain that was pulsing from his left leg.

Hearing Sanjay's voice, Agent Mosur jumped from his seat in the corner of the small room and ran to the side of the hammock. He grabbed Sanjay by the hand, "Welcome back, buddy! You must have been right. God was watching out for you. You could have been killed."

"Where is Singha?" Sanjay grimaced in obvious pain. "Did you get Singha?"

"What do you mean? We never saw Singha," agent Mosur was perplexed but curious.

"They were together. I mean...." Sanjay gritted his teeth and wrinkled his brow. "Man, my leg. It really hurts, sir."

"Yes. I know. Your leg is broken. We are waiting for the paramedics to arrive." Agent Mosur carefully lifted the sheet covering Sanjay, so that he could see the temporary splint that had been placed on his leg for protection. "There is no way to get an ambulance back this far into the slum. There are no streets capable to handle such a vehicle. They are walking with a stretcher and should be here soon. Just stay still and relax."

Sanjay closed his eyes and took several deep breaths "Yes. Singha and Giri stole some bikes and I jumped from the roof and knocked Singha off of his cycle. He hit the wall hard and I think it knocked him out." He took two more deep breaths, "Giri was coming at me on his motorcycle, and I had no choice. I shot him. Is he dead?"

"I know. I know. Yes, Giri is no longer." Agent Mosur stated this with very little empathy. "Where did you get your gun, Sanjay? You realize that carrying a weapon like this is illegal, right?"

"Yes sir. But he was evil. Pure evil," Sanjay pushed himself into a sitting position and scooted back against the wall, "Am I in trouble?"

"Don't worry about that right now. We will sort that out later. Actually, having that weapon may have saved not only your life, but countless others at the hands of that morally corrupt animal."

Sanjay closed his eyes as an intense bolt of pain shot up from his lower leg. "Singha must have escaped. Did you see two bikes or just one?" Sanjay grimaced, as he continued to think about the situation. "They both had bikes. I didn't see what happened to them. Giri rammed into me. I don't remember anything after that."

"No, only one bike. The front wheel was completely flattened, and the frame was bent. Based on your recollection of events, looks like the bike we found was the one Giri was riding. At high speed, and without a driver, I am sure it ricocheted back and forth like a pin ball down the narrow alley. It was totally destroyed. Scratches and dents all over the bike."

"I know where he is going," Sanjay's eyes lit up as he grabbed Agent Mosur by the arm, "I know where he is headed and if he thinks that I am still alive, he won't be there for long."

"Alright, can you give me specific directions?" Mosur grabbed a pad of paper and pen out of his front pocket.

"Yes. Absolutely. It is near Roorkee. About a two and a half hour drive. He will either be at the training center or his personal residence. I know the directions to both."

"Excellent!" Agent Mosur took down the directions provided by Sanjay. The route suggested by Sanjay seemed very easy to navigate, mostly highway for the majority of the trip. Although Sanjay was unable to recall the exact address from memory, the best route to the Roorkee area would ultimately be determined by Apple Maps. Once there, Agent Mosur would refer to the very detailed directions given by Sanjay that he hoped would lead he and the team to the compound.

When Sanjay had finished, Mosur excused himself politely, addressing the ladies of the house along with Sanjay. "I need to radio this information to the authorities. You are in good hands, Sanjay. I will be heading to Roorkee to meet the others." He placed his hand on Sanjay's shoulder. "Well done, my friend. You are a brave young man. We will see each other soon." He wrote down his cell phone number on one of the sheets of paper and handed it to Sanjay, "Don't hesitate to call if you think of anything else or if you need anything."

Triskal hovered above the small dwelling as Agent Mosur wove his way back through the twisting paths and cluttered walkways toward the main thoroughfare where he would be picked up by other agents. Mosur had been instructed to meet the agents in the parking lot of the Jawaharlal Nehru University, a large public university immediately adjacent to the Munirka slum.

With no demons in sight and with Sanjay's safety ensured, Triskal rocketed back into the Delhi night sky on his way to join the others near Roorkee.

After twenty minutes of weaving through the slum maze, and after another ten minutes of searching the crowded parking area, Mosur noticed two gentlemen in matching blue suits at the back of the university parking lot. Agents Manjar Shah and Himanshu Sandajar were leaning against the hood of their Suzuki Vitara smoking Gold Flake Kings cigarettes, Agent Shah's preferred brand, when they saw a slightly winded Agent Mosur jogging towards them.

Both men flicked their cigarettes to the side of the car in unison. "Hop in, Mosur. Let's get on the road."

"Thanks for the lift, boys," Mosur rattled off the initial directions as he struggled to gain his breath, "Roorkee...head to Roorkee." He sucked in another huge breath, "Will give more directions...give me just one second."

The driver, Manjar, plugged in his cell phone and quickly typed in Roorkee, India into the Apple Maps App as he drove towards the main gate. The female voice of the GPS system instructed him to take a right turn as they exited the parking area. The display screen in the Vitara indicated that the total trip duration was estimated at three hours and fourteen minutes.

The Tiger's Den

"My God sent His angel and shut the lion's mouths, so that they have not hurt me, because I was found innocent before Him; and also, O king, I have done no wrong before you. Then the king was exceedingly glad for him, and commanded that they should take Daniel up out of the den, and no injury whatever was found on him, because he believed in his God.

- **DANIEL 7:22-23 (NEW KING JAMES VERSION)**

Do not forget to entertain strangers, for by so doing some have unwittingly entertained angels.

- **HEBREWS 13:2 (NEW KING JAMES VERSION)**

46

trevor was abruptly wakened from a deep sleep by the wail of a siren just outside the building where he was being held captive. The high pitched screams of the many sirens strewn across the campus caused him to reflexively cover his ears.

After putting his pants and shirt on, Trevor shuffled his bare feet across the dark room to the door and placed his ear against the cold steel that separated him from the rest of the world. He could hear feet thumping up and down the hall outside and doors being opened and shut.

Trevor banged on the door, "Help. Please let me out. Is there a fire? What is going on?"

No response.

He continued to bang on the door. He slammed his fists together on the door, harder and harder, until the sides of his palms were throbbing and demanding that he quit.

He heard the sound of footsteps coming his direction. He could hear people yelling and screaming at each other throughout the building. The doorknob on his door was being jiggled back and forth but the door didn't open. He could hear two men yelling something in Hindi. The knob was being man-handled again. The thud of a body slamming into the door caused Trevor to jump back a few feet into the darkness. After four or five attempts to break down the door, Trevor could hear the two pair of feet bounding back down the hall.

Trevor stood staring at the door for a couple of minutes. The frantic yelling and door slamming in the building was now replaced with complete silence. Trevor moved forward and slid down the door into a sitting position and cried out to God. "Lord, please deliver me from this place. Please deliver me from this evil. I pray that you have great purposes still in store for me in this life that I might still impact this world for the benefit of your Kingdom and that many more will come to know you."

After another few minutes of silence and without hearing any steps or movement outside of his door, Trevor heard the locking mechanism next to his head turning.

"Hello? Who's there?" Trevor jumped to his feet but was careful not to open the door himself without knowing who was on the other side.

"Fear not, Trevor. It is Maritius. Stay here for a few minutes. It is far too dangerous to leave right now."

"What do you mean? Why is the alarm sounding? Is there a fire? Are we in danger?" Trevor peppered Mari with anxious questions.

"Faith, my friend. Be still. Quiet your fear. The Lord has you in his capable hands." Maritius spoke softly and slowly, "I must go now but will see you again very soon. You will know me by my actions."

Again, a riddle that confused Trevor. Know me by my actions? What did he mean by that? He turned his back to the door and stared blindly into the darkness of the room. He would heed the advice of this all too wise and kind stranger.

47

स even mighty Angels hovered directly above the compound. Less than one thousand feet below their outstretched wings, they could see three creatures in frantic flight around Commander Singha, demonic entities seeking to influence Singha in his decision making.

A line of vehicles was headed for the exit of the compound when Singha ran out of the main building waving his arms for the small convoy to stop. "This camp is compromised. Do not return here for any reason. Will call with further instructions tomorrow. Get off the property as fast as you can. We don't have long before they get here."

One of the drivers called out to Singha. "Commander, what are you doing? You have to leave with us. Now! We have Rajiv. What should we do with him?"

"I don't care. Just get rid of him. Dump the body in one of the rivers on the way to Delhi." Singha kicked the dirt in front of him with his work boot. "What about Trevor. Where is Trevor?"

"Boss, we couldn't open the door. It was jammed, I think..."
The reporter of this news, a young man in the second vehicle,
almost choked on his own words.

"Don't worry. I will take care of Trevor myself. I have to tie
up a couple other loose ends. Did you idiots forget about the
recruits? Once I am finished, I will catch up with you." Singha
turned and headed away from the main building in the direction of the bathing area. The angels watched as Singha paced
back and forth in front of the crude huts that housed the current crop of trainees.

From the angel's sky high vantage point, the demons surrounding Singha appeared very much like hungry sharks in a
feeding frenzy, darting back and forth around him, poking him
ever so slightly whenever they came close enough to touch
him. Singha swatted at the air as if he were being attacked by
mosquitos. He appeared to be completely out of sorts and dis-
gusted with the situation. A single streetlight that had been
stolen from one of the businesses in Roorkee by his morally
corrupt camp personnel dimly lit the courtyard area where
Singha was pacing.

Singha paused for a moment, looking in the direction of
the small cubicles that housed his future mercenaries. He
walked resolutely to the door of one of the hovels, lifted his
45 caliber Ruger, and fired two rounds into the small space.

The angels could hear the screams of the only inhabitant. A
shriek of pure terror came from the adjacent cell. Singha took
two steps sideways and fired through the door that held the
shrieking recruit. The shriek turned to a painful howl. Singha
fired one more shot through the door and silence returned
to that particular unit. The loud cries from the first cell had

turned to raspy whimpers and slowly diminished until no more sound could be heard.

Singha marched down the line of mud and thatch huts, firing two or three shots into each unit, until his gun was empty. He replaced the empty magazine with one that was fully loaded and continued on his murderous path, until all prisoners had been executed to his satisfaction. The band of demonic spirits were in a lather. They howled and applauded, as they continued to circle around their personal tool of evil.

Orion and Maritius watched in horror as the scene played out. They had not experienced anger like this since the day of the massacre in Mumbai. They could make out the grins on the faces of the demons as they danced in celebration of the carnage that they had encouraged.

The Angels turned towards each other in a formidable circle of Holy power. Without the need for human language, the orders were telepathically delivered by Orion to all gathered. They all bowed their heads in reverence to the Father's plan and, one by one, they dropped out of the sky in flight towards their respective reports already on the Earth below.

Maritius and Triskal made it a point to soar by the demons surrounding Singha as they headed towards the building that housed Trevor. The whoosh of the Angel's powerful wings flung the three demons headlong into the dirt next to the bathing area. They made no attempt to follow the Angels, satisfied to focus their attention on Singha and the havoc that he might bring to the chosen.

Orion and Leshyra took their places next to the tiger cages. Their orders were clear. This was to be the site of the final showdown between good and evil on this day.

48

ROORKEE, INDIA
1:07 A.M.
JULY 9, 2022

The trip from Delhi was much easier than expected, taking them less than three hours in total, probably due to the light traffic this late in the evening. As they passed a road sign that indicated only 10 kilometers to Roorkee, Agent Mosur took out the directions that had been provided earlier by Sanjay.

"Once we pass through the main city center, we will be looking to make a left onto Bharti Marg." Agent Mosur read through the directions again. "Sanjay said that the entrance will only be a couple kilometers down this road on the right. We should see a large steel cattle gate next to a small guard house. He said that the gate was typically unlocked but was always manned by two guards. Next to the gate, there is a large flagpole that flies two flags. The top flag will be the Indian flag and the smaller one below it is a black flag with ILRO in white block letters. Below these letters is a red, white, and blue map of America with a large black hammer and sickle stamped across it. Evidently, this flag represents the Indian Liberation Resistance Organization."

Agents Shah and Sandajar nodded their understanding.

"One more thing, Sanjay said that the guards would be heavily armed and that they both had radios if backup from the compound was needed. At any given time, there are no less than ten armed militia members on the property and many more recruits."

As Agent Shah made the turn onto Bharti Marg, four military grade jeeps coming from the opposite direction flew past their Vitara, spewing dirt and dust as they rounded the corner in the direction of Delhi.

"Looks like they got the warning from Singha. Hope we aren't too late," Agent Mosur clapped his hands together in disgust, crumpling the notes that he was holding in his lap.

"When will the others arrive by helicopter?" Himanshu asked Mosur, who had been in constant contact with the Intelligence Bureau during the drive from Delhi.

Local law enforcement was not equipped for this type of conflict and the IB intended to coordinate instead with the Indian military. A plan was formulated to have Mosur, Shah, and Sandajar scout the property before flying in a group of twenty four soldiers that had been assembled at the Roorkee Cantonment, the headquarters of the Indian Army's Bengal Engineering Group and home of the Bengal Sappers, a group affectionally referred to as "God's Own." The Bengal Sappers had the unique distinction of being the only group in the Indian military affiliated with both the Navy and Air Force and were viewed by American military leaders as an accomplished, commando style fighting unit. The Sappers were the oldest and arguably the most respected Army unit in the country and based on the base's proximity to the ILRO compound, they were identified immediately as the perfect complement to the Bureau's team, a well-armed group of military professionals that would be necessary in taking down this radical and dangerous organization.

Three De Havilland Canada DHC-6 twin otter airplanes had been immediately inspected and fueled. The team would parachute in groups of eight when the orders were given, so that the team could maximize the element of surprise. With the base nearby, the whirring of the twin turboprop engines would likely not raise any eyebrows.

After continuing down the well-worn and mostly dirt road known as Bharti Marg for a couple of minutes, the headlights illuminated the gate and flags that had been perfectly described by Sanjay. The gate was swung wide open and the guard house was completely empty.

Agent Mosur pointed towards the open gate, "Let's go, boys. We may be too late."

Plans had changed. There would be no time for scouting the property. If they didn't move now, there would be no chance of finding anyone on the compound. Agent Mosur picked up his cell phone and placed the call to the Army General at the Roorkee Cantonment. Once connected he gave the simple order, "Send in the birds."

"Roger, Agent Mosur. Roger that. Birds are in flight. I repeat. Birds are in flight." The general ended the call on his end.

49

Roorkee, India
1:11 a.m.
July 9, 2022

revor had slowly counted to sixty twenty times. Without a watch or cell phone to mark time, this seemed the best way to gauge the minutes. Trevor placed his ear against the door. Not a sound. He reached down and gently turned the doorknob and slowly pulled the door towards him. The brightness of the hallway light caused him to squint with all his might as he looked in both directions. No one in sight. Still not a sound.

Trevor took a couple of steps into the hallway, shielding his unaccustomed eyes from the bright ceiling lamps overhead with his right hand. At the end of the hall, he carefully peered around the corner. The desk where the guard usually sat was empty and the front door had been left wide open. With more confidence, Trevor skipped across the room and opened the door to another hallway. All the doors seemed to be open, with papers and clothing items strewn across the hallway, as if everyone had left in a hurry. Where was Rajiv? Did they kill him?

The building was completely empty. The hair on the back of his neck stood on end. Trevor could sense that this might be an opportunity to regain his freedom. He quickly ran to the front door and looked out at a completely deserted camp. No movement. Where had the gunshots come from just minutes earlier?

Trevor took two deliberate steps toward the road in front of the building, his head swiveling back and forth searching for any signs of danger. He would follow the road until he reached the gate. He started to jog down the dirt road in the direction of the main building. If he could make it past the building and into the darkness beyond, he might have a chance. As he picked up speed, he could hear gunshots coming from beyond the main building, close to where the recruits typically bathed each day. One of the bullets ricocheted off the dirt in front of him.

Trevor stopped in his tracks and dropped to his hands and knees in a shallow drainage area adjacent to the road. He looked back in the direction from which he had just come and quickly surveyed the camp for better cover alternatives. He could barely make out what looked like another building at least a half mile from where he was crouching. The next gunshot indicated that the person that was firing at him was getting much closer.

Trevor jumped out of the culvert and ran in zigzag fashion across the courtyard. The five additional discharges of the gun came in rapid succession and then stopped. Misfire? Reload? It didn't really matter. Trevor was determined to find some sort of shelter. He changed direction and ran in the exact opposite direction from where the shots were being fired. The blackness of night and rocky landscape made running much more difficult. He tripped and fell every few steps, catching his feet on unseen rocks or plants. He continued moving until he ran headfirst into an eight foot tall, barbed wire fence, ripping a large gash in his forehead before the taught wire bounced him back in a heap. He pushed himself onto all fours and tried to catch his breath. He stood and walked back to the fence. The sharp barbs covered every wire, and the crown of the fence was made up of large circular bales of razor wire. Not a chance.

He heard a breaking branch. Looking back in the direction of the main camp, he could see the beam of a flashlight dancing awkwardly through a small grove of trees that had to be less than a few hundred feet from his position. After grabbing several massive breaths, Trevor started to jog down the fence line, looking for a gate or some breach in the fence. He found neither.

As he approached what he had thought was a small building, he noticed that it was actually a collection of large commercial grade cages. He could see the ominous shapes of three large tigers prancing back and forth as they watched his approach. Behind the cage complex, there was a ten to twelve foot tall fence with the same rolls of razor wire crowning the top. He had come to the end of the line. This was a dead end. Trevor let out a huge sigh of desperation and disgust.

One of the tigers circled around to the front of the cage, stood on its hind legs, placed his large front paws on the steel framing and roared out what Trevor took to be a clear warning that humans were not welcome.

Trevor looked back towards the main building and could see a dark figure running directly towards him. Trevor looked in every direction but seeing no reasonable option for escape, dropped to his knees, and prayed for protection.

Commander Singha stepped out of the cover of darkness and into the brightly lit area under the spotlight attached to the shed. Trevor watched the red laser dot from the sight on Singha's handgun dance on the dirt in front of him, until it was trained on his chest. Singha looked over at his prized Tigers. The fear of their ruthless owner, now in full view, had silenced the roars of intimidation. With heads now bowed in fear, but with eyes still on their nemesis, all three retreated to the back of the cage.

"What a treat. Who knew that this was feeding time for the cats? And lucky, you." Singha inhaled deeply to regain his breath after the chase. "You have the great honor of being the main course. Nothing they like more than American food." His face contorted into a sadistic smile, but there was no laughter. "Go on. Get in the cage, before I lose my patience and shoot you instead. Tigers love it when they have new visitors. I would hate to steal that pleasure from them tonight."

Completely invisible to Trevor or Singha, Orion placed his arm on Trevor's shoulder and whispered a clear but inaudible message into Trevor's mind. "Fear not, brother. The Lord is with you. Do not fear these animals. They will protect you today."

Trevor walked to the door of the cage and slipped the large bolt out of its housing. His hands shook as he gently opened the heavy steel reinforced gate. He closed it behind him and turned to face three of the fiercest, yet most beautiful creatures that he had ever seen.

Trevor took several deep breaths in and out as he watched these gorgeous, yet intimidating animals parade back and forth in front of where he stood. In and out. In and out.

All three tigers were careful to maintain eye contact with this new visitor to their enclosure. A large boulder sat in the middle of the caged area. Trevor took slow, but faithful steps toward this rock and sat cross legged in front of it. The tigers continued to march around the cage in concentric circles until, one by one, two of the majestic cats sat down on either side of Trevor. The largest of the tigers jumped to the top of the boulder and laid down on its flat surface just above Trevor.

While Trevor remained completely still, the two tigers that now flanked his position on the ground stood angrily on all fours with their haunches visibly puffed up and roared in Singha's direction.

Singha took two steps toward the cage and raised his gun in Trevor's direction. "So, I guess you are now a tiger whisperer, Trevor? Isn't that special!" Trevor watched as Singha pulled on the trigger. He looked down at the gun and tried to pull the slide back. The gun was obviously jammed. Orion, with his angelic hands keeping the slide from being pulled back to rechamber a round of ammunition, watched the anger overtake Singha. The demons that swirled behind Singha's back were completely helpless, mere witnesses as their nemesis took charge of the situation.

The Commander slammed the gun into ground. It bounced into the side of the cage with a tinny thud. The tigers all stood at attention with their sturdy legs in a wide and ready-for-battle stance. "Sit tight, tiger lover, I have everything I need in the shed." Singha turned and started to walk back to the door of the shed.

Without saying a word, Trevor stood up and started to walk to the cage door. The words heard just minutes earlier kept ringing in his ears. "Do not fear these animals. They will protect you today…. Do not fear these animals. They will protect you today."

Trevor pushed the heavy door outward, until it rested against the outside of the cage, creating an unobstructed pathway both into and out of the cage. Trevor turned and walked back into the cage, the intense fear he had felt earlier, now somehow abated. He took a seat in the same position. The three Bengal tigers stealthily moved to the front of where Trevor was seated, the largest of the tigers jumping off the boulder and taking the lead position with the two others just behind him on either side. The hunter instinct in these great beasts had been ignited.

The tigers took slow and deliberate steps toward the open gate, each looking back at Trevor before each step, as if asking for permission. As they left the enclosure, they came together, shoulder to shoulder, only twenty feet from the open shed door.

Singha slammed the door to the shed as he reemerged holding a rifle. He was staring down at the gun with ammunition in one hand obviously trying to figure out how to load the magazine. The bellowing roar of the lead tiger caused Singha to frantically jump back against the wall of the tin building, dropping the rifle and shells in the process. All three tigers stood on their back legs with large paws raised in the air as they let out blood curdling roars in perfect unison. Singha moved sideways down the side of the shed wall, careful not to take his eyes off the angry cats.

As he reached the end of the front wall section, he slowly reached up and removed the electric prod that was hanging from a nail on the side of the building. The Tigers dropped back to all fours and took one cautionary step back towards the cage. Singha pulled the trigger over and over as he took a more emboldened step toward his prized animals. "Stupid cats! You thought this might be your lucky day, did ya? Forgot about my magic wand, maybe?" He fired the buzzing electric current again, as he made a rapid and more threatening step towards the Tigers. This time, the tigers stood their ground and dipped their shoulders in a ready-to-pounce position. The lead tiger let out what sounded more like a bark than a roar, obviously signaling to the others that the shock of this electric prod was a risk worth taking.

The trio of skilled hunters spread out like a fan in front of the increasingly nervous Singha. Each cat was now hunched low to the ground with their heads only inches from the dirt, eyes looking straight up at what had now become their prey. Singha watched as the tiger on the right side of the lead cat took two calculated steps sideways. The huge animal slowly scratched the hard dirt with his front claws, digging deep cuts in the earth before charging directly at him. Commander Singha caught the tiger in the chest with saber like precision, the long crackle of full voltage stunning the huge animal enough to cause him to fall on his side and clumsily stumble back a few feet out of range of Singha's wand of submission. The second cat's attack from the right side was perfectly timed, catching the middle of the electric prod in its teeth as Singha swung it around in the second cat's direction. The weight of the tigers' rear end slammed Singha back against the poorly constructed shed, bending the sheet metal inward like a shiny, oversized clam shell. Singha slid off the metal and started running in the direction of the camp.

Singha was no match for the speed of these master predators. The lead tiger, still crouched in the hunter position, assessed his tased feline partner, now standing more firmly on his feet, and then returned his attention to the fleeing Singha. He bolted into the darkness and covered the eighty to one hundred yards that now separated him from his targeted prey in less than ten seconds. With his massive fangs, he grabbed the fleeing commander by the neck and slammed him into the ground headfirst. The other tigers, only a couple of tiger strides behind their leader, pounced on the body and took their own bites of flesh. Singha cried out in agony as justice was being served by his brutally mistreated and anxious for revenge trophy animals. He clawed and screamed as the tigers continued to dole out their justice. The lead tiger continued to apply pressure with his jaws to the neck of their captor until Singha's body was limp and quiet.

The showdown between captor and captives lasted only a matter of seconds but seemed like an eternity to Trevor. He stood and exited the cage, finding a seat on a stump next to the shed. He placed his head in his hands and wept, both out of relief and out of the horror of what he had just witnessed. Why had he been spared?

The three tigers, in order to be fully satisfied that they had killed their prey, poked at the lifeless Singha with their bloody paws before laying down in the dirt next to the body.

Trevor heard the crackling of underbrush out in the darkness just behind the shed. He stood up and craned his neck in the general direction of the crunching of grass and leaves, wondering if Singha had somehow escaped death or if the tigers were headed back in his direction. Something or someone was headed directly towards him from the camp. Trevor looked around, but there was nowhere to run or hide. In a matter of seconds, a very tall man with broad shoulders and strong arms stepped into the only lighted area next to the shed. He was dressed in a white tunic over white pants and sandals. His white hair flowed back over his shoulders to almost the middle of his back. Trevor stood and was just about to warn him about the tigers when the man lifted his hand in front of him to let Trevor know that a warning was unnecessary.

For the first time that evening, a bright moon appeared from behind the clouds and Trevor could see the three tigers laying in a circle around Singha's motionless body. The man walked back to where the tigers were seated, knelt, and placed his hand on the lead tiger's head. The large cat purred in a show of respect and admiration. The man stood and started walking toward the cage. The three tigers, one with flowing white and two with brownish-orange coats, followed the man in single file, until they were back inside the enclosure.

He turned back and closed the gate behind him as he walked towards Trevor.

"Your faith is great, Trevor. Faith is a gift for those that are willing to receive it. You are called to do great things, my friend."

"Maritius? Is that you?" No answer. "Thank you." Tears clouded Trevor's sight as he spoke, "Who are you? Where did you come from? Where is Rajiv?"

"Rajiv will be fine. He is in Triskal's capable hands."

"Who is Triskal?" After an uncomfortable pause, Trevor raised his voice with a trace of laughter, "*Who is Triskal, he asks?*"

Maritius simply cocked his head to the side and then looked up into the heavens. He glanced back at Trevor, took two large steps forward and then nodded in the direction of Orion and Leshyra. Trevor looked to where Maritius had just nodded and saw nothing but the tigers and the blackness of night behind the cages.

"Wait.... Who...?" Trevor stopped himself, "I don't understand. I have so many questions."

Maritius didn't say another word. He placed his hands together in the traditional praying, or namaste position in India, and bowed in humble admiration of the brave servant in front of him.

He turned and started to walk back towards the center of the camp alone. Trevor, feeling somewhat weak in the knees, sat back down on the stump and thanked God for his protection, for Maritius, and for the precious, often underappreciated, gift of faith.

50

After sitting on the stump for close to half an hour, Trevor could hear the whirring sound of turbo prop airplanes overhead. The moon had broken through the clouds just in front of him and the moonlight illuminated at least a half dozen parachutes of jumpers that were already halfway to the ground. For the first time that evening, his heart rate slowed, and an overwhelming feeling of peace swept over him.

Trevor decided to wait under the spotlight until someone found him. Walking back through the darkness might place him in danger. He moved the stump closer to the tiger cage directly under the beam of light. The three tigers stood in unison and moved closer to where Trevor was sitting. The lead tiger placed his large black nose through one of the openings in the steel mesh. Without fear or hesitation, Trevor reached into the cage and gently petted the large cat on his soft forehead. "Thank you, big fella. I will never forget you."

The cat purred loudly as Trevor continued petting, "I will find a much better home for all of you. That is my promise."

His promise of a better life for these animals was not simply a pleasant idea. He would make sure of it.

From the shadows behind the shed, a voice rang out. "Trevor, is that you? Trevor?" The man was holding a gun pointed in his direction.

"Yes, sir. I am Trevor." Trevor stood and looked in the man's direction while placing both hands behind his head to make it clear that he posed no threat.

"Glad to see that you are safe. I am Agent Mosur." He stepped closer to where Trevor was standing. "You can put your arms down, sir." He holstered his weapon and retrieved something from his front pocket. He raised his badge as he approached.

Trevor whispered a quick prayer of thanks. "Thank you, God."

"Come again, sir?"

"No. Nothing, Agent Mosur. Just thanking the man upstairs that I wasn't on the menu this evening." Trevor let out a nervous chuckle.

"Gotcha. And by the looks of it, I don't think Mr. Singha was quite as lucky." Agent Mosur looked to his left at the body of Commander Singha and then back at Trevor. The massive lacerations that could be seen in the neck area and the copious amount of blood that had pooled around his head clearly indicated that Singha had succumbed to the massive injuries inflicted by the tigers.

Another man appeared from the shadows and called out to Mosur. "You guys OK? Were you able to locate, Mr. Haas?"

"This is Agent Shah. We need you to come with us, Trevor?"

"Yes, sir. Couldn't be happier to see you guys."

They started to walk back to the main building. As they crossed through the recruit bathing area, Trevor could see several men in military uniforms placing bodies in body bags next to the crude huts that had served as their quarters. Trevor turned his face away and kept walking behind the two agents.

Once in the main building, Agent Shah grabbed a chair for Trevor and pulled it closer to the table where he and Agent Mosur had set up a temporary command center. "Have a seat, Trevor. Water?"

"Yes. That would be great."

As Mosur left his seat in search of the water, Trevor sat down and scooted the chair closer to the table. He crossed his arms on the table in front of him and rested his head on his forearms.

"You alright, buddy?" Agent Mosur asked when he returned to the desk with two bottles of water.

Trevor raised his body with some effort and leaned back in his chair. "Yes, sir. Sorry. Long day."

"Long day, indeed." Agent Shah pulled his chair closer to Trevor. "Got some good news and some bad news. Which one do you want first?"

"Surprise me." Trevor answered with very little enthusiasm or emotion.

"Evidently, the entire camp got the warning to evacuate. We just missed them. That is the bad news. The good news is that as the three of us were headed here from Delhi, we saw a caravan of vehicles fly past us as we rounded the corner towards the compound. Being the middle of the night in the absolute middle of nowhere, it was a little curious to say the least." Shah looked down at the paperwork in front of him and scanned some of the information. "Fortunately, one of the elite units from the Roorkee Cantonment had already barricaded the highway only a few miles outside of Roorkee in case anyone was able to escape from the compound. In total, they apprehended over a dozen of the militia operatives. Remarkably, no one was killed or injured during the capture. When they realized that they were completely outmanned and outgunned, they surrendered without firing a shot. The best news is that Rajiv was with them and we were able to remove him from the vehicle without incident."

Trevor stared at Agent Shah as he contemplated this information. "How is he? How is Rajiv? Was he hurt?"

"Rajiv is in good shape, except for that leg of his. We flew him by chopper to Delhi so that we can perform all of the required medical checks. And by the way, you are booked on the next chopper in the same direction."

"That is great news." Trevor wiped a tear from his eye. "I hope that this ends their reign of terror here in India. Did you find the gentleman dressed in all white, you know, the one that put the tigers back into the cages?"

"What man in white? What do you mean he put the tigers back into the cages?" Agent Shah cocked his head in confusion. "No. There was no one on the compound when we arrived except for you. Not sure who you would be referring to, Trevor."

The corners of Trevor's lips turned up slightly in a smile of wonderment and thankfulness. "Never mind, guys. My mind could be playing tricks on me. Been a rough week." He leaned back further with his hands behind his head. His chair teetered on its back legs and almost tipped over before Trevor reflexively shifted his weight in order to steady himself. The chair slammed forward back onto all four legs. "Or, maybe, just maybe, it could be as simple as the man upstairs watching out for me here in India. Whatever the case, I was certainly glad to see him take charge of those tigers."

Freedom

For you, brethren, have been called to liberty; only do not use liberty as an opportunity for the flesh, but through love serve one another.
- **Galations 5:13 (New King James Version)**

Then I looked around, and I heard the voice of many angels around the throne, the living creatures, and the elders; and the number of them was then thousand times ten thousand and thousands of thousands, saying with a loud voice: "Worthy is the Lamb who was slain to receive power and riches and wisdom, and strength and honor and glory and blessing!"
- **Revelation 5:11-12**

51

Visitation hours at the Mumbai Central Prison started in less than ten minutes. We were given very detailed instructions by Aswani Kumar, the prison visitation proctor, regarding the rules that applied to non-family members for visits with an inmate. Mr. Kumar was a muscular, two hundred pound plus, no-nonsense individual. He used a large, black Billy club as a pointer as he motioned to where we would be seated in the visitation center. The rule that impacted both Rajiv and me the most during the visit was the prohibition of any steel objects during such a visit, which meant my crutches and Rajiv's cane would need to be left in the waiting room.

"Don't worry, buddy, I will give you a piggyback ride to the table." Trevor winked at me, only half kidding. "Alright, maybe not. Just put your arm around my shoulders and we can make the twenty foot walk together."

It had only been two months since the attack in Mumbai that had shattered my leg. Although last week's x-rays showed that the steel rod holding my Tibia together was in perfect position, the doctor demanded that I remain on crutches in an air cast for the next eight weeks. I had initially protested this directive, but Trevor quickly cut me off, shooting a commanding glare at me before assuring the doctor that the orders would be followed completely. No further discussion on the topic would be needed.

Using Trevor's right shoulder for support, I hopped my way across the room to our meeting cubicle. I took my assigned seat behind the plexiglass divider that separated us from Sanjay who was already seated on the other side of the see through wall. Hayward and Sanjay pulled up two steel fold-up chairs and sat just behind the bench that only accommodated two visitors.

With his hands bound in shiny cuffs, Sanjay grabbed the old school phone receiver from its cradle on the wall to his left and pointed towards where the same unit on the visitor side was mounted.

I reached up and grabbed the phone, as Trevor scooted his chair across the concrete floor closer to the bench where I was sitting. "Good morning, Sanjay. How are you holding up?"

"Great boss. Never been better," Sanjay smiled as if he had just won a marathon, "You seem to be getting around pretty good on that bad leg of yours."

"Yeah. I guess. Thanks, Sanjay." His mention of my leg reminded me that the doctor had recommended that I keep it elevated whenever possible. I readjusted my weight so that I could swing my leg cast up on top of the bench. "We just finished meeting with your attorneys. I realize that a twenty five year sentence may seem harsh, but we will do what we can to convince them to release you much earlier." Without thinking, I bowed my head just slightly, communicating a lack of real confidence in my statement to both Sanjay and Trevor.

"Boss, please don't worry. I have gained far more than I have lost. God has found me. Even though I didn't deserve it. He found *me*! That is a reward for eternity. I will gladly pay my price." Sanjay placed his palm on the glass, "I am forever grateful for your trust in me. My loss of freedom in India for the next twenty five years is nothing in comparison to my eternity in Heaven now being secured. Don't forget that the Apostle Paul was imprisoned for quite a long time. It didn't stop him, did it? So, why should it stop me? Right?"

"Oh, that reminds me. Speaking of finding something." Trevor reached into his briefcase and pulled out Sanjay's Yankees cap and his sister's Tiger Eye necklace and handed them to the guard.

Sanjay stood up with his hands covering his face. Fighting back the rush of tears he said, "Oh, man. I can't believe you found it. Thank you."

"I know. That hat is quite a collector's item." Trevor gently poked at Sanjay.

Sanjay cocked his head in amusement and smiled. "You got me, brother Trevor. You got me good."

After a long conversation with our new brother in Christ, I placed my palm opposite of Sanjay's on my side of the glass. "You have an amazing story and a powerful testimony, Sanjay. Simply amazing. Your future is bright. Thank you for what you have done to stop Singha, Giri, and their entire organization. You are a blessing to India and to the world." I started to choke on these final words as Sanjay placed his hand on the glass, mirroring mine. No more words needed to be spoken today.

Sanjay's full conversion, his obvious repentance, his strong faith, and his new relationship with God was remarkable to behold. Very disappointing to realize that the celebration of this life changing event would, at least for the next twenty five years, be limited to a prison visitation chamber. I placed the phone handset back in the cradle.

Rajiv and Trevor stepped towards the glass partition, one on each side of the bench where I was seated. They placed their hands on top of mine in a show of support for Sanjay. The glass divider meant nothing at this point. The show of love and support, on the other hand, meant the world to all of us.

Sanjay pulled his hand away from the glass, stood proudly, and took two steps back from the partition. He placed his hands together in front of his chest, bowed gently, and started to walk back towards the door where Mr. Kumar was waiting to escort him back to his cell.

52

In typical Hayward form, Jaworski pulled up to the Caravela Café riding a fluorescent pink and lime green Vespa. He was sporting a two sizes too small leather jacket with yellow block letters across the chest that said, "Built for Speed.'" A yellow lightning bolt was etched above the word Speed. I was still shaking my head as he walked through the door of the restaurant. Most of the patrons turned to watch our six foot seven inch, middle-aged child as he hung up his prized jacket on the coat rack next to the cash register and then slowly removed his bright blue helmet as if he was trying out for a low budget movie role. He waved to the crowd as if he was a national celebrity. When many of the customers waved back, our table burst into laughter. Harold truly saw every social situation as a comedic opportunity. Beth would always remind me that his never ending twisted, yet harmless stunts were the main reasons we kept him around.

"What is happening, SUV drivers?" Hayward grinned and punched Trevor in the shoulder, as he walked around to the last open seat at the end of the long table.

"Glad you could make it, you nut case." I shook my head once more for his benefit, "Alright, I'll bite. What's with the new ride?"

"Oh, you saw Bessie, huh? She's a rocket ship, that one." He placed his napkin in his lap.

"I'm sure she is. You know that you are not driving that to church services in old Goa this morning, right? You would either arrive sometime midafternoon or spend the entire day on the side of the road when that old scooter breaks down. She definitely looks like she is on her last set of tires." I waved at our server who was now pointing and laughing with the hostess about the highlight-of-the-morning entry made by Jaworski.

"Come on. Give the girl some credit. I got her up to at least twenty miles per hour on the straight away driving to the restaurant." He gave a defiant snort. "Only wobbled a tiny bit but mostly purred like a kitten, maybe with a bit of asthma." The table busted out laughing again.

As our server approached the table with pen and order pad in hand, Beth, Cade, Alisha, and Trevor looked back down at their menus. "Nice to be serving you all today. Except for maybe that one on the end." She pointed at Harold and the table erupted again, "Just kidding. Are you all prepared to place your food orders?"

After polishing off our breakfast choices, we piled into Trevor's SUV, leaving Bessie in her choice parking spot directly in front of the restaurant. I am sure that the owners of the

Caravela Café were thrilled to babysit, for all to see, quite possibly the most hideous scooter in all of greater Goa.

All six of us had been looking forward to this Sunday morning for weeks. Most Sundays were spent at our home church just north of Panjim where Trevor, Beth, and I took turns preaching and leading worship while Cade and Alisha helped Arun and Shilpa Reddy, local lay leaders, run the children's and youth programs. Jaworski would occasionally provide the sermon, but he much preferred the more socially engaging job of church greeter and hospitality chairman. Today, the typical 9:30AM and 11:00AM worship services would be held in the evening so that we could spend this morning visiting one of the oldest Christian churches in all of India, a Portuguese basilica, which had been built in 1594.

After the twenty five minute drive from Panjim, we made the final turn into the church complex of Old Goa, an amazing UNESCO World Heritage Site that houses many of the historic Churches and convents of Goa. Trevor looked at his watch and instead of turning left into the church parking area, he turned right, into the parking lot for the Archaeological Museum of Old Goa, a large building across the street from the Basilica of Bom Jesus.

"We are a full forty minutes early." Trevor looked over at Harold in the passenger seat and then at the rest of his passengers in the second and third rows, "Let's check out the museum. Rajiv said it takes about twenty minutes and it is well worth the thirty rupees for admission."

"Sounds good to me," Harold was already out the door, "What are you guys waiting for, a formal invitation?"

"Funny, Harold," Beth said from the back row, "A little easier for those of us that didn't call 'shotgun'. We're coming."

Rajiv was right. The museum tour was worth the effort, even if only for the short history lesson of Portuguese Christian influence in this part of India. We learned that the Basilica of Bom Jesus was considered one of the seven wonders of Portuguese origin in the world. The downside of the tour was the obvious lack of air conditioning. As we finished the tour, I could have easily wrung out my shirt like a used shammy. I offered a short prayer under my breath that Bom Jesus had better ventilation than Bom Museum.

After learning more about the area and the historic significance of the buildings on this property, everyone seemed more excited to attend the services this morning. As we took the short walk to the basilica, the temperature was already in the mid-eighties, but the gentle breeze helped to dry my damp clothing just enough to make sitting through and hour long service bearable.

We reached the front of the Church about ten minutes before the service was slated to begin. The windows were propped open and gigantic oscillating fans lined the outermost aisles pointed in the direction of the four large rows of church pews. To say that I was thrilled with this observation would be a massive understatement. My unspoken, yet top priority, would be to find a seat nearest one of the mega-fans. Trevor, Hayward, and my family could thank me later.

As I stepped through the vestibule doors into the sanctuary, I was struck by the simplicity of the interior. Except for a sparkling marble floor etched with precious stones and the gilded statue of St. Ignatius of Loyola, the building was fairly plain compared to other cathedrals from the fifteenth and sixteenth centuries. The pews were beautifully hand made in dark stained teak wood, and although somewhat plain themselves, served to be very comfortable for both sitting and kneeling during the services.

Once everyone was seated for the services, a powerful organ prelude signaled the beginning of the service. The entire service was a beautiful mix of English and Konkani, the official language of the state of Goa. Although no one in our group could join in singing when the music was offered in the local language, the worship experience of hearing a familiar Christian hymn overlaid by the beautiful Goan language was uplifting in a way I had never experienced. It was simply beautiful.

After the service, one of the church elders gave us an abbreviated tour of the Church. Alisha, because of her love for all things Tuscan, was most captivated by the mausoleum where an ornate silver casket, a gift from one of the last Modicis, Cosimo III, the Grand Duke of Tuscany, held the mortal remains of St. Francis Xavier. We then toured the rest of the Church complex, visiting the Church of St. Francis of Assissi, a beautiful Catholic Church attached to the Archaeological Museum and briefly peeking through the front doors of the Se Cathedral Church just behind St. Francis, where afternoon Mass was already underway. The Christian history in this beautiful part of India was far beyond anything that I had ever imagined.

"Alright, Dad. This place is amazing but isn't it time for lunch yet? Just sayin'." Cade's all too predictable empty stomach was leading him down the gravel path in the direction of Trevor's SUV. He looked back as he continued his negotiation for an early tour dismissal, "The architectural tour must come to an end, you guys. I think three churches and a museum is quite enough, right Leesha?"

"I am going to side with you on this one, big brother." Alisha winked at me and started jogging to catch up with Cade.

53

ROORKEE, INDIA
10:52 A.M.
AUGUST 17, 2022

he flight to Delhi had been uneventful, but sleep had not come easy for me. We were all extremely excited about the trip to Roorkee that would allow us to relocate Trevor's feline protectors, even though we were not sure what to expect.

After a very late meal that ended after midnight, we went to the lobby, ordered decaf coffees, and continued talking for the better part of three more hours. At 3:15AM, after looking down at his watch in obvious disbelief, Trevor stood and started making his way towards his room. "You guys are nuts. If we don't head up now, we will be here all night. The cars will be here in less than four hours."

"Right behind you, boss," Hayward hopped out of his seat and started to follow Trevor down the hall.

I yelled jokingly to them, my voice growing into a loud crescendo as they disappeared around the corner, "Don't worry freeloaders, I will get the check. *Again!*" I shook my head, signed the bill, and headed for my room.

The cars arrived at 7:00AM just as requested and we were on the road in less than five minutes. The drive to Roorkee was a bumpy three and a half hours, allowing only cat naps for those of us that were sleep deprived.

As our small caravan entered the gate to the Roorkee compound, the vivid descriptions of violence and carnage that Trevor had shared with me over the last several weeks played in my head like a gratuitously explicit and exceptionally violent, wartime-action movie trailer. The torture, the mud, the heat, the sights, the smells, the sleepless nights, the constant verbal abuse, the animal cruelty, the overwhelming fear. Trevor now referred to this terrorist training ground as 'Camp Abaddon', a reference to the Angel of the bottomless pit described in the book of Revelation, because of the overwhelming feelings of doom and despair he experienced while being held captive here. My overactive imagination was flooding my brain with unthinkable images. I could only imagine how revisiting this site might be affecting my good friend in the back seat.

Our animal rescue inspired motorcade of two Suzuki Marutis, one Honda HR-V, and one Toyota Fortuner followed the large animal transportation vehicle that was driven by two young Wildlife Rescue and Rehabilitation Center professionals down the rutted and muddy road in the direction of the tigers that we were here to liberate. The rains during this monsoon season had definitely taken its toll on any non-paved road in the area.

Trevor was tapping his feet on the floorboard of our Maruti as he scanned the camp in all directions. It had been little more than a month since Trevor had regained his freedom, but I could tell that the return trip was causing my friend some significant anxiety. "You alright, Trev?"

"Yeah. Yeah. I guess," he adjusted himself in his seat as he turned towards me, "Just weird being back here. A lot of not so great memories, if you know what I mean."

"Gotcha. You ready to stretch your legs? We have some tigers to relocate." I could see Beth, Rajiv, Alisha, and Cade getting out of the car in front of us.

"Yeah. I'm good. Wouldn't miss this for the world." Trevor opened his door and took a deep breath before joining the others just outside of the main entrance to the cage. Harold crawled out of the back seat and followed me as I made my way around the front of the eighteen-wheeler, on the opposite side of the main entrance from the others.

After opening the large rear doors to the trailer, Mansing and Sunit, the two tiger relocators that were sent to help with this mission, carefully backed up the large trailer until it nearly abutted the main entrance to the cage. Sunit, after giving the hand gesture for Mansing to stop, squeezed between the chain links of the cage and the bumper of the vehicle, and after surveying the positions of all three tigers to ensure appropriate distance from his position, placed a makeshift staircase in front of the lift gate and then carefully opened the cage. With a large electric prod in hand, an important precautionary measure, but without any twisted desire to inflict pain as had been the case with the now deceased previous owner or his power hungry minions, Sunit slowly walked around the perimeter of the cage until he was directly behind the nervous and very inquisitive animals.

Sunit used the three-foot-long rod to motion in the direction of the trailer. He was careful to make very deliberate and smooth movements with the wand and never lost eye contact with the lead tiger. The cats appeared more curious than frightened of this new visitor. Fortunately, Sunit did not need to pull the trigger that would provide a menacing and well understood crackling message to the tigers. "Good girl. Good girl." He took one step towards the animals. They backed up one step. Step by step, Sunit and the three magnificent creatures moved closer and closer to the waiting vehicle. Their fluffy white and orange-brown hair stood tall on the backs of their powerful necks. Once they were about ten feet from the steps that led up to the bed of the trailer, they turned their attention away from Sunit and rambled up the steps into the trailer, sniffing wildly as they tried to assess this new environment.

Sunit calmly closed one of the two swinging doors to the trailer as Mansing closed the other. Mansing grabbed the makeshift steps and headed back to the cab of the truck.

Everyone outside of the gate stood in awe of these animals without speaking a word. Watching these regal tigers being motioned towards the luxury transport vehicle by seasoned professionals was mesmerizing. Their love and care for these animals was obvious. The WRRC had spared no expense to make sure that the twelve-hour trip to the chosen relocation area would be as comfortable as possible for these magnificent creatures. Each animal had its own separate enclosure inside of the customized eighteen-wheeler. In each enclosure, four-inch-thick foam matting had been secured to the floor and then covered by plush, yet sturdy, commercial grade carpeting.

The soft and spongy addition would act more like a cushy mattress than the floor of a truck trailer.

After they were finished loading the animals, Sunit and Mansing shared pictures of the inside of the truck's cargo bay. Large benches and walkways had been erected throughout the space to allow the animals area to move around freely during transport while exploring their temporary home on wheels. Large flood lights lit up the area, turning the usually dark trailer into a large cat's playground. There were two large tanks of water and two large bins of food at the front of the trailer. Sunit indicated that the cats typically refused to eat or drink while being moved, but in case there was an unexpected delay, the cats would have plenty of water and would be well fed. No animal cruelty concern with this group, that was for sure.

"You guys hungry?" Beth asked the collective group. "We have plenty of sandwiches, bags of chips, samosas, naan bread, chicken, and lamb curry. Take your pick."

After polishing off an early lunch, we piled back into our respective vehicles and headed out of the compound in the direction of the Sundarbans area in Bangladesh. My excitement to watch these animals be released back into the wild continued to swell with each passing mile of our trip.

Our GPS estimated arrival time at our hotel in Kolkata was around midnight. We would eat, freshen up, and try to get a few hours of sleep before heading to the drop-off location in the morning, hopefully leaving sometime before noon. I was overjoyed and giddy that we would be able to fulfill the promise that I had made to these amazing tigers, but my pounding headache reminded me that it was time to get some much needed sleep.

54

After an hour and a half drive from Kolkata, we arrived at the edge of a large stand of mangrove trees deep inside the Sundarban National Park. Over twenty members of the Global Calling Organization had made the trip to join us for the release of these amazing animals back into their native environment.

Sunit and Mansing informed us that the park, which is shared by India and Bangladesh, covered over five hundred square miles, and serves as a sanctuary for the Royal Bengal Tiger along with other endangered species such as the estuarine crocodile and the Ganges River dolphin.

We were asked to gather as a group about one hundred yards away from the trailer, an appropriate distance from where the tigers would be released. These beautiful and majestic creatures were still considered dangerous, and our expert tiger handlers were committed to ensuring the safety of our team. As we approached the still ocean water, a peace settled over me that felt like a warm blanket on my soul. The quiet mangrove beaches were both beautiful and tranquil and seemed to stretch for miles in every direction.

The back of the trailer was parked to face a large grove of Sundari trees that would act as the tiger's entryway into one of the mighty jungles that covered the Gangetic Plain. Although we were still in the heart of monsoon season, the sky was clear, and the temperature was in the low eighties. We could not have asked for a more perfect day for the release.

Mansing and Sunit carefully opened the large bay doors on the back of the custom tiger transport truck, making sure that they were relatively obscured from the tiger's line of sight. One by one, the three massive cats jumped from the trailer onto the sand, their heads on a swivel as they surveyed their new surroundings.

"Dad, they are huge!" Cade walked forward to get a better look at the tigers.

I grabbed his arm gently, "Whoa, buddy. We were asked to keep still until they entered the jungle, remember?"

"Yes, Dad. Sorry."

The three tigers moved in unison towards the tree line. The first steps were deliberate as if they were not sure that they were truly free. Once they were clear of the truck by forty or fifty feet, their pace quickened, and they pranced toward the stand of Sundar trees.

Two of the cats disappeared into a thick area of mangrove trees nearest the water. The largest tiger, the one that I had perceived to be the lead cat, stopped only yards before the jungle entrance. Without turning his body, he craned his powerfully thick neck back in our group's direction. I could sense that he was looking for someone and I watched as Trevor made his way to the front of the crowd of twenty five witnesses.

The tiger bowed its head just slightly, as if to give his version of a thank you and then gave a mighty roar before pouncing through the same opening in the mangrove stand that had been used by the others.

Mansing turned his gaze away from the tiger and looked back in my direction. "I have never seen anything quite like that, and I have handled tigers for years."

A tear ran down my face as my family appeared by my side. I looked at Beth and smiled. My eyes were not the only eyes filled with tears on this day. I grabbed her soft hand in mine and put my free arm around the shoulders of my son and daughter as we all stood in contemplation of the tiger's newfound freedom.

After about five minutes, I broke the silence. "Alright, let's head to the cars and go grab some lunch."

"Great idea, dad. I'm starving.

What else could I expect from my always famished teenage son. I ruffled his hair and laughed. "Let's get you some food, son. We are just getting started. There is much more to do here in India."

Author's Note

I have a special place in my heart for India. The history, the people, the tradition, the beauty, along with amazing memories of many trips to the subcontinent inspired me to write a book that would allow readers to see this amazing place through my eyes, while allowing me to paint a picture centered around God's love, promise, and hope for this wonderful country even amid significant Christian persecution. For those that are afforded the opportunity to travel to India, you should absolutely place it high on your travel priority list.

2020 turned out to be a challenging year in the United States and around the world. The COVID-19 pandemic impacted the way we work, travel, eat, socialize, vacation, purchase groceries, use media, and spend time with family. Many of the impacts, but certainly not all, have been negative. One of the most profoundly negative for me was my inability to travel, both in the United States and abroad. For the first time in twenty five years, I was unable to visit key customers, I was unable to attend important industry conferences, there were no vacations for the family, and I was not able to visit India for over twelve months. Today, as I write this note, I remain unsure as to when the opportunity to travel to India might avail itself again. After over thirty trips to India since 2009, I feel a tremendous void in my life that will only be filled when we are able to travel again safely.

The people in India are remarkable. Yes, there are parts of India that are more third world than first world, but there is a distinctive beauty even in these regrettable and sometimes forgotten parts of India. The people across India tend to be very content. They are typically content in their own situation. Content in where they live. Content with very little in many cases. But joy runs deep in India. There is a celebration at every turn. A smile on almost every face. A deep longing to be helpful and hospitable to visitors. There is also a genuine curiosity about most things. When in India, I am constantly being questioned about the United States. Do I live near New York City? What is my favorite food? What is my family like? Do I play cricket? Am I a Dallas Cowboys fan? The list goes on forever and I always enjoy the interrogation. Please understand that I am in no way suggesting that India is a special "nirvana" that only exhibits good, but I will say that in my experience, the good far outweighs the bad.

With respect to religion, India is truly a melting pot. The Hindu faith is the practiced by 80% of the population. (14% Islamic, 1.7% Sikhism, 0.7%, Buddhism, 0.37% Jainism, 2.3% Christian) Other religions that have a history in India include Judaism, Zoroastrianism, Yungdrung Bon, Sanamahis, and the Baha'i Faith, each represented by thousands of followers.

As Christians, we are called to take the inspired Word of God out into the world, to all people, so that all may hear. Everyone deserves to hear this message and deserves to make a personal decision regarding this message. In this way, I am hopeful that the book will be a reminder to all of us regarding our responsibility as Children of God. No matter the dangers that the world may place in our path, this purposeful willingness to share the Good News is our global calling. Below, I have included a few verses from the Bible that clearly lay out this responsibility.

But sanctify the Lord God in your hearts, and always be ready to give a defense to everyone who asks you a reason for the hope that is in you, with meekness and fear.

1 PETER 3:15 (NEW KING JAMES VERSION)

And He said to them, "Go into all the world and preach the gospel to every creature."

MARK 16:15 (NEW KING JAMES VERSION)

Therefore, we are ambassadors for Christ, as though God were pleading through us; we implore you on Christ's behalf, be reconciled to God.

2 CORINTHIANS 5:20 (NEW KING JAMES VERSION)

Evangelism can be tricky business in certain areas of our world because of fear, local law, politics, or even religious persecution. It is no different in India. In the first half of 2020, even with a three month lockdown in place, hate crimes against Christians rose by over forty percent, according to the Persecution Relief Organization. The group reported two hundred and ninety three incidents in the first six months of the year. Although troubling, Persecution Relief went on to say in its half-yearly report that, "there is hope, as God's eyes are upon this blessed nation and the Christian minority in India is on their knees praying for the current situation." I remain hopeful that there remains a hearty appetite for the Word of God in India.

Personally, I have never experienced any type of persecution and have been fortunate to engage in many deep conversations regarding faith. I have spent countless hours comparing the theology of Christianity with the foundational ideas and beliefs behind Hinduism and Sikhism. It has proved to be an amazing learning experience for me and has truly solidified my faith.

At the very core of our calling to take the Word of God to all nations, we must have the courage and faith to follow through on this mandate. Most importantly, we are required to bring this life changing message with love and compassion. I pray that this book will cause people to think about the many evangelical opportunities and missionary possibilities that exist across the globe and that many will take time to pray for those that are currently serving in ministry positions throughout the world. I would also encourage readers to study the Word of God with an open mind, allowing for Him to move mightily in their hearts and lives. With a great deal of confidence, I can say that He will open doors that you could never even imagine or knew existed.

May you truly be blessed by God in all ways. Open your heart and mind to his amazing promises and perfect plan for all people, each one created and adored by Him. May God continue his mighty work in India and here in the United States of America.

Of course, I would be remiss if I failed to mention those spiritual protectors that work in fulfillment of God's plan on a regular basis; a special nod to the mighty angels all around us. Thank you for your constant watch and care over all of us.

Acknowledgements:

My thirty plus trips to India made writing this book both an honor and a pleasure. I am forever grateful to my current and former employers, especially the three that are based in India, and for many of my Indian friends and colleagues that have made these trips far more than just your average business trips.

Every book is made better by engaged and committed beta readers. This book is no exception. I am thankful to have an amazing Christian mother that painstakingly goes through every page with a fine toothed comb, always providing me with helpful comments and suggestions with a heart of love and support. She is one special mom.

For my good friends, Kerry Sutton, and Travis Roberts. Your consistent support and excitement keep me motivated to continue writing Christian Fiction. Kerry, from our days at Trinity Baptist Church in Kerrville, Texas during the crazy eighties until today, we have remained close friends and accountability partners, and I can't tell you how much I appreciate all of the history that we have created together. Travis, you are a rock for me in business and in life. Starting with our days at URL Mutual and continuing with our time at Cadista, we have shared many amazing memories together in both India and the U.S., and I sincerely expect that many more will be a part of our future.

To my team at Unichem Pharmaceuticals, thank you for your unwavering support and interest in this book and for all your amazing comments and suggestions. Sam Goodman, thank you for the thoroughness of your edits and the thoughtful criticism. Would I have expected anything else? Abhi Bandela and Rajaram Pai, you truly are my secret agents from India. Your advice and suggestions regarding all things India have been invaluable. From the explanation of neighborhood cricket rules to the spelling of words that are unique to India, you guys have truly been sent by God as the perfect editing eyes for this book.

I am truly grateful to my new friends at Xulon Publishing. The team at Xulon has made this process both seamless and smooth. I can't emphasize enough how important it is to work with Christian brothers and sisters that all share the same love of God and desire to impact the Kingdom of Heaven in a positive way. Thank you, Todd Bullington, for being a great sounding board and for all of your feedback regarding my first two Christian Fiction novels. Kim Small, you are a Rockstar! Your openness and sense of urgency, along with your impeccable turnaround times during the production process makes you one of the best in the industry. Don Newman, I have enjoyed our conversations about faith and look forward to a great relationship moving forward.

And, to my wife Jenny (the true reader in our family). Thank you for your love and support throughout the years. Through life's ups and downs, we have always figured out a way. I thank God for being the glue that keeps us together in a very special way. He has truly blessed us beyond measure. I love that you challenge me in positive ways that make me a better person and a better writer. Many of your amazing ideas found their way into this book, and in the author's opinion, it made The Tiger's Eye a much better story. Thank you.

Additional Note from the Author

I hope that you enjoyed The Tiger's Eye, Angels in Mumbai, the second book in the Global Calling Series. There will be at least one more book in the series that should be released in the next couple of years.

A positive review on Amazon would be fantastic and greatly appreciated, as it affords me the opportunity to focus more time and energy on my writing and helps to persuade others to read my work. I read every single review. Although, I typically do not respond to reviews, I certainly will respond to all Facebook posts (ScottDelaneyAuthor), Facebook Messenger texts and messages that I receive via email.
Contact Scott at: sdelaney0522@yahoo.com

Please do not hesitate to reach out. I would love to hear from you. Thank you and God Bless!

Scott B. Delaney

CPSIA information can be obtained
at www.ICGtesting.com
Printed in the USA
BVHW042147240521
608070BV00015B/341